AGE OF MONSTERS

JOHN LEE SCHNEIDER

SEVERED PRESS
HOBART TASMANIA

AGE OF MONSTERS

WWW.SEVEREDPRESS.COM

ISBN: 978-1-925840-95-7

"Thou mighty city, in one hour has thy mighty judgment come. And the light of a single lamp shall shine no more."

Revelations 18

CHAPTER 1

Everybody remembered where they were when the world ended.

When you met them, that was always the first thing people told you – where they were – what they were doing. What it was like.

Jonah certainly remembered where *he* had been – out fishing.

He'd almost missed it.

He had just come in from a day on the river, smelly and wet, stopping by the old general store, with nothing more on his mind than frying up his catch, and maybe stocking up a few supplies for the rustic mountain cabin he kept just north of town. He lived nestled high up in Oregon's Siskiyou Forest, and the market was the last post before open wilderness.

The end of the world had been on TV.

Jonah had been idly checking out the woman standing in-line in front of him – noticeably attractive, despite the deliberately frumpy flannel, heavy jacket, and worker's boots. Her hands were in her pockets, hiding her ring-finger, but the obvious effort to cover it all up suggested a married woman. Jonah was guessing a soldier's wife – a military bride accustomed to being on her own while her husband was deployed. You could tell she was used to fending off approving stares – although the one sideways glance she had spared to Jonah, with a brief, up-and-down appraisal, had also added the unconditional qualifier 'and out of your league'.

The clerk was absent. They had been standing in line for a couple of minutes, and the man waiting at the counter, a big burly guy in a hunting jacket and a beard, was becoming impatient. He rapped his knuckles loudly on the counter.

"Hey!" he shouted. "Anybody here?"

The door to the back suddenly opened, and the elderly gentleman who ran the place on weekends looked out at them wide-eyed. Behind him, a small portable TV was blaring the news.

"Oh Lord, I'm sorry folks," the clerk said, making no move towards the register. He looked at the three of them blankly.

"Oh my God," he said. "You don't know what's *happening*?"

Jonah exchanged glances with the other two standing in line, answering for the three of them with a bewildered shrug.

The clerk pulled the TV cord from the wall, and brought the little set out onto the counter, plugging it in underneath the cash-register. He turned the tube to face them.

The screen blinked to life.

Images of a war-zone.

Jonah's brows furrowed. "What is this?"

The old clerk eyed him grimly.

"This is live," he said. "This is New York."

Jonah blinked, uncertain whether to believe the images coming through on the tiny little screen.

On the day of the 911 attacks, Jonah had been a college kid working at a local department store. He'd shown up early, before dawn, driving an old clunker with no radio, and his supervisor – a rather stern, normally-composed older lady – had met him at the door, her eyes wide, vulnerable and frightened.

Jonah still remembered the moment vividly – he had followed her over to the TV & Electronics department – and there it was – on fifty different screens, from sixty-inch to table-top.

He felt a strange doubling back as he stared at the tiny little bulb-tube antique.

911 had been one thing – graphic – horrifying.

But it had been a couple of buildings.

This was...

Well..., the New York City skyline was burning.

Beside him, the woman in flannel was checking her phone, shaking her head, muttering under her breath.

"It can't be," she said. "My husband's in the Navy. He would have called."

She tapped at a couple of buttons on her phone, apparently getting no response. She looked around. The burly hunter pulled out his own phone, and tapped the screen.

"I've got nothing," he said, "It's fully charged. There's just no signal."

The clerk shrugged. "Service is spotty out here," he said. He nodded at Jonah, who pulled out his own antique, bordering-on-obsolete, flip-phone – which he'd actually got almost twelve years ago because it was done up in the old-style Star Trek 'communicator' design – and he still felt very futuristic with it in his pocket.

A technological caveman, Jonah had sent one text in his life – it had taken him ten minutes.

"Don't look at me," he said.

The woman was frowning at the TV. "Is this a cable station?"

"Broadcast," the clerk said. He tapped at the monitor behind his counter. "The Internet's down too."

For the moment, their only window to the outside world seemed to be the little black and white screen – with its thirty-pound chunk of glass stretching out bizarrely behind it, the thing had probably been in the back break-room for over thirty years – even Jonah had a flat screen.

The images were dark and indistinct. But it was clear that whole buildings were coming down – 911 a hundred times over. The Manhattan skyline was crumbling before their eyes.

"What's happening?" Jonah said, shaking his head. "Is it terrorists?"

The clerk glanced at him. "No. Not terrorists."

Jonah frowned. A hermit by nature, he had actually been holed-up just recently. He worked most of the season as a guide-pilot, but the recent rains had grounded any prospective charters – his trip out on the river today was his first time out of the cabin in two weeks. He hadn't even been on-line.

The audio feed on the little TV abruptly cut out, leaving only the strobing black and white images.

It was late dusk where they were – with three hours difference, New York was in darkness – a complete black-out.

Except where the city burned.

The view onscreen was from a chopper – a rough and broken POV – blinded by plumes of smoke and buffeted by strong winds.

And then suddenly the picture was staggered and spinning.

There was one brief shattered image – indecipherable – as if the chopper had somehow been physically struck in mid-air.

The video-feed went dark.

There was nothing else after that. The little screen went blank.

For several moments, the small group of them stood, staring at each other.

"Okay," the big burly fellow asked aloud, "what the hell was that?"

The clerk was shaking his head. "All I know is that it all went down literally within the last hour – and it was the whole damn city. And before the audio cut out, they said it was starting to happen everywhere."

"What do you mean everywhere?"

"*Everywhere*," the clerk said. "New York. L.A., Chicago... London, Paris – fuckin' Beijing."

But the big guy was shaking his head stubbornly.

"Oh come on. This doesn't even make any sense. What? Did every country in the world just go psycho overnight and suddenly decide to blow each other up?"

He turned to Jonah, as if for confirmation. Jonah stared back doubtfully.

"Wait a minute," the woman-in-flannel said. "*What's* 'happening everywhere'? What exactly did you see?"

The clerk blinked back at her, hesitant to put it into words.

"I... don't know *what* I saw," he stammered helplessly. "There were... *things*."

The big guy snorted derisive laughter.

"'*Things*'," he repeated. "Great."

He tossed twenty bucks for gas and groceries on the counter,

"My sister lives in L.A.," he said, "I've got a land-line at home. I'll give her a call."

Now he actually chuckled. "That's one of the benefits of living in the Northwest – no one ever wants to bomb Oregon."

He hiked his grocery bag over one shoulder and walked out, still tapping his phone, trying to raise a signal.

Jonah flipped back his own Star Trek screen to see if he could at least access voice-mail. Walking with his head down, he nearly tripped over the woman-in-flannel standing at the door, who was likewise trying to activate her own dead phone.

She looked up with a neutral shrug. "Nothing."

Jonah held the door for her and followed her outside.

He almost bumped into her again as she suddenly stopped cold, her breath catching in an abbreviated gasp.

Nearly stumbling, he reflexively caught her shoulders in his hands, before he looked up to see what was the matter.

Standing in the parking lot, just between the store and gas-pump, was a dinosaur.

In fact, it looked like a *T. rex*.

It was eating the burly gentleman who had walked out before them.

The five-foot head tossed back the still-kicking mouthful the way Jonah had seen a pelican toss down a flopping fish.

There was a wet, gulping swallow, and then the beast turned its attention to them.

Its head cocked, fixating like a hawk.

Jonah froze, unsure whether to move.

Beside him, however, the woman-in-flannel pulled a pistol from her deceptively frumpy jacket. Feet spread, demonstrating obvious training, she began to shoot – firing off an entire clip.

The first sting startled the beast – it snapped at empty air after each successive shot.

Then with a low growl, it turned to them again, apparently making the association – and appearing displeased.

Jaws gaping, it charged.

CHAPTER 2

That was another thing different from 911 – the impression that it was all very far away.

This was right here and right now.

Jonah was flashing instant recalls of recent headlines – the latest batch of UFO/Bigfoot stuff that had been making the rounds – the sort of stuff that always popped up during slow news-weeks, whenever no one particularly important was shooting at each other.

Not that he had been paying attention, anyway. Sequestered up in his cabin, Jonah had mostly hidden himself away from all that – as he liked it, world events tended to pass him by.

That is, until one day they came right up to your door.

The teeth moved towards them at startling speed.

Jonah had read that Tyrannosaurus possessed a particularly destructive bite – several tons of bite-force, an almost mechanically-reinforced, shock-absorbing skull and neck, with a jaw lined by armor-piercing teeth that bit out huge holes.

Three steps and it would be upon them.

The woman-in-frumpy-flannel, her smoking pistol still in hand, turned and ducked back inside the store.

Half a heartbeat later, Jonah followed.

The clerk turned wide-eyed as they burst back inside – he'd heard the gunshots – and Jonah started to shout a warning. But the point was almost instantly moot as the beast struck the doorway behind them.

Jonah had seen footage of elephants rampaging through towns in Africa – drunk off of fermented fallen mangos – four and five-ton animals that bulldozed human-constructs like paper.

T. rex weighed what? Eight tons? More?

The entire store-front collapsed as the beast crashed through. The clerk was crushed right along with the architecture, even as the store alarm blared its warning.

Pinned under a collapsed cross-beam, the old man struggled briefly.

Then the massive jaws came down, rooting him out, yanking him free of the debris like a crow grabbing after the early-morning worm.

The jaws snapped the clerk in half. Another pelican toss, and both pieces disappeared down the cavernous gullet.

Then the beast's eyes turned to where Jonah and the woman-in-flannel had been knocked to the floor. The crocodile-jaws seemed to *smile*.

"Out back," Jonah said, his voice a terse whisper. "My truck."

The woman gave him another quick appraisal, but nodded, and the two of them scrambled out through the stockroom, stumbling in the dark for the rear exit.

Behind them, there was a loud crash – the rex moving to follow.

And above them, the timber began to creak. The primary support post had been taken out with the front wall, and now the roof was starting to pull apart.

That was actually what gave them the break they needed. They burst out the rear exit into the parking lot, just as the store collapsed.

The tumbling lumber piled on top of the hapless rex itself.

For the first time, it ROARED – a foghorn blast of pain and outrage, as it was abruptly buried in wood and sheet-rock.

Jonah had a good-sized four-wheel – a Bronco – built for the rough terrain where he lived – but it was not exactly known for speed, and he still had his boat hitched to the back.

But there was no time to unhook it now. Jonah slid into the driver's seat and cranked-up the engine.

The woman-in-flannel stared at the trailer dubiously. "My car's out front..."

But she was cut off by another foghorn bellow as the rex was rising to its feet behind them.

Muttering and cursing, she climbed into the passenger seat.

Looking over her shoulder, she slapped a fresh clip into her pistol.

Jonah eyed her as he shifted into gear. "How many of those do you carry?"

She locked the clip into place. "Just drive."

The rex was irritably shaking free of the collapsed rubble and there was a decided impatience in its posture as its eyes found them once again.

Jonah squealed tires as the truck dragged the trailer out of the parking lot.

Beside him, the woman leaned out her window and opened fire.

She apparently had pretty good aim – based on the rex's reaction, every bullet hit.

And it clearly didn't like getting shot.

With another ear-splitting roar, it launched after them, jaws agape.

"Hey, lady...?" Jonah ventured.

"Naomi," the woman answered, slapping still another clip into her pistol.

"Okay, 'Naomi'? Maybe you wanna stop shooting at it? I think you're pissing it off."

She glared. "I was trying to hit its goddamn eyes."

But she nevertheless pocketed her pistol.

Which might have been too little, too late.

As Jonah looked in his side mirror, all he saw was a jagged, widening maw.

And with the drag of the boat, it was gaining.

With a sudden lurch, the teeth latched onto the trailer, biting through the stern of Jonah's   fishing boat like a shark hitting a surfboard – the wood shattered into kindling.

The jaws clamped down, and the sudden tug-and-jerk felt like their trailer had been hit by a freight train.

For a moment, Jonah thought they were simply going to be tossed off the road.

But like the tail of a lizard, the trailer-hitch snapped, and the truck broke free.

The rex shook its catch side-to-side like a bulldog, before realizing its real quarry had escaped.

Stamping its feet, it came after them again.

Heart pounding, Jonah floored the accelerator – without the weight of the trailer, they picked up speed.

Naomi was looking over her shoulder. "Step on it," she said. "It's following."

Jonah stomped the gas, taking the road into town.

CHAPTER 3

For a massive tank of a beast, the rex kept pace with the Bronco quite nicely, thank you – especially as Jonah was obligated to slow down around the tight mountain curves, sliding precariously over sheer-drops in the dark.

Siskiyou Pass, Oregon, was a small township hidden in the forest along the Rogue River – but it had a Sheriff's Department – presumably with weapons. Beyond that, Jonah really had no plan.

Coming out of the woods, you hit a couple of miles of flat road before you reached the small ridge that overlooked the residential areas – and also where you found most of the official city offices.

When they touched-down on level ground, Jonah stomped the accelerator, at last gaining distance.

Naomi was leaning out the window, looking back.

"This guy's stubborn, isn't he?"

Although losing ground, the rex showed no signs of stopping. Jonah would have figured such a big animal would have gassed out by now, but it charged after them single-mindedly, like a galloping rhino, even as they finally began to pull away.

They had left the beast almost a mile behind when the glow of streetlights signaled the town of Siskiyou Pass just ahead.

Except, as they turned off the mountain road onto the ridge that comprised Main Street, they realized that it wasn't the streetlights at all.

The town was on fire.

Just like New York – just like on television.

"What the hell?" Jonah eased up on the gas, glancing nervously over his shoulder for their pursuer.

Naomi suddenly screamed aloud, "Watch out!"

Jonah turned back just as the dark shape suddenly jumped out in front of them.

Adrenaline shot through him and his foot jerked to stomp the brakes – it was the size of a man – but then he saw the teeth – and the claws.

Instead, he floored the gas again.

They hit the thing dead center and drove over, the Bronco's heavy wheels absorbing the shock like a speed bump.

Naomi had her pistol out again. "What the hell was THAT?"

But Jonah knew – he'd recognized it readily enough – the sickle-claw on the foot was a dead giveaway – a dromaeosaur – like Deinonychus, or Velociraptor – a dinosaur.

Another dinosaur.

A moment later, two more came leaping in from either side.

Jonah swerved, knocking one of them aside, but the other latched on to the passenger side of the cab.

A fanged muzzle peered inside and a clawed talon reached in through the window.

Naomi shot the thing twice in the face. With a stuttered, bird-like screech, it fell away, and Jonah swerved again, catching the falling body with the wheel. There was another squawk and a wholly satisfying crunch as they left the thing flopping in the road behind them like a run-over cat.

The two of them exchanged a wide-eyed glance.

"Are you okay?" Jonah asked.

Naomi nodded, holding up her still-smoking pistol.

There were more of the things on the street now – attracted by the sound of their engine, they came bounding in from between the burning buildings.

"Jesus, that's the Sheriff's office," Naomi realized. "It's trashed – it's gone."

The import struck them together. There was no help to be found here – they were on their own.

They had to run.

"Get us out of here," Naomi said.

The problem now, however, was that they were trapped.

As they reached the end of Main Street, Jonah skidded to a stop.

The sickle-claws were blocking the road.

A lot of them.

Jonah nodded at the pistol in Naomi's lap.

"How many bullets have you got left?"

She frowned. "This is my last clip," she said.

And with that, she leaned out the window and began firing away.

Once again, her aim was remarkable – she dropped two of them in quick succession, causing the others to scatter.

Naomi pulled back into the cab, cranking up her window.

"Go!" she said.

Jonah hit the gas, lurching through the intersection.

The reprieve, however, was too short. Within seconds, the sickle-claws were back upon them.

As a kid, Jonah's parents had taken him upstate to the drive-thru 'Wild Life Safari' – they had stopped on the tour, and a lion had briefly climbed up on the hood of their family Sedan, hopping over the roof in two quick bounds – Jonah remembered the animal's thudding weight as it padded above their heads. He remembered thinking how easily it could get in if it really wanted to.

There was a heavy blow as one of the foot-claws struck the Bronco's windshield, starting a long spidery crack.

A second set of claws hit the passenger window. Naomi simply shot through it, even as a third creature joined the first on the hood, banging away at the windshield.

Another couple of blows and the protective glass would cave in.

Jonah hit the brakes, sending both creatures tumbling out into the road.

Revving the engine, he leaped the Bronco forward, over the top of the both of them – two speed bumps this time.

The rest of the pack, however, had regrouped and surrounded them.

There was a momentary pause as both sides waited on the other.

And then, apparently satisfied with their advantage, the sickle-claws began to advance.

Jonah had heard they were supposed to be smart – and it did seem they actually *savored* the moment – as a group, they seemed to pause, spreading their claws, hanging on the instant before the strike.

But the strike never came.

Abruptly, the sickle-claws simply vanished.

In a heartbeat, they disappeared into the surrounding dark like a school of fish.

Jonah struggled to see – the flame played tricks with the shadows.

The things had scattered – sort of like how small predators will abandon a kill when something larger came along.

From around the burning buildings, came something larger.

A LOT larger – even bigger than the *T. rex*.

Another sickle-claw – only this one was pushing thirty-feet tall.

And where the eyes of the others reflected back the yellow firelight like a pack of wolves, this creature's irises glowed emerald green.

Jonah glanced at Naomi, who looked glumly down at her diminutive pistol with its few remaining shots.

Not to be outdone, the *T. rex* chose that moment to finally appear behind them on the main road.

The big rex had settled into a walk, but now that it saw them, it stepped back up into a charge.

Instantly territorial, the giant sickle-claw snarled, letting out a hooting bellow – a base rendition of the birdlike screech – stamping its feet and brandishing four-foot claws.

The rex never slowed.

Shifting targets, it charged teeth-first into its challenger.

The sickle-claw leaped forward to meet it, the vicious foot-claw digging for the belly.

The two beasts crashed together right over the roof of the cab.

Naomi smacked Jonah smartly across his shoulder – right at that spot where the tendons meet the bone.

"Go!" she said, fiercely. "Go *now*!"

Nearly dead-armed, and momentarily blinded by the involuntary sting of tears, Jonah punched the gas again, shooting the Bronco out from under the two battling brutes, turning off Main Street onto the ridge that overlooked the entire town.

But as he pulled up to the edge, Jonah was forced to stop.

The fire was worse down below.

The residential district was basically gone.

And in the streets, they could see more of those *things*. They were everywhere.

Naomi was shaking her head, as if physically rejecting the image.

"My God, I *live* down there."

Behind them, however, their escape window was fading fast – the rex had the sickle-claw by the neck, and it seemed as if that had already settled the matter.

Jonah would have actually expected the clawed beast to make more of a fight, but the rex had simply bulldogged it – he'd once seen a coyote do the same thing to a large bobcat – the thick canine neck shaking the more-slender feline like a rag-doll.

Then there were those rex jaws – what it bit, it bit *out*.

The sickle-claw was down, and clearly done, but the rex's jaws remained locked around its throat.

Jonah backed the Bronco up from the ridge, looking over his shoulder into the woods.

The town below was impassible.

But his cabin was high up in the mountains.

If they could just get past this little road-block.

Without another word, Jonah turned the Bronco back around. He clicked on his brights and revved the engine, leaning on the horn and charging back the way they had come – face-first into the snarling rex.

Naomi's nails dug into his already-wounded shoulder. "What are you *doing*?"

Ignoring her, he simply swerved up onto the sidewalk. The Bronco scraped the side of the burning building as they passed.

The rex reared up, a chunk of meat in its jaws, and stared balefully after the retreating taillights.

Jonah could see it in his mirror, looking after them – he waited to see if it would follow.

Instead, it swallowed its mouthful, bent down and took another bite of its fallen rival.

Jonah let out a breath – but stepped on the gas anyway.

The road led up into the mountains – his cabin several miles beyond.

As they put distance behind them, he slowed enough to rub his throbbing arm.

Beside him, Naomi's eyes narrowed. "That didn't *hurt*, did it?"

Jonah glanced at her sideways. "I'm fine," he said.

Naomi pocketed her pistol.

"So," she said, "what's *your* name?"

CHAPTER 4

That was how it started out in the sticks.

In the cities, it was much worse.

Per-capita, there were a lot fewer survivors.

New York was first – a preamble – late night on the East Coast – pre-dawn in Europe – a declaration of war before hostilities erupted almost simultaneously across the entire world.

In context, what went on in the sticks, was rather like screaming at a mouse, right before being trampled by a herd of elephants.

But in both cases, it was all of a sudden – no warning – and no one saw it coming.

In San Francisco, Doctor Rosa Holland, MD, *had*, of course, heard recent rumors, and she knew all the most popular urban legends had been resurfacing – the Bermuda Triangle, Area 51.

In this case, 'Monster Island' – supposed leaked footage, purporting to show living dinosaurs.

On the news, various 'experts' had widely discredited its authenticity. Inundated at work, Rosa had only caught it in passing, but personally suspected some Hollywood promotion, and found it rather ridiculous that the item had made the news at all – it was ironic that, in a day of such increased possibility, you could no longer even be sure of reality. Coverage like this on TV didn't help.

'Genetic engineering' had been added to the lexicon of the tin-foil-hat crowd – 'Monster Island' dated back to the era of the first cloned sheep.

Rosa remembered 'Daisy' – pictured standing next to its genetic parent/twin – ostensibly, just a regular-old sheep. But it had ignited excited conversation at the time – at least one well-known pundit had suggested that this could mean the end of extinction – or at least put it within the reach of human hands.

For herself, Rosa had considered more practical applications. She had volunteered in a lot of third-world countries, and she had seen a lot of war, disease, and atrocities of all kinds. But it was starvation that was always the worst – the most inexorable, the most insidious – the most awful to witness. There were places on Earth that were like nothing less than never-ending death camps.

Of all the atrocities, it was also the most unnecessary.

Ironies abounded. One of the primary motivators in early genetic research was to create better, more plentiful food – larger crops and livestock. Certainly a sensible enough goal – something that might actually go a long way towards *solving* some of the horrors she had witnessed.

But in her own home town, the entire concept had become paranoiac fodder. And drip-fed through the press, activist-style – salaciously, with buzzwords like 'growth hormones' and 'Frankenfish' – it had become its own conspiracy theory.

Rosa found it amazing how scientific efforts that had extended human lifespan well into the seventies – higher in the healthiest Western countries – were now being blamed for the ill-health of those seventy-year-olds – everything from cancer to heart-disease.

Or Rosa's favorite – 'obesity'.

As a Doctor, she recognized that you had to die of something. She would take obesity in old-age over starvation as a child.

It was easy to get angry over pretentious Western sensibilities and priorities.

Rosa had been questioning a lot about her life lately.

Her job *hurt* her.

She was in the business of helping people. But when you did that for a living, all you ever saw were people who needed it – people who were injured, sick, or dying.

Rosa had, of course, known about all the divorce, alcoholism, and suicide rates associated with her chosen profession. But she hadn't *appreciated* it. You never do when you're not living it.

She was still a young woman – and a pretty one – but the frown on her face rarely faded anymore. Whether angry or sad, or just exhausted, her life was a litany of second-hand suffering every single day – even for people she *could* help.

And then she would come home alone.

No time for anything else.

Was she really ready to spend her life this way?

All this had been on her mind while she was walking home that day – taking the walkway from her hospital to the public parking garage across the street. She crossed with a couple coming from the hospital – a man who was not quite old enough to be the father of the rather rough-looking woman who walked beside him – who might have been showing early signs of being pregnant.

A new welfare-mother-in-waiting.

Rosa sighed. Boy, was that cynical.

Still, she knew the type – her dress once would have been called 'Earthy', but in modern days, it had morphed into something darker – some weird Wiccan-offshoot, counter-culture of the sort most heavily predominant in L.A. – but was clearly migrating north.

Los Angeles was Charles Manson town, after all. Weird, acid-induced cults had always lurked in the background. And judging by this particular woman's Manson-family style-statement, it was a fashion that was coming 'round again.

Rosa tried not to look over her shoulder as they walked just behind her in the parking garage.

As they reached the elevator, the girl that worked the coffee stand looked up from her I-pod.

That was another daily depressant – the sight of that poor mousy girl, locked-up all day in that tiny little booth right next to the elevator on the ground floor.

She always looked up at you like a puppy in a kennel – desperate for any kind of attention – practically daring to be robbed – surrounded all day by car-exhaust and concrete.

Okay, Rosa thought, stepping into the elevator, there were always worse jobs.

It was almost dark – nearly nine o'clock. She had put in almost fourteen hours. And she had also had to blow off a date – a set-up from one of those Internet sites, pushed on her by a friend.

When she realized she would be working late, she sent the guy a text.

Before she even finished, she got a message from her friend – a college roomie named Suzy, who she hadn't seen in six-months – one of those life-support relationships kept in stasis by a series of e-mails and text-messages.

Suzy's message was accompanied by a frowny-face: "You blew him off, didn't you?"

Rosa sent a frowny-face back, to which Suzy replied, "You're a workaholic control-freak."

"Yeah, but I'm hot," Rosa responded.

Suzy: "You're also over thirty. Sell-by-date."

Rosa hadn't answered. Suzy wasn't exactly psychic – this would be the third time she'd broken dates with this guy. They'd been exchanging messages for three weeks, and she still hadn't even met the man.

But now she saw she had gotten a text back from him.

"Have a nice life."

The elevator reached the roof-top floor of the parking lot and Rosa stepped out with her head down, looking at her phone, debating whether to respond.

Thus preoccupied, she didn't immediately notice what loomed right over the horizon.

She saw it first out of her peripherals, not yet grabbing her full attention – she simply had the impression of a really dark cloud, indicative of an oncoming storm. And in a way, that's exactly what it was.

She even ignored the reverberation in her feet at first. Living in San Francisco, she had adapted a blasé attitude towards even fairly rough tremors – anything below 3.5 didn't warrant anything other than a louder speaking-voice until the rumbling passed – to even mention it was to label yourself a tourist.

Human compartmentalization, Rosa thought, as she steadied her footing. More irony. The entire West Coast was a volcanic runway – one that scientists insisted would inevitably erupt – maybe in ten-thousand years, or maybe tomorrow – but there really WAS a dragon under the mountain.

But people that lived there – herself included – put it blithely out of their heads. Her grandparents had lived their whole lives in the shadow of Washington State's Mt. Rainier – rated the most dangerous volcano on the continent.

And everybody always looked shocked when the volcano finally blew.

In her hand, her phone seemed to have lost its signal.

She was standing there, tapping at her screen when she felt another heavy tremor vibrating up through the street.

Rosa paused.

This felt... different.

Another rumble.

It wasn't like a 'quake', really – it was more like an impact tremor – heavy – staccato – repeating. There in the parking lot, a number of car alarms started going off.

Rosa actually stumbled off balance. Reflexively, she grabbed the railing that overlooked the thruway below.

People in the street had started to run.

For the first time, Rosa looked up – directly to the black cloud that blocked out the sky.

That was when she realized that this storm was alive.

It stared down at her from better than twenty-stories high – with bright, glowing green eyes.

And damned if it didn't *look* like a dinosaur – just like out of all that discredited leaked footage.

But Rosa shook her head defiantly – *rationally* – it simply couldn't be – it was too BIG.

Way, WAY too big – there was nothing like that – no dinosaur – no *animal* – that ever *lived*.

Therefore, that meant 'nothing' was walking west on California Avenue towards her right now.

She felt the very real impact of its steps, shaking the ground.

The impossible skull suddenly split – opening into a yawning, ragged fissure, ridged in blades, like razor-sharp lava-rock.

From the volcanic maw came a ROAR.

Stumbling back from the railing, Rosa held her ears against the deafening bellow.

Through the ringing in her ears, another sound echoed, small and helpless beneath the false thunder – the sound of screams.

The crowds had panicked – people were running blindly in the streets.

In the roads, traffic was paralyzed, and Rosa could actually hear the metallic crumpling of cars, crunching like peanut shells beneath the creature's tread – their unfortunate occupants pulped like grapes.

And towering above it all was...

... what...?

The Dragon under the Mountain?

A monster.

Absurdly, Rosa almost laughed – because the image she summoned up from her childhood was 'The Beast' – The Beast from The Pit.

She'd been raised traditional Catholic, but she'd thought college and medical training had erased most of that. Yet standing there, struggling for less than a minute with the impossible apparition that confronted her, she was already going Biblical.

Then, Rosa turned and looked across the rest of the horizon.

It was the view she walked by every day – high from the hillside, looking down into the city – she was used to the low hum and the lights – city sounds she tuned out like crickets.

Tonight, the glow of city lights was not neon – tonight, San Francisco burned.

And the burning skyline had been joined by a range of living mountains.

Some were long-necked giants, with heads careening a thousand feet into the sky – others were horned and armored dreadnoughts.

But most of them were like the dragon-beast that loomed before her now.

She couldn't guess how many – they were spread across the entire city.

To her credit, Rosa remained calm – detached, even – just as she would when slicing into a human abdomen – delivering an otherwise ghastly mortal wound under carefully controlled conditions.

From her vantage atop the parking garage, her observations were professionally cool and collected.

Rosa was strictly an indoor-girl, but she loved animals – as a kid, that meant a lot of trips to the zoo, and she remembered the first time she saw a live elephant.

As a tiny person then, herself, she specifically recalled the way it moved – sort of an odd slow-motion – but that was actually an illusion created by greater mass moving at a living speed.

She had noticed the same thing years later, driving in the mountains, when a herd of elk had crossed the road in front of her – in contrast to the sprightly deer that darted between cars along the outskirts of the urban areas, *these* animals were the size of horses, carrying their weight in that same illusory slow-motion – yet moved with the same bouncing spring, tossing eight-hundred pounds in the air in a fawn-like bound.

But the closest analogue to what she saw now, was the slow rumble of an avalanche she had once seen skiing – fortunately from the opposite ridge – it was as if the mountain had suddenly shaken itself like a wet-dog, and a layer of snow had simply dumped off its back. You could see it coming for a mile, racing at breakneck speed.

Or perhaps the eruption of Mount Saint Helens – another active volcano in the Cascade chain – in a single blast, a quarter of the mountain had simply collapsed off to one side, rolling down into the valley.

What Rosa saw today was like that.

Only it was in something alive.

And it could SEE you.

It was AFTER you.

That was the second thing, Rosa realized.

This was no rambling amble through town.

Make no mistake, THIS was a rampage.

These living mountains were smashing the buildings in front of them to dust. They were destroying everything in their path.

Rosa was reminded of rhinos on the Savannah, which were known to stamp out fires – there was more than one evening campsite that had their dinner rudely interrupted – rhinos could exceed two or three tons – and they were known to do the same thing to nests of stinging ants.

This was the same sort of deliberate effort.

Anyone inside any of the crumbling skyscrapers would be crushed into nothing. On 911, when the World Trade Center had come crashing down, it had not even left bodies.

The Twin Towers had fallen in that same false-slow-motion. Rosa remembered reporters on the street starting to run as they realized the concrete avalanche was cascading down on top of them.

Like a Tsunami – charging across miles in moments – and then suddenly it was upon you.

Rosa had met a young man who had survived the Thailand Tsunami of 2004 – he had been laying on the beach and then suddenly he was being crushed by something like the weight of a house. He had somehow popped to the surface, and been pulled out of the rushing wave by a woman perched on a third-story roof – together they had fielded other survivors out of the backwash. Rosa had treated the young man for part of a finger he had lost in the incident.

He said the wave had been upon him in seconds.

Rosa looked around in sudden realization at the concrete tomb she stood on top of – even as the colossus was now towering directly overhead, staring down with its glowing green eyes.

The tsunami was upon her.

She turned, staggering, as the worsening tremors threatened to knock her from her feet.

Ignoring the elevator, she ran for the stairs.

She had just made the second story when the parking structure was hit from above.

Around her, the concrete and steel began to crumble.

She made one more story before the floor beneath her simply gave way.

For one crazy moment, she clung, dangling from the railing, before that tore away as well, dropping her into the basement-level below, along with the collapsing stairwell.

Something struck her head and the world went dim.

Her last thought before successive blows knocked her unconscious was that she was going to die.

She actually took a second to get ready – that Catholic upbringing again.

Then for an indeterminate time, the world was simply dark.

The next thing she was aware of was hands upon her, and the sound of grating rubble.

She felt herself carried, and remembered being gingerly sat down between two parked cars.

When she finally blinked awake, she recognized a nurse from her own ward – a young, painfully-dedicated woman named Julie – 'Nurse Price' – whose heart bled for every skinned knee – who Rosa herself had predicted would never last.

Julie was tending to her cuts, apparently with a first-aid kit stashed next to the fire-extinguisher, dabbing alcohol and applying gauze.

"Doctor Holland? Are you okay?"

Rosa sat up painfully, looking around the small circle, sitting among the assorted rubble.

The entire garage had collapsed. The basement level was underground, and now a cratered opening nearly forty-feet above their heads was their only window – that and the remaining stairwell, filled with rubble from the four stories above.

Rosa turned to the group of eyes that blinked back at her in the dark – she recognized the girl from the coffee shop, as well as the young security guard that worked nights at the garage. There was an older couple – likewise battered in the collapse, and who Julie was tending to beside her.

Also among them, was the couple Rosa had seen crossing the street – the guy with the future welfare-mom.

"Bud and Allison pulled you out of the rubble," Julie said. "They saved your life."

Rosa blinked, still a bit groggy, and hoped her own finished thought didn't show on her face.

She regarded the two of them sincerely. "Thank you," she said.

The man – 'Bud' – nodded, but said nothing, simply huddling back, glancing nervously up at the still-crumbling ceiling.

Overhead was darkness – Rosa could see stars.

She could also still feel the staccato quaking in the ground – impact tremors from massive weight – and the roar of thunder that was not thunder – echoes of primal rage.

This storm was not passing – it had settled on the city, growing in strength.

Rosa wondered what must be going on in the streets.

By some miracle, the little group of them had fallen through the cracks. In terms of survivability, there were critters that survived in a field under a rototiller – bugs, worms, mice – fragile life-forms that had somehow missed the churning blades.

But that wasn't the way to bet.

"What's *happening*?" Rosa whispered, as if the sound of her voice would bring the beasts down upon them.

She looked at the blinking circle around her.

No one answered.

But whatever it was, it wasn't over.

CHAPTER 5

In San Francisco, it lasted for ten days.

The small group of them hunkered down in their little impromptu bunker, waiting out the blitz.

San Fran was one of many big military hubs along the California coast – the invasion of dragons did not go unanswered.

The counter-strike was prompt, and soon enough, there came the sound of jet-engines.

And with the roar of the war-birds, came the bombs.

Officially, all hell had broken loose.

For better than a week, America's Finest battled the Beasts from The Pit for possession of the city.

By the third straight-day – feeling every impact, every explosion, breathing the stench of burning smoke – hearing the gale-storm roars of the outraged beasts – Rosa was beginning to wonder if anyone in the city *besides* themselves might have survived.

Really – how *could* they?

Rosa had been waiting for a lull – that was the part when the aid-groups came in – just like the ones she had done so much volunteer-work for – they waited until the principals took a break from killing each other, and then she and her fellow bleeding-hearts would go scrape up all the human wreckage.

This time, however, there was no lull.

Sometime early on, Rosa stopped believing in rescue either – and actually felt a touch of resentment – she had spent her life giving aid, but there would be no FEMA coming for *her*.

Ten days eating out of vending machines, breaking into cars – the coffee-girl had a week's stash of cookies and crackers. They had stored water from a fire-hose in janitorial buckets.

And all along, they could hear it – all around – just above – waiting for the moment when the eye of the storm might finally decide to descend directly down upon them.

Whether dragon-beast behemoth, or stray missile – the blades of the rototiller were still turning.

In the main part of the city, once the skyscrapers had started cascading down, for most people, it was simply over – it was not a question of waiting out the storm.

And if you made to the street, all there was left was to run.

The screaming in the streets, however, had not lasted much past that first night.

There was the difference from a Tsunami – once it rolled over, the wave didn't circle back to finish the job.

Another seemingly deliberate action – like rhinos stamping out ants.

Rosa knew their little group had somehow been missed, but didn't yet realize how near a thing it was.

In fact, they knew almost nothing at all – they didn't even have radio after the second day – and all they got from the initial reports was that things weren't any better anywhere else.

And so the group of them hid away in the cracks.

Go back far enough, Rosa thought, and humanity's humble roots were not much more than that – tiny mice, hiding in their little holes. And in the course of a single day, they had come full circle.

Eight of them – out of a city of eight-hundred thousand.

Or initially eight. The older couple had both been injured badly – the husband had gotten the worst of it, having thrown himself on top of his wife as the stairway above started to collapse.

He had only lived for a short while, dying sometime before dawn after that first night. He had lain discreetly, under a plastic seat-cover for the next two days – that is, until he began to stink in the heat, and they had carried him up the surviving steps to the street level, where he had lain ever since.

The old man's name had been 'Larry' – or 'Uncle Larry' to the children in their neighborhood, since he and his wife couldn't have children of their own. Rosa knew this because his wife – 'Aunt Rita' – sporting two broken legs, and a great deal of pain to go with her fresh grief, had spent a lot of time talking about him in the days since.

Julie had been in constant attendance to the old lady – she was a nurse, and here were people to help. Here in a crisis, she was the very caricature of Florence Nightingale, right there in the garage.

Rosa had worked enough disasters to recognize the psychology – people took on roles – shielding themselves with the balm of activity and purpose – that all-important distraction. Rosa watched, semi-amused as Julie all but duplicated her morning rounds at the hospital – tending to the old lady – to all of them, including Rosa herself – checking on every last scrape and cut.

Then there was the poor girl from the coffee shop – with her pathetic little label-maker name-tag – 'Jamie'. On the second day, Rosa had found her in the corner, crying.

Her cat, she said, was home alone – and then apparently unable to continue, had burst into helpless tears.

Rosa had almost laughed – in the face of the world literally exploding around them, it was at once absurd, yet at the same time, the thought nearly brought tears to Rosa's own eyes – the tiny, helpless little thing – a much-loved pet that depended on you for everything – frightened and wondering where to find you when the end came.

And then throw in the fact that a cat was apparently all this young girl had.

On the other end, there was the kid – the security guard – 'Jeremy' – also with an identifying name-tag – Rosa could tell he was just dying to save the day.

"No," he had told her, when Rosa asked, "they wouldn't let me carry a gun."

Mostly, he simply moved around a lot – evidently from an urge to be proactive – he just didn't have a clue what to do. So instead, he burned all that energy pacing back and forth in the small space. He seemed to hover over the rest of them, like a self-appointed guard dog – an attentive fox-terrier.

He had also expressed particular concern over Nurse Julie – who had rolled her eyes in Rosa's direction.

Rosa sighed. Men were always men.

The quietest member of their little group – excepting a few loud bouts of morning sickness – was Bud's lady companion, Allison.

She was an attractive woman, albeit in a hardened, dangerous way. Rosa couldn't guess her age – she bore the sort of dark circles under her eyes that would make a nineteen-year-old look forty.

Of course, being pregnant didn't help. Rosa recalled her own uncharitable thoughts right before she'd learned the woman had saved her life.

Still, Rosa had seen a lot of the type – trashy and knocked-up – the kind that brought *all* the drama. It wasn't surprising she would be cool in a crisis – she probably wasn't afraid of a fist-fight in a bar, either.

And they always seemed attended to by a certain type of guy – usually after a long line of the other kind.

Rosa felt a moment's pity for the man who sat beside her – the one *not* responsible for those dark circles – but who would certainly be paying for them.

Rosa had seen a lot of Bud's type too.

She wondered, but did not ask if he was the father.

Cynical, she thought.

But she supposed it was something to think about – better that, than the reality around them.

Because the reality was, pretty soon they were going to die here.

In all the disasters Rosa had worked – even in hurricanes, even in the floods – even war-zones – she had operated out of protected areas – always just a chopper-flight away from safe-ground, far away from demilitarized madness.

This was something different. There wasn't even any direction they could reasonably *go*.

The bombing raids alternated with missile strikes. There was no effort to preserve the architecture – the city was a total loss – they were just trying to take the beasts down.

From the bottom of the collapsed basement of the garage, they couldn't see much of the battle – they didn't know how many planes – how many creatures – or even what effect the missiles had on them.

And somewhere in the middle, Rosa wasn't sure if the behemoths weren't just killing each other as well.

At least one plane had crashed within their view – almost right above them. There were monsters in the sky as well – nothing they could clearly see – but things that were bat-winged and very BIG.

The jet had landed nearly on top of them – it sounded like it hit the tarmac somewhere beyond the neighboring block. In the garage, they could smell smoke from burning fuel.

That had been on the last day of the bombings.

All at once, the air-campaign ceased. The military retreated.

And whether that was cause or effect – Rosa wasn't sure which came first – whatever had hit the city, seemed to have receded as well.

Just as abruptly as the siege had started, the storm above seemed to have abated – no more thundering roars – no more earthquake-footsteps.

As suddenly as it began, it all just stopped.

But it wasn't until the second day after that, when they first dared creep back up towards the surface.

CHAPTER 6

The stairway to the street level was mostly preserved – the elevator shaft had deflected the bulk of the collapsing upper-stories off to one side.

But looking up the narrow path that remained, Rosa was still reluctant.

She recognized that psychology too – the paralysis that kept you from acting to save your own life.

As if to spite herself, she finally brought it up to the others.

"We need to at least see what's up there," she said. "Maybe we can get out of here." She looked around at their little group. "Anyone with me?"

Bud had started to rise but Allison's hand latched onto his shoulder, pulling him back down.

He had glanced at Rosa, who nodded understanding.

Julie stood up. "I'll go," she said.

Upon hearing that, Jeremy stood as well. His eyes were wide and nervous, but he swallowed determinedly. "Me too," he said.

Running over to the fire-house, he broke the glass canister next to it, pulling out the fire-ax. Wielding it like a club he turned back, his teeth-set.

Rosa and Julie exchanged looks.

"You know," Rosa said, "we're just going to take a quick look – maybe just the two of us."

Jeremy started to protest, but Rosa reached out and took his ax.

"Here, I'll just take that with me, thank you."

Jeremy frowned uncertainly, but subsided.

Allison, however stepped forward. In her hand was a semi-automatic pistol.

"Here," she said. "Take this with you."

Rosa regarded those dark circles once again.

"You didn't mention you had this," she said.

"It didn't come up," Allison said. She eyed Rosa seriously. "I want it back."

"Here," Julie said. "I'll take it."

She tossed her nurse's ponytail, cocking the pistol. "My dad made me take lessons." She glanced at Jeremy meaningfully. "I've also got a brown-belt in Kenpo."

Rosa looked up to the empty sky, summoning courage.

"Okay," she said. "Let's go."

The stairway was narrow, with the weight of rubble held in check by crossed girders – but Rosa knew any slight shift in weight could quite easily shake the rubble loose and they would be crushed.

She wondered if they were being foolish, and again felt that impulse to just sit tight.

But their little hidey-hole was only the illusion of safety and she knew it.

Even so, stepping out onto the street-level, out from the shelter of their stairway, she felt incredibly vulnerable and exposed – the morning sun was like a prison spotlight.

Julie climbed up beside her. Perched on the pile of rubble that had been the parking garage and the thruway, the two of them looked out upon the ruined city.

That was when Rosa realized how truly fortunate they had been.

The shattered skyline no longer even resembled San Francisco – no structure over five stories remained standing.

They stood there, just absorbing the TOTALITY of it – a city of eight-hundred thousand people – utterly wiped away.

You couldn't get rid of cockroaches so completely.

And as they made their way to a vantage point atop their little mountain of rubble, Rosa saw the monsters actually had *not* gone.

They lay scattered among the ruins – massive bodies, torn and cannibalized.

Nothing seemed to be living in the entire city.

Rosa wondered what it was that had killed these beasts. She could see damage from munitions fire – bombs and missiles.

But the majority of the wounds seemed to be caused by tooth and claw.

And while, certainly, these giant corpses had been fed upon like carrion, Rosa could see that many of these wounds had bled.

They HAD been killing each other.

It didn't even make sense – no animals behaved this way – this was rabid.

Whatever made them, made them mad.

Looking out on the city-scape of scattered carcasses, Rosa wondered if it was all of them, or if these were just the ones left behind.

And for the first time, she wondered what might be happening beyond the city. Until now, that had been a psychological investment she simply couldn't afford.

Just like wondering what the cause of it all might have been.

There had been nothing in the leaked 'Monster Island' footage to account for all this. Even a *T. rex* would have been biting at the ankles of the creatures that had descended upon her city.

Of course, Aunt Rita had her own ideas – in her world, it was just a simple, old-fashioned, religious-style Apocalypse.

For Rosa's part, the Catholic schoolgirl in her was perfectly willing to accept that the descriptions matched. Monsters and abominations? What else would you call them?

Despite her injuries, and despite the loss of her husband, the old lady actually seemed the most composed of the lot of them.

If they were facing Last Times, she said, that just meant it was time to rise up.

She seemed quite at peace when she had finally passed, six days in. In the minutes before she had gone, the old-lady had held Rosa's hand, as if to comfort *her*.

"A doctor sees too much pain," she had told her, giving Rosa's hand a squeeze. "And you hate it so *much*. A girl as young and pretty as you should smile more."

They had laid her to rest next to her husband near the top of the stairs.

"They're gone," Julie said.

Rosa turned. "What are?"

"The old-lady," Julie said. "And her husband. They're gone."

Rosa looked where they had lain and saw nothing but a torn plastic seat-cover.

She looked around cautiously.

Among the rubble, something skittered just out of sight.

After a moment, that skittering-something hopped up on top of the piled concrete.

It was about two-feet tall – gangly like a plucked emu.

The slender limbs were adorned with vicious-looking claws – almost like fishhooks – and its sharp, beak-like snout was lined in lizard-like teeth.

On its foot, toe-tapping like a drummer, was a lethal-looking sickle.

The thing bobbed in jerky, bird-like motions.

Its jaws were slathered in blood, and in its claws, it held what looked like a rib-bone.

After a moment, several others hopped up beside it, all of them staring with goggly eyes.

One of them had a piece of Rita's black shawl.

In sudden anger, Rosa picked up a piece of concrete and threw it.

The little lizards scattered but bounced back promptly. And now a few more appeared, bobbing their heads like prairie dogs.

Julie raised the pistol and picked the closet one off its perch with a single shot, sending it spinning like a tin-can off a fence.

Now the others retreated for real, vanishing into the cracks like scurrying rats.

Rosa and Julie examined the twitching corpse left behind.

It was covered in a thin, pale plume – not feathered so much as quills, giving the creature the appearance of scales rather than a pelt.

"Is this a dinosaur?" Julie asked, still pointing the pistol, warily.

Rosa nodded slowly. The pediatric wing had recently redone the playroom with wall-paintings of dinosaurs, and she clearly recognized the hooked sickle-claw – albeit a smaller version – the domestic cat versus a cougar. But that murderous hook was intimidating on the miniature model as well.

Behind them, there was the sound of tumbling rock.

The pack of little lizards had regrouped several yards away, still eyeing them interestedly. Julie took another couple of shots at them and they scattered once again.

The shots echoed in the streets.

Rosa had never heard an echo in the city before.

Or more correctly, a single echo, because the sounds were constant.

This was all by itself.

Rosa had heard it said that if you turned off the sprinklers, every city on the California coast would be a desert in two weeks.

It actually rather looked like that. The ruined buildings were covered in dust – almost appearing fossilized, like some ancient ruins.

Looking around, it was amazing how fast a despoiled city returned to the land.

The footprints of humanity were not so deep as imagined, after all.

In the eerie silence, Rosa and Julie made their way up to the crest of rubble and looked down upon the city.

One of the cars in the parking lot had yielded a pair of binoculars, and Rosa took a quick scan of the skyline.

There was literally nothing standing – not even the beasts themselves.

But as she focused in on one of the carcasses, she now realized its flesh seemed to be moving – rather like dead animals on the Savannah sometimes roiled with scavengers. But the things that had come out of the nooks and crannies were not your local coyotes or raccoons.

This was more like watching an elephant corpse swarmed by Nile monitors, digging into the stomach, climbing on its back, rooting around inside the cavernous chest-cavity.

Rosa did not particularly know her dinosaurs, but she knew one when she saw it.

While diminutive next to the giant carrion, they were quite impressive in their own right – Rosa estimated many of them scaled upwards of ten tons.

Darting in among them – wolf-sized – were packs of sickle-claws – skittish of their larger cousins, but emboldened sufficiently by the mountain of free carrion to risk proximity.

Oddly, as she focused in with the binoculars, she didn't see any of those *little* scavengers on any of the giant carcasses – perhaps chased off by the larger carnivores.

But then as she panned down onto the streets, she found them.

Those little guys seemed to be focusing on the leftover *human* wreckage.

Scavengers were, by nature, opportunistic. Why risk confrontation with the big predators, when all these travel-size meals were just as plentiful? Some of the decadent little lizards actually lounged and snoozed luxuriously on half-devoured corpses.

Rosa was already beginning to hate those little bastards.

Worse, as she adjusted the binoculars on the far horizon, she realized the giants weren't all gone either.

It was difficult to see in the distance – dust from demolished concrete drifted like fog – but gathered along the far-side of the city, apparently, in repose for the moment, at least three of the mega-beasts had gathered around one of the giant carcasses.

And as she adjusted focus, Rosa could see what at first looked like birds lined up along the giant beasts' backs.

Then she realized it was more of the little sickle-clawed scavengers – apparently discovering yet another niche for themselves – like birds picking parasites off the hide of a buffalo – they scurried over the giant scales like lice.

The giant beasts were standing, but seemed almost dormant – like a horse sleeping on its feet.

Their eyes were slitted like a dozing cat's. Rosa could see just a sliver of that strange green glow spliced under the lids.

Then Julie was patting her urgently on the shoulder. When Rosa turned, she pointed over past the ruined hospital.

The plume of smoke reaching over the make-shift ridge of rubble was not a random fire.

Turning her binoculars, Rosa saw the fighter jet that had crashed two-days before. The engine was still smoking.

"You think that guy's alive?" Julie asked over her shoulder.

Rosa lowered the scopes.

"Only one way to know," she said. "It's not far."

She nodded to the pistol in Julie's hands. "You've still got bullets, right?"

Julie nodded. "Six. I think."

Rosa hefted her ax, setting her feet like any good cavewoman who had never swung an ax in her life.

"Okay," she said. "Let's go take a look."

CHAPTER 7

The jet had not exploded, but had left a trail of fuel that continued to smolder. The plane was perched at the end of an impromptu runway that had taken it over nearly three city blocks.

Fortunately, the architecture in its path had been mostly single buildings and strip malls, catering to the hospital and commuter area that bordered on the nearby park – not exactly a runway, but better than the side of a skyscraper.

Rosa could see the pilot, still in the cockpit.

He wasn't moving – either dead or unconscious.

"The hatch is open," Julie said. "That means he tried to get out."

"And couldn't," Rosa finished. That didn't bode well. Nevertheless, they began to climb the slope of broken concrete.

Their first efforts sent loose debris rolling and bouncing noisily into the street, sending more echoes ricocheting into the eerie, dead silence.

This time, the ruckus attracted gawkers.

A quartet of sickle-claws appeared on the ridge behind them.

No little scavengers here – these were the big wolf-sized beasties – and neither did they waste time once they spotted them – all four came bounding like sprinting greyhounds.

Struggling for balance on the chancy slope, Julie fired her remaining shots.

And perhaps she was a little rattled, because they all missed.

The claws would be on them in seconds.

Feeling almost ridiculous, Rosa brandished the fire-ax.

Then four shots rang out in quick succession, ringing in their ears.

All four beasts pitched over forward into the gravel, blood and brain-matter spurting out the backs of their lizard-like heads.

The largest of them flopped spasmodically at Rosa's feet.

She turned, and above them, the pilot was sitting up in his seat, his pistol muzzle still smoking.

"Evil sons-a-bitches, ain't they?" he hollered down.

Rosa and Julie exchanged glances. All four bullets had hit targets less than four inches across – fired within seconds.

The pilot smiled winningly.

"Lieutenant Lucas Walker, US Navy, at your service."

He pulled the clip from his handgun and tossed it over the side.

"I hope you ladies are friendly. Those were my last bullets."

He tapped the raised hatch. "I don't suppose you could help me out here? My foot's stuck."

Climbing underneath the fuselage, Rosa and Julie began pushing where the nose of the jet had been pinched, trapping the man's leg.

Rosa wedged her ax handle between the plane and the broken concrete, and both women – who together didn't weigh more than two-hundred and fifty pounds – jumped up and down, trying to rock the weight of the jet just enough.

The mangled metal groaned, matched immediately by Lucas inside the cockpit.

"Just so you ladies know, that *really* fuckin' hurts."

Rosa had patched a lot of field injuries – ignoring Lucas, as soon as she felt the first give, she leaned harder. She and Julie were now matching Lucas' strained curses as the fuselage finally moved.

'Ohhhhh you BASTARD!" Lucas blurted as the metal groaned again.

But then his foot pulled free.

And like an animal released from a snare, he hiked himself out of the cockpit, his easy air belying the hollows in his eyes after two days spent trapped. With a nearly imperceptible shudder, Lucas planted both his feet out onto the semi-solid pile of broken concrete.

His left foot was swollen and purple – as if to spite it, he stomped hard on the rubble.

Rosa saw the bolt of pain flash through his eyes, and the squirt of a tear dotted his cheek.

He flicked the tear away, with an affirmative nod. "Yep. *That's* gonna smart for a while."

With that, he turned to the two of them with a formal salute.

"My thanks to you, ladies. I'm in your debt."

And with that, he began to root around his crashed plane, pulling open a compartment below the cockpit – walking on his wounded leg in utter deliberate defiance.

"Here," Rosa said, moving forward, "let me take a look at that foot."

Lucas smiled reassuringly, as he tossed bags from the compartment – supplies and weapons – and extra bullets. He popped a fresh clip into his pistol.

"I'm fine, Ma'am," he said.

"It's *'Doctor'*," Rosa said, irritated. "Now sit down and let me look at it."

With an indulgent sigh, tossing his last bag out on the crushed concrete, Lucas acquiesced, taking a seat on the wing of his downed plane.

"So," Rosa said, in by-rote bed-side manner, "you're a pilot. I suppose you have one of those 'call-signs'. Like Maverick?"

Lucas nodded mildly. "I do."

"What is it?"

He smiled innocently. "It's the name I go by when I fly."

Rosa took a patent breath, as she poked at his swelling, purple ankle – making sure to highlight the spots she knew would hurt.

Her prodding produced the barest twitch in Lucas' brow, and an even broader, more deliberate smile.

"Well," she said, somewhat begrudgingly, "it's not broken – just kind of crushed. You've probably got some pressure fractures – especially in the smaller bones." She looked up. "It's good and purple, too. That means you're hurt."

Lucas nodded. "I knew that much."

And with that, he pulled his boot back on, and hopped back to his feet.

"That must hurt," Rosa said, deliberately unimpressed.

'Oh *yeah*, it does," he said, but loaded up his heavy packs on both shoulders anyway, apparently determined to experience as much discomfort as possible. "Back in high-school, my wrestling coach used to call it an 'owie'."

"That's a bit more than an 'owie'," Rosa said.

"Well," Lucas said, again stomping his foot experimentally, grimacing at each bolt of pain, "you may be right. But we gotta suck it up anyway, don't we?"

With that, he turned and began climbing up over the ridge of rubble where the sickle claws had appeared.

Glancing at each other, Rosa and Julie followed.

Once he reached the top, he pulled out his own binoculars and scanned the broken skyline.

He settled quickly on the stuporous giants poised on the horizon.

"They've just been standing there like that," Rosa said. "It's like they're asleep."

"It's mental deterioration," Lucas replied. "Whatever makes them giants, it also eats their brains."

Rosa shook her head. "It's... a dinosaur, isn't it? Like a *T. rex*?"

"Actually," Lucas said, "that one's a Carcharodont – probably Giganotosaurus – a carnosaur – kind of a big allosaur."

He tipped a sage, informed eye over his binoculars.

"They gave us a list of what we were shooting at," he said. "Apparently, these guys don't get along with *T. rex* at all – in fact, they seem to have driven the tyrannosaurs out of this area.

"In fact," he said, "that's what was mostly going on here – the city was gone in two-days – they were just fighting over it." Lucas shrugged. "We were shootin' at 'em, but I don't know how much they cared."

"But they're... so *big*," Rosa said. "I mean there's never *been* anything like that – not ever."

"Yeah," Lucas said, "about that."

He handed his binoculars over – military-issue with zoom capabilities.

"This might shine a light," he said.

He directed her towards one of the carcasses, where packs of the smaller creatures – carnosaurs and sickle-claws alike – were devouring the fallen giant.

"They're really going to town, aren't they?" Lucas said. "Take a closer look."

Rosa zoomed in, focusing in on a single sickle-claw as it perched upon the massive carcass.

In the high resolution, she could see the blood on its lips.

She could also see its eyes.

They glowed emerald green.

CHAPTER 8

There was one man who saw it all.

From a vantage point two-hundred and twenty miles above the Earth, staring down from orbit, Major Tom Corbett had heard all the nicknames – 'Buck Rogers' 'Rocket Man – burning out his fuse up there alone' – but plain old 'Major Tom' was the one he liked best – he used it as his call-sign.

Sometimes in the pure deadpan of the military, people would call him Major 'Major Tom' – he didn't know what he'd do if he got promoted.

Truth to tell, he never wanted to be – space was the final frontier, after all. Any higher rank, he'd be looking at a desk job.

And pretty much anything would be a come-down after this.

You floated up here.

Last time down, he'd submitted to an interview – a pretty, perky, and painfully ambitious young reporter, who spoke her name like a catchphrase – 'Rebekah Adams, KAB News, Houston' – probably all of twenty-three. Young Miss Adams seemed torn between producing a puff-piece and 'penetrating journalism' – acting out her own version of good-cop/bad-cop – tossing her blond locks like a runway model, while holding her microphone like a taser gun.

Reciting questions as if for a full-page in the Campus Confidential, this young reporterette, had asked if there was anything he missed on Earth.

"Nothing," Tom had replied. "When I'm up there, I don't care if I ever come back."

In recent days, THAT little comment had come back to bite him.

The young reporterette had been on one of the last network feeds to go dark.

He didn't precisely know what had happened to her, but those last moments hadn't looked good.

None of it had – and he had seen it all.

That was his job. He was the watchman – the Eye in the Sky.

The EITS space-station was a relatively new addition to the reinvigorated space-race – part of the new space military. It had only been up a year, and was specifically designed for intelligence – possessing its own internal database that could theoretically access any outlet on Earth.

Major Tom was also currently the only human being in space.

The International Space Station was presently running on automation – debris from a Chinese satellite had compromised the structure, and it was scheduled for repair later this month.

Tom had actually picked up a lot of the ISS's duties himself, rerouting communications from other satellites – he'd actually been a little irritated, and had been hoping they'd be getting back on line sooner than later.

Besides the tedium, it was also a bit high-profile for the EITS – the buzz among those that talked about such things in the civilian sector, was that this was a communication/espionage project. His perky little reporterette had asked a couple of penetrating questions along just those lines.

Tom understood the truth of it well enough. It was not, in fact, an espionage project – it just absolutely enabled it – no, we're not listening in your living room – we're just setting up a bug so we can do it whenever we want – or clone any database we can tap into.

Obviously, he couldn't tell that to his oh-so-serious young interviewer, so he just talked about his daily duties – about fifty hours a week performing necessary functions – didn't really do weekends.

"What do you do the rest of the time?" she had asked.

Unable to resist, he had said, "Oh, I just like to tap into people's phones and TV sets – you know, watch what everybody's doing in their living rooms."

Rebekah Adams – KAB News, Houston – had not laughed. His comment proceeded to go on a rotating news-cycle for weeks afterwards.

Tom's commanding officer had actually, formally, ordered him not to crack any more jokes.

"Don't be funny," he had said. "The press does not have a sense of humor that we are aware of."

Currently, however, this communications juggernaut was having difficulty raising a walkie-talkie. That was a fundamental flaw – there had to be a signal to read, and it seemed that the grid itself had gone dark.

There had been a few initial reports coming in from Houston, but since then, the digitized communications channels had been gone.

One of the more commonly asked questions Tom had gotten about satellites was 'could they function in a crisis?' – specifically in regards to the world-wide web – the disaster-scenario being something like a global emergency.

Tom's personal pick as the best way to take out the digital-grid, would have been some sort of invasive super-virus, but the most commonly cited, of course, was always 'nuclear exchange' – and the potential electromagnetic pulse – the semi-mythical EMP.

His answer was always yes, the network should function – assuming the database remained, and every tower on Earth wasn't taken out too.

Remarkably, something very close to that seemed to have actually happened – everywhere, all at once.

Initially, he picked up a lot of extraneous images – mostly local TV and radio-stations – particularly in the sticks, where they were more likely to still be using open broadcast – although the bulk of these blacked-out quickly as well.

At the moment, he was trying to raise contact with one particular tower – a new installation just north of Eureka, California, built in conjunction with the launch of the EITS station.

Most of the towers that had gone down were in the urban areas – where the infrastructure had been the hardest hit – the Eureka tower was fairly remote.

But that too was down. Tom didn't know if it had been destroyed as well, or was simply off-line.

As for what had happened to the world...

Well... the images he *could* get told him that.

At the very beginning, there had been news reports – he played and replayed images from all over the world. From his vantage, he could see it all – he could collate it, even run graphics-extrapolations and simulations based on it – but contact with his chain of command was cut-off alarmingly early-on.

That by itself should have been impossible. If they were broadcasting anything, unless literally every frequency was somehow being jammed – also impossible – he should be picking *something* up. He knew for a fact that they were still out there – in some of the bigger cities there still maintained military resistance – albeit, ineffective and token – but Tom was getting nothing.

In the meantime, he watched the world destroyed in real-time. Live.

Ostensibly, most of the footage was of the destruction itself – but between it all, was the people.

There were a lot at first – survivors of the initial blitz, mostly in the surrounding areas immediately outside the cities – but these faded fast. After the first few days, most of what he got was from the outlying areas – particularly in the higher-elevations.

Some of them were people trying to talk to their families – sending out messages in video bottles – many in foreign languages – others were simply reaching out – is anybody out there?

The bulk of these began to flicker and fade as the world went dark – but there were a few echoes. Armageddon or no-Armageddon, people apparently still pod-cast, as a few remaining towers bounced images randomly off satellites – sometimes making sense of scrambled programming.

And although no one could hear him, or had any idea that he was even there, Tom listened to their stories, one by one.

There was one guy in the Midwest, who had managed to fire up an old radio-station transmitter. That one hadn't worked out so well – something about the signal attracted the attention of the 'new wildlife' and the place had been stomped flat – all described in moment-by-moment detail by the apparently semi-deranged operator as the beasts had stampeded down on top of him.

A group of teenagers – among the last survivors in any of the urban areas – somewhere in downtown Tokyo – exchanged a video diary in a language Tom couldn't understand.

There was a young woman living somewhere in Alaska who had barricaded herself in an old hunting cabin – she had been fighting off packs of sickle-claws like wolves.

She periodically turned the camera from herself to the shadows skulking out beyond her fence – she was talking about polar bear season – her place was already well-fortified, with spiked mats on the steps and windows – only this year, she explained, as she fired intermediate shots out the window – most of the polar bears seemed to have been eaten.

She panned to a view of the sickle-claws prowling outside, the peaks of the Yukon directly behind.

Some survivors had even retreated off-shore. There was footage from a boat – a yacht of some kind, apparently broadcasting from its own antennae –

where the last thing you saw was the mouth of a large shark – resembling a Great White with a mouth seven-feet wide – sufficient to take out the boat's hull in a single bite.

One broadcast actually showed some idiot climbing on the back of what looked like a three-horned Triceratops, attempting to ride it – evidently with another person filming. The clip had ended with the beast charging off over the hill with the guy still clinging to its back.

Even in the face of Armageddon, there were still Darwin Awards.

But Tom took a moment to watch every bit of it – trying to hear all of it at once, and at the same time, all of it individually.

That was how you did surveillance.

No detail was inconsequential – but it must be dealt with on its own scale, or you run into the systemic problem of 'preoccupation with inconsequential details'.

It also served to steel himself, as he played and replayed the testimony of people recording their own epitaphs.

In particular, Tom had listened to their reasons 'why?'.

The guy in the mid-west with the radio station had spent two days broadcasting a lot of wild conspiracy-stories before he was stomped flat – deep-government stuff mixed in with a lot of Biblical hugger-mugger.

That one had resonated with Tom, who had spent a lot of time as a kid listening to the UFO/Bigfoot hours on early AM tin-hat radio.

As an adult, he still found it all fascinating – the circular logic, always starting from a given premise, was often ingenious – and could be remarkably convincing, especially coming from otherwise intelligent minds.

Something about conspiracy-theories satisfied that human need to apply meaning – or at least 'reasons'. It was sort of like religion in that way – perhaps that was why followers always believed so fervently.

All those conspiracy-stories.

Tom had to admit, at one time, as a kid – hell, even into his early twenties – part of him had believed every one of them.

These days, he believed in precious few.

It was disappointing in a way. As an adult, he knew, for example, that there could be no Bigfoot – not because the animal was impossible, but simply because of the kind of animal it would have to be – a breeding population would be visible – especially in the day of cell-cameras and the populated areas where 'squatch was supposed to live.

Ditto the Loch Ness Monster. In fact, 'Nessie' was the subject of one of Tom's personal favorite long-term hoaxes – the famous 'plesiosaur' photo – which learned scientists claimed showed an object better than thirty-feet – and continued to do so well into the millennium, despite a local newspaper story identifying the beast as a foot-tall model – literally two weeks after the incident, when the pranksters themselves came forward and fessed-up the gag.

There was even a Bigfoot hoax where some guy had actually been killed – he had been laying in the road, pretending to be a Sasquatch hit by a car, and he had been run over twice.

In a way, Tom could almost understand the hoaxes – it was an effort to preserve the magic – even if it was the magic of a charlatan.

And that seemed to be true of all the good monsters. All the good conspiracy stories too – where there wasn't deliberate fraud, there was the suspension of disbelief – 'the fact that there's no evidence is in itself suspicious'.

That last one was a particular favorite in the 'we are not alone'-crowd.

That had been Tom's crowd. 'We are not alone' had been where his first interest in space had come from.

In his tenure, he had seen precious little alien life.

At least, he hadn't until now.

It was ironic – that same scientific education that had dispelled all those childhood myths, stood in utter defiance of what he saw before him now.

He was belatedly reevaluating what he believed to be possible.

On his screen, was a complicated computer mock-up of cell reproduction.

The details of the formula were classified – even to him.

The file's code-name was "Food of the Gods'.

CHAPTER 9

Tom didn't pretend to understand all the details – even some of the abstracts were above his head – he was a glorified pilot, after all.

The 'Food of the Gods' – named after the Wells novel – because it was exactly that.

At its most basic, the summaries described a chemical-compound related, among other things, to the pituitary gland – the gist being that, rather than genetically engineering an animal for size, the chemical was simply introduced into the system of a living creature.

According to this simulation, that organism would grow.

It was rather like injected energy – a tiny little fusion reactor for DNA.

Theoretically, you could order DNA to produce any result you desired – in this case, growth – via the activation of any number of contributing systemic mechanisms – from pituitary and other hormones, to genetic predisposition, to cell-reproduction and regeneration.

It was, of course, easy to get wrong.

The chemical had two substantial flaws – the first being that it only seemed to work on genetically-engineered organisms.

Secondly, when it *did* work, there were a couple of pesky side-effects.

The first thing was that the infected organism's irises would actually begin to glow – perhaps a reaction to the sheer energy being forced through its system – and always emerald green.

More problematically, however, the chemical *killed* any organism it infected – but only after causing mental deterioration similar to rabies. The rate of deterioration was related to both dosage intensity and volume.

Tom couldn't find it explicitly stated how long a subject might survive in this rage-infected state, but it was clearly long enough.

It certainly explained a lot of what he'd seen below.

As he followed the research down the rabbit-hole, Tom was discovering how limited his security clearance really was – *him* – literally, the Eye in the Sky – the files he was attempting to access laughed at his attempts to hack past.

What he *could* get, however, was telling.

Most of these reports seemed to have been compiled literally within the last six months – very much in catch-up fashion – a lot of them referencing files he could not access directly.

It was as if someone had kicked over the Lost Ark in the warehouse, and they were now reviewing old records.

Nor was there any direct indication of the 'why' of it. Original funding was apparently outside government – initially stemming from humanitarian, and most particularly conservation groups – the idea of resurrecting extinct species dated back to the sixties.

But evidently something had happened – sometime before the turn of the century – Tom didn't know if it was accident or breakthrough – and the government had stepped in.

Tom sighed – that was always right about the time things went south.

If he remembered right, it was also right about the time that Daisy the cloned sheep had made the headlines – kind of an imperfect duplicate – among other defects, it had aged prematurely, as if its genes were responding to the actual age of its parent.

Sitting where he was now, the former conspiracy-theorist in him wondered if Daisy herself was the hoax – a sub-par, VHS copy of an organism – a sad, boring reality for the public to absorb – and thus not worry about.

Further tin-hats were raised when he discovered the scientist who was apparently the primary subject of the government-acquisition – a name Tom actually recognized from his AM-radio days – a geneticist named Nolan Hinkle.

That *really* took Tom back – Hinkle had been a fixture-subject on early-morning conspiracy AM since the days of the earliest modern genetics research.

This had been back in the day when the mainstream world hadn't even fully accepted the process of evolution. Hinkle was considered more than a bit of a kook – or a bit of an Einstein, depending on what books you read.

Based on what he was looking at now, Tom couldn't call it.

At best, you were stepping into Frankenstein-level moral-ambiguity.

Hinkle's research boiled down to the chemical manipulation and mutation of DNA – based on the very simple principle that all life is a chemical reaction – from conception, to development, to growth, photosynthesis, to respiration – an exchange of energy, activating chemical responses – intake of air, the digestion of food.

There was a particular focus on gigantism, both in individuals and evolved species. Many evolutionary branches produced giants – it was certainly heavily in evidence in dinosaurs, but achieved by almost every major group – fish, mammals, reptiles – particularly in the oceans.

In evolutionary terms, gigantism in species was limited by biomass – with the somewhat undersized flora today reflecting the modern Earth's rather arid environment.

But the Mesozoic through the Cenozoic routinely saw animals three and four times the mass of the largest animals today.

In simple terms, it came down to what the biosphere was prepared to feed. The higher levels of CO_2 had created the lush environment of the Cretaceous, and the resulting giants lived off the increased biomass.

Which was also why an environment where the most plentiful giants were predators was an ecological anomaly.

While the Earth had produced animals over a hundred tons before, these had generally been herbivores. Giant carnivores like *T. rex* had topped out around ten tons – it was a simple matter of ratios – a predator population couldn't outgrow the food source that sustained it – and where herbivores lacked size, they existed in large numbers.

Meat-eaters were not, however, limited by biomechanics – there was no reason a theropod *couldn't* attain such titanic sizes – provided the necessary energy to sustain it.

The Food of the Gods solved that.

And if saving the world had been its stated goal, it was safe to say it had been radically re-purposed.

Because as near as Tom could tell, it had destroyed it.

And it was not over.

The Apocalypse came in waves.

Over the ten days since detonation, the initial violence had abruptly calmed, as the chemical ran its inevitable cycle and the infected animals simply died – and at the onset, the Food of the Gods seemed to have manifested almost exclusively in the cities. Computer simulations clearly showed the bloom of infection – in time-lapse, it rather resembled the explosion of tactical nukes – spreading outward, playing out, in real-world time, for days and weeks instead of seconds.

What happened in the cities, however, was only the final manifestation of a much larger infestation – because there were also the uninfected animals – what the literature referred to as 'normals' – and, out in the sticks, they seemed to be everywhere.

And there were a hell of a lot more monsters out there than just *T. rex.*

While Tom's role was intended as a gatherer rather than an analyzer of information, that still gave him clearance to high-level chatter – including the initial breakdown provided for the troops – simple procedure to prepare them for what they were facing.

Once he'd accessed *those* files, Tom had found himself simply astounded.

He remembered the 'myths' of 'Monster Island' – always one of the more unlikely of urban legends.

But even for a conspiracy-theorist, this was delusional madness.

The write-ups were very detailed – very concise – and all in plain-text, military dead-pan.

The creatures had been given code-names – and 'Big Rex' was just one entry out of several *pages* – there were a dozen species of carnosaur, alone, including the big Carcharodonts – code named 'Shark Tooth'.

But there were also sauropods, ceratopsians – as well as listings for sharks, plesiosaurs, pliosaurs, mosasaurs – a whole bestiary.

In its own way, the groupings were very orderly – rather like putting together a zoo – or more accurately, a preserve, filling in artificial niches – even down to those skittering little sickle-clawed scavengers – top-predator down to cockroach.

And very much like dead elephants on the Savannah, the carcasses of giants didn't last long – and just like on the Nile, what was left always made it into the river, where scavenging lions gave way to crocs.

San Francisco harbor was crowded with massive floating bodies, branching out into the ocean.

God only knew what critters might be lurking off shore. The breadth of monsters undersea dwarfed those on land.

He'd already seen one boat taken by a giant shark – likely a Megalodon. That meant they were out there – just waiting to chow down all that infected carrion – just like a pack of Great Whites after a dead whale.

The pattern had already begun to repeat, world-wide.

Once the giants died, they were devoured – and a new infection bloomed.

It explained why the infected organisms tended to be predatory species.

The chemical was introduced through ingestion – it was simply too potent for direct injection.

As it played out on the ground, observation confirmed the literature – it only seemed to affect genetically-engineered animals, as if some key ingredient in their creation was somehow absent in natural life forms – and the higher the dosage, the more rapid the effect.

The balance point where it killed the organism varied from individual to individual – a rex that gorged itself on a whole carcass would obviously be affected faster.

As it was presented in the official intelligence report, "In cases of ingestion, the growth effect takes a period of weeks, with the rate of the effect directly influenced by the amount consumed. One could speculate on what effect direct injection might have."

Tom looked down at the screen, re-reading the paragraph – all printed in that same deliberate deadpan.

'Speculate'.

He glanced at his other screens – all playing and replaying devastation and smoking ruin.

Yes, he thought, one *could* indeed speculate.

Sitting up there, quietly in space, floating before his computer screen like a feather – there was not a hell of a lot else he *could* do.

And better to speculate on what was happening on Earth rather than on his own possible alternate futures – not a one that Tom could think of where the carnage below left any possible way for him to get back home.

Assuming, of course, home still existed.

So he read his files, he ran his simulations, and he searched for patterns.

On the third day, he found one.

During the heart of the initial blitz – in *all* the cities – something had abruptly changed.

Three days in, and suddenly there were factions. The beasts had turned on each other.

Nor was this random – the battle-lines seemed to have broken down into pack-warfare.

Which was strange, Tom thought, if the mental deterioration was like rabies.

A closer look, however, suggested there was something more at work than just the Food of the Gods – something more basic.

Carnosaurs and tyrannosaurs would naturally be at odds – placed into the same geography, both occupying the same niche, without prey animals to complement their numbers, that was nothing but a declaration of ecological warfare.

Tom noted something else interesting – in terms of demographics, the tyrannosaurs seemed largely out-numbered in the conflict – at least as infected giants – but at the same time, were particularly aggressive.

Carnosaurs would mingle with ceratosaurs or megalosaurs – *T. rex* walked alone – there was no instance in any record of a rex tolerating a rival predator species in its territory – and every instance was a death-fight.

They even seemed to go after those tiny little sickle-clawed scavengers – it didn't seem to like *them* at all. Or maybe 'like' wasn't the word, because they were eating those little guys just like popcorn.

And none of it seemed to be an effect of the Food of the Gods – the 'normals' out in the sticks clashed along party-lines, and tore at each other every bit as savagely as the infected giants.

The pattern endured – three days in, and they had been at each other's throats.

Just territorial aggression? Aggravated by steroid-rage?

In any case, it was apparent that the global war wasn't over, just because humanity had cashed their chips in early.

Tom's eyes turned to a particular screen he had reserved for the young woman still trapped, barricaded inside her cabin in Alaska – where sickle-claws continued to make periodic raids.

She talked to her camera a lot.

Tom could relate – it was the sort of thing you did when you were isolated and alone.

The young woman was currently in relatively good-spirits – she was obviously capable, and well-supplied – but Tom knew that eventually her resources would be spent – even if she'd been stocked for the entire winter – and how much ammunition could she possibly keep on hand?

To Tom's knowledge, there wasn't even anyone left to help.

He hadn't heard from his own command since almost the moment it all began.

Still, if he could just connect with that Eureka tower – constructed specifically to function as liaison to the EITS station.

If he could get that activated, he might actually be able to restart the Internet out of his own database – most satellites should still be operational.

If lines of communication could be opened up, that might change things.

It could at least change the fortunes for a few survivors – the kids in Japan – the young woman in Alaska.

Her name was Kristi.

On short acquaintance, Tom found he liked her. And he very much did not want to watch her die.

Like he had, Rebekah Adams, KAB, Houston.

In the days since it all went down, Tom believed he had personally seen more death than any human being in history had ever witnessed.

Perhaps it was optimistic that he still found himself fearing for a few remaining lives.

Or perhaps it was just a defense mechanism to keep from thinking about his own.

That was better, he decided – it was colder – rational and scientific – at the immediate moment, detachment was his only friend. He consciously knew he was six-ways-from-Sunday past section-eight trauma and would have to adapt his behavior accordingly.

So he ran his simulations and he collated his data. He looked for patterns, and tried to raise towers on Earth.

And he continued to read files – following further and further down the rabbit hole.

CHAPTER 10

In the hills just south of Siskiyou Pass, there was a new King under the Mountain.

It was not a matter of vote, or even primitive ritual. It was simply existential reality.

The rex stood on the hill, framed by the flickering light of an oncoming storm.

It towered well over sixty meters. Its eyes glowed green.

At its feet, the creatures in the valley simply fled.

A predator would not normally be so high-profile – when stalking, *T. rex* could move with surprising stealth.

Today, however, the rex simply announced its presence. It had quickly learned that, these days, that was enough.

In the valley basin below, lay the corpse of another infected giant – a large sauropod, stretching nearly half-a-mile from head to tail – a mountain of meat that was currently being gnawed on by every critter in the forest.

The rex uttered an impatient grunt and the scavengers broke like flies, vanishing into the trees.

Less than two short weeks ago, he had been one of them – skittering around the ankles of the giants. It had sorely tested his tyrannosaur-pride.

But things had changed. And while the rex itself did not directly associate this change to its battle with the infected sickle-claw back in Siskiyou Pass, or devouring its opponent's corpse, that *was* when he had felt the first slow onset – similar to the way alcoholic euphoria sets in after ingestion.

Initially, the sensation was simply an over-caffeinated feeling of power and energy.

Once its growth topped out, however, all that energy would have nowhere to go, and deterioration would begin. Along with it, would come madness.

For the moment, however, the rex was only aware of a mild-buzzing in its head.

At the perimeter of the basin, some of the smaller scavengers were back, and had started to encroach.

There was no native fauna among them.

Even all the lions and tigers and bears who might have dared to directly contest the new wildlife, pound-for-pound, soon discovered the toxic taste of these giant, seemingly free mountains of carrion.

As somewhere up space, Major Tom had listed among its primary flaws, the chemical *killed*.

And while there was nothing in the available text that specifically described the effect of the chemical on a normal, non-engineered organism, there *was* reference that it was always fatal – and it wasn't pretty – something about that DNA fusion-reactor going into meltdown.

The rex, of course, knew none of that, but did take note of the remains of a bear, lying along the dead sauropod's haunches, that had evidently tried to scavenge the infected meat.

Visually, the effect was rather like a systemic, full-body allergic reaction – like every cell swelling into a zit, and then popping all at once.

The bear was an unrecognizable mess.

That mostly took care of any competition from the indigenous local predators. And of course, the rex had his own rivals in check – it had already chased most of the sickle-claws out of the area, as it had any lingering carnosaurs. The Siskiyous were solidly tyrannosaur-territory.

But right now, trespassing stealthily from behind, were a small pack of those little cat-sized beasts – those scurrying, clawed little lizards – no more than ants compared to the infected rex.

They stayed guardedly away from the downed sauropod, but snapped at some of the scavenging birds – cawing back at them in a mimic of their own squawks.

The rex jerked at the sound – snorting with a touch of irritation.

On the ground below, the little lizards turned and hissed.

The rex actually paused at the cheeky affront, its nose wrinkling.

Then the rex blinked, its eyes briefly tearing, like with a dose of smelling salts in the sinuses – perhaps some chemical musk.

Whatever it was, it sparked an instinctual temper response.

Turning from the carcass, the rex began to stamp the little lizards like yellow-jackets at a barbecue.

The tiny creatures darted in every direction – one actually made it under a log, hissing balefully, screeching its oddly birdlike warble – but the rex simply stomped the log flat too.

It turned, somewhat disgruntled, back to its meal, wiping its foot disgustedly on the rocks.

At the perimeter of the basin, the other creatures faded back.

And now, along the ridge, in the same direction the rex had come, more giant shadows loomed – a pack of them, framed by the strobing lightning, eyes glowing green.

His 'gang' – the big rex was not the only tyrannosaur wandering slumber-mountain.

A procession of a dozen or more – all infected giants – spread out across the crest of the hillside, looking down into the basin.

The group of them had been more or less traveling together. And they had taken to following the big rex as sort of a defacto-leader.

They hung back respectfully, of course – mostly females at the moment – although a few scattered males prowled at a distance.

Dominant females would sometimes tolerate adolescent and even adult offspring – but these were also almost exclusively female – male aggression made them incompatible in a pack.

In mating season, the dominant female would pair-bond with the dominate rogue.

The big rex regarded his entourage – particularly the males that postured along the perimeter – alert for any potential challenge. A couple of them *had* tested him in the recent past – both attempted coupes had been quick and total failures.

But no one was feeling particularly sparky today – the rex's would-be rivals simply stood down, waiting in regimented formation – and therefore he allowed them to remain. They would chase off any competing predators while they waited their turn at the banquet.

If Major Tom could have observed this small scene, he might have gained new insight.

This was ritualized social-structure at work – born of pure behavioral instinct.

The strictness was a necessity when one was born with evolutionary super-weapons – just existing among your peers was an uneasy state of détente. Fossil tyrannosaurs often showed scars from inter-specific battles – a LOT of inter-specific battles. The breed had, in fact, been described by researchers as honky-tonk bar-brawlers on a Saturday night.

For the moment, the big rex was in charge, and the others would follow, according to a simple hierarchy, based on the fairest system in the world – anyone who could kill him got to be in charge.

There were no 'betas' in *T. rex* socio-biology – once any one of the young males reached sufficient size, they would try for the alpha spot.

It was not even a real choice – just pure instinct – and because there were very few non-lethals in a rex-fight, they would either be the new alpha or they would be killed.

But until then, they would follow the rogue – always at a safe distance – and he would tolerate them. Smaller rex were good for rustling up prey, similar to the strategy of modern lions, where the smaller, faster females corralled big herd animals right into the claws of the larger, heavier males, who killed them.

All this structure had evolved over the hundred and fifty million years it took therapods to *get* to *T. rex*. And any violation of these strictures would be met with full-on ferocity, whether the transgression came from giant carnosaur, or tiny scavenging lizard.

Satisfied his court was in order, the rex bent to the carcass and began to feed, the massive jaws, calving out massive chunks of flesh, biting cleanly through bone, and swallowing mouthfuls whole.

On the hillside around him, the pack waited patiently.

At the perimeter, a few *T. rex* normals also waited in the wings – likewise spoiling at their own wounded rex-pride – 'Tyrant Kings' reduced to scurrying around a giant's ankles.

When the rex had eaten its fill, it stood from the much-diminished carcass with a carrion-belch that echoed in the basin.

Along the ridge, the others all paused to see if the rex would guard the carcass, as he had done in the past, sometimes curling to sleep right up next to it – practically daring anyone to wake him.

But instead, the big rex slowly turned, staring off in the direction of the coast, its nose curling as if with that sulfur whiff once again.

Now that its hunger-urge was momentarily appeased, its simple-behavior now directed it to follow its next instinctual impulse.

In this case, a territorial instinct.

T. rex did not think things over – it responded to stimuli – and whatever it was, it activated that buzzing kernel that was just beginning to gnaw at its simple mind.

After a seeming moment of reflection, the rex began to walk.

Respectfully, the Earth shook in its steps as the Tyrant King under the Mountain left the basin behind.

Almost as a group, the other rex moved in, swarming on the relinquished pile of meat, and began to tear away massive chomping bites, like a school of Great Whites stripping blubber from a dead whale.

After another moment, the 'normals' began to sneak in from the perimeter, picking at the long neck and tail that stretched beyond the reach of their giant, rage-infected fellows.

The massive corpse of the sauropod began to disappear at a remarkable rate, as even the bones were consumed – a gluttonous feeding-frenzy that continued well into the night.

When the morning came, less than a third of a corpse was left behind.

In the basin, the predators slept off their over-indulgent debauchery – snoring, belching.

And as they lay in decadent slumber, the green glow of the Food of the Gods glinted through their slitted eyes.

CHAPTER 11

Rosa had never met anyone quite like Lieutenant Lucas Walker.

That by itself was not so unusual – she had lived on campus for ten years – her jobs had been in the immediate local community – bartender and waitress – something sufficiently demeaning to subsist on, as she worked her way through school, and ran her student loans up into the National Debt. Rosa's contacts with the military had been drunken furloughs at the bars, trolling for women.

Either that or her forays into the third-world, cleaning up after them after they blew one town or another to bits.

Much to Rosa's irritation – and Jeremy's as well – Nurse Julie had been fawning over the handsome Lieutenant since the moment they'd led him down to their shattered shelter – with Lucas deliberately bouncing on his damaged foot as they descended the stairs. Julie had gone to work on his every scratch and abrasion.

Mildly amused, Lucas tolerated her indulgently.

The others had gathered 'round like cave-dwellers – Lucas was the first contact with the outside since it all began.

Rosa could see him taking professional note of the shell-shocked eyes staring back – the coffee-girl, Jamie, sat huddled, clutching her own knees to her chest like a stuffed animal – the young kid in the security badge showing way too much upper eye.

And of course at least one of them had to be pregnant – Rosa saw Lucas' eyes pause on Allison – just as Rosa's own had that very first day. This was followed by a quick appraisal of Bud, as the man looking after her.

Tactical assessment complete, he turned to Rosa, identifying her as tribal head.

"How long have you all been here?" he asked.

"Twelve days," Rosa said. "Where the hell were you?"

Lucas raised an arched eyebrow, smiling dryly. "Jeez. You sound like my wife."

"You're married?" Julie asked, crestfallen.

Lucas smiled gently. "*Very*," he said.

Rosa glanced sternly at the young nurse. She, herself, had noticed his tagged ring-finger right away – something that came with experience – and *certainly* nothing to do with any reflexive attraction on her part – just as it was only as a medical professional that she had noticed the near-perfect physique of the almost quintessential alpha-male – muscles cut with a chisel – MMA-style tattoos sleeved down both arms. And even with two days beard-growth, he presented that cut of military cleanness – absent the sloppiness she always associated with frat guys.

There was also his blatantly chauvinist good-nature – Rosa was irritated to find herself responding to it, just like some bimbo-brained cheerleader.

She reminded herself, this was one of the ones she was mad at.

"Lieutenant Walker," she began...

"Don't be so formal," Lucas cut in. "You can call me 'sir'."

He offered up a big, cheeky, excruciatingly-confident grin.

"Oh, come on," he said. "Just once. I wanna hear how it sounds coming from you."

For a moment, Rosa actually had the impulse to hit him – for all the nearly cauterized-emotional patience her job's discipline required, she actually felt her hands curling into fists.

Then she looked down at her own pampered doctor's hands next to his rocked-hide. As if she could hurt him with a baseball bat, let alone her knuckles.

Maybe she could stomp on his broken foot. Or yank out a couple of his stitches.

"Okay," Rosa said, icily, "*Sir...*,"

Lucas' brows raised.

"Brrrr," he said. "That was pretty good. Scary."

He learned forward as if with new interest.

"What was your name again, ma'am?"

"Rosa," she said. "Call me Doctor Holland."

Lucas grinned.

"So," Rosa said, "where the hell have you people been?"

"Well," Lucas said, sitting up attentively, "WE – and I'm using the royal 'WE' – have been in LA. *And* Chicago. *And* in New York. And personally, I've been right here."

"Dropping bombs on us," Rosa said. "So the military's plan was just to let us die?"

Lucas smiled patiently. "Ma'am, I don't think you understand. We *lost* in LA. *And* Chicago and New York. And in case you missed it, I got *my* ass kicked right here. And while we were trying to save all *these* places, a LOT of other spots – all full of people waiting to get rescued – all got left to burn."

He tossed a piece of the surrounding rubble dismissively.

"Or got stomped flat."

"San Fran," he said, "got off easy. You had us right here on-site. And we still got our asses kicked."

New York, Rosa thought – LA. and Chicago – those were questions she hadn't been asking yet.

While she was working up the nerve, Bud asked for her.

"What's been happening up there?"

Lucas eyed him seriously, and then the others.

"Don't ask if you don't really want to know."

The group exchanged furtive glances, but Bud nodded for all of them.

Lucas shrugged. "Well," he said, "what you see is what you get." He tossed a thumb in the direction of the smashed-in ceiling and the devastated city beyond.

"*This*," he said, "*everywhere*."

There was a long, sober silence.

"Locally," Lucas continued, "once things went south in L.A. and here in San Fran... well, we kinda had a lot of bases clustered right around here – and damned if they pretty much didn't get taken completely out."

Rosa took quiet note of the word 'completely'.

Again, Bud asked the question she didn't want to.

"What's left?"

Lucas shrugged. "West Coast? Militarily, pretty much the land bases are gone. Fortunately, this was a big Navy area and we've managed to relocate off-shore. The anchor-point is just off Fort Hunter – about a hundred miles south.

"Other than that," he continued, tapping a rim-shot on a smashed car-bumper, "it's all gone."

He waved his hand slowly, as if wiping it all away.

"*Everything*," he said.

The little circle stared back, blinking in the dark. Julie's eyes were wide and mollified. Bud reflexively pulled Allison close. Jamie squeezed herself tighter into her little ball. Even Jeremy paused in his incessant pacing.

So," Lucas said, slapping his hands with by-rote, gung-ho optimism, "that's the score as it stands. Obviously, that's a number we're going to try and improve on."

He hiked his wounded leg up on to the rubble like an easy chair and reclined, as if dismissing the subject altogether, and ready to simply settle down for a nap.

Rosa cleared her voice.

"Well, Lieutenant Walker," she said, "what's the military's master-plan now?"

Now Lucas grinned. "That's classified. I could tell you, but then I'd have to kill you."

Rosa felt her knuckles curling again.

"Okay," she said patently, "what's YOUR master-plan?"

"Well," he said, waggling his injured foot, "as soon I can get along a little better, I'm taking us all out of here, and we're gonna reconnect with my base just a hop south of here."

"Define 'a hop'."

"Fort Hunter. Like I said. A hundred miles or so." Lucas tapped his bum leg. "That's why I want my foot working better."

"And you expect us to just follow you through a hundred miles of monster-infested war-zone?"

Lucas shrugged, then nodded.

"Best not to linger," he said. He made as if to check his watch. "My wife's probably already expecting me. And she gets really testy when I'm late and don't call." He offered Rosa a confidential wink. "You know how women are."

"I do," Rosa said.

Lucas reached for his wallet. "Here," he said. "This is her."

He pulled out a well-worn photograph and handed it over.

Suitably gorgeous, Rosa thought – a bombshell in a boob-shirt and a thong – a perfect complement to Lucas' own chiseled musculature.

The kind of woman that even Rosa – who could turn heads in her doctor's fatigues – reflexively hated.

"She won that wet t-shirt-contest, by the way," Lucas informed her, as if baiting her with her own just-finished thought – while she sat there with two-weeks of hairy pits, furry legs, and no bath.

Lucas was briefly lost in his own moment – smiling to himself as he took back his photograph – holding it with the care of a fragile antique.

"This was the very first day we met," he said, "We were just kids. I was just out of boot. Met her on the beach."

When he looked back up, his eyes were, for the first time, unguarded, and just a little bit wistful.

"I like photographs," he said. "We always fight about that – my wife, she's gone one-hundred percent digital." Lucas held up his own cellphone. "But this stupid thing hasn't worked once since all this shit started."

He held up the worn Polaroid. "I still got this."

Then he paused, considering. "You know, if I told her that, it'd piss her off, just for my being right."

Rosa said nothing. But she could see that happening.

Lucas very carefully folded the picture back into his wallet.

"And speaking of that," he said, making another show of checking his watch, "all this shit going down and I haven't *called*? I know she's *already* fixing to kill me."

He held up his forehead to the light. "I was out late on poker-night with the boys once. Tried to sneak into bed after curfew. She gave me this, with her ring finger."

Just at his hairline, was the scar from a row of stitches – the kind of injury that might be caused by a knuckled-up diamond.

Despite herself, Rosa smiled – okay, now she was beginning to like her – maybe she could forgive the thong-bikini.

"What's her name?" Rosa asked.

"Naomi," Lucas said.

And then, with just a slight puff of his chest, "MRS. Naomi Walker."

CHAPTER 12

As it happened, Lieutenant Walker was right on both counts – at that very moment, Mrs. Naomi Walker was at once swearing violence and cursing his name.

After twelve days alone with her up in his cabin, Jonah was beginning to fear for the guy if she ever found him.

They hadn't been bothered by the beasts – not this high up – not this remote. But the radio reports had not sounded good – and even those had not lasted for long.

Naomi had been marking each day off on the kitchen wall-calendar – it was a point of irritation for her that the days accumulated with no word from her husband – and she didn't care if it wasn't coming from her dead cell-phone, the defunct post-office, or singing goddamned telegram – all she knew was that he was very goddamn late and she was getting pretty goddamn mad.

"This sort of thing is *just* like him," she said, glaring at Jonah, as if he were in on it.

Jonah gritted his teeth – not for the first time or the hundredth. He had learned that was her way.

In the last couple of weeks, he had learned a lot about Mrs. Naomi Walker – who still sometimes thought of herself as Naomi Kathryn Anderson – a military brat – raised on bases – valedictorian of her high-school class, but never went to college – met her soon-to-be husband while partying on her twenty-first birthday.

Jonah knew this about her – he had learned a *lot* about her. Among other things, he learned she had high-standards – standards that he wasn't *near* living up to.

She had been utterly appalled at his cabin: "You *live* here? Are you a transient, or an alcoholic or something?"

It also turned out Jonah shared a lot of her husband's faults – 'man-faults', she called them – but apparently none of his virtues. Or if he did, she hadn't mentioned one yet.

A lot of it was certainly cabin-pressure, but Jonah wondered if this was how she always handled her husband's absence during deployment – talking aloud to him as if he was right in the room – actually getting angry over things he *would* do if he was – and then seemed to hold it against him that he wasn't.

Or maybe she was simply nuts.

Either way, those were conversations Jonah had learned not to get involved in.

You might have thought just by looking at her that, if you *had* to be trapped for an extended period in an isolated cabin, it might as well be with *her*.

You would have been wrong. It was actually a good deal worse than being stuck up there alone. Jonah had never experienced cabin-fever in his life, before two weeks ago – this place had been his refuge.

They hadn't gotten off to a good start – as he had let her into his single-bedroom dwelling, she had set *that* boundary immediately.

"Look," she said, "I'm married. Don't be getting any ideas."

In light of current circumstances, that had knocked Jonah's nose just a little out of joint.

"Little presumptuous? I didn't exactly slip you a roofie to get you here, you know."

She smirked. "Please. You're a guy. I look like *this*." She eyed him knowingly. "I saw you eyeballing me back at the store."

Jonah colored briefly – he'd thought he'd been more subtle.

"I'm not that type of guy," he said.

She gave him another one of her appraising up-and-downs.

"No," she agreed, "probably not. Forget I brought it up."

That one almost sparked his temper. She knew how to touch a nerve.

Did girls just sense it, he wondered? Did they just instinctively know how to twist that knife in just the appropriate way to really *dig*?

Jonah *almost* said it to her – see, there were guys who would nail your wife, and those who wouldn't. And just because you weren't a rat-bastard, didn't make you a fuckin' beta-male.

He wasn't that type of guy because he HATED that guy.

His marriage had ended over THAT guy.

A wife of ten years – who he had married young, and expected to be with for the rest of his life.

He remembered very clearly the moment that he *knew*.

He also remembered thinking some very dark thoughts about THAT guy – and he understood very clearly crimes of passion.

'Anger' was not even the word – it was more primal than that – it just sort of *melted* over him, like lava meeting ice – the ugly, black, choking anger of a cuckold – pretty much the same instinctive/chemical response you got all down the animal phylums – it didn't matter whether you were a man or a wolf – if you mess with thy neighbor's wife, you better expect some teeth in your ass.

They had been living in Portland then, and Jonah remembered loading up his rifle and climbing calmly into his Bronco – and he had found himself wondering how many men had felt just like this throughout human history – all the way back to the caveman marching purposely out of his cave, armed with a wooden club. He seemed to be moving on autopilot – acting out an almost involuntary, socio-evolutionary response – cause and effect.

He had driven to the end of his street... and then, instead of driving into town, he had turned south, gotten on the highway, and come out to this very cabin.

And he had never really come back.

When he got there, he had sent that one text he had ever sent in his life.

"I want a divorce."

Poking out one painstaking button at a time – it took him another two minutes to figure out how to send it.

He never saw her again – he never spoke her name – the proceedings all got handled through the lawyers. No contest with any of the property. Her new guy had money.

She *had* eventually called him – after she and new-guy had split.

Jonah hadn't answered.

That had been ten years ago.

Naomi's from-the-hip judgment lanced a lot of old wounds.

"You don't have to worry about me," Jonah told her. "Once bitten, twice shy."

The subtly of their dynamic was not improved by the fact of the man she *did* have – not just a 'man', but a MAN. It wasn't overt – or even intentional, Jonah believed – but she could not help but look at Jonah, himself, with a touch of contempt for what he wasn't.

And Jonah, for his part, couldn't help but acknowledge the comparison. He'd met a few fighter pilots during the course of getting his own license, and they were all ripped arms and cage-fighter tattoos – cut with military discipline.

From her point of view, he could understand her lack of enthusiasm at being stuck with *him*.

He was embarrassed even to tell her he was a pilot – he hadn't even brought it up until she found one of his business cards, which read simply, 'Jonah Kirkland Charters'.

"Captain Kirkland?" she had asked doubtfully.

She was even less impressed after she saw the little buckets he flew – one archaic old chopper and a single-engine plane.

And truth to tell, he was even a little afraid to fly *those*. He simply didn't have the nerve or coordination to handle something like a fighter-jet.

He'd watched those guys practice – half-a-dozen planes, separated by a meter in formation, at twelve-hundred miles an hour – *that* kind of precision. It actually gave him the shudders.

Jonah had wanted to learn to fly since he was young – enough to pursue it to a license – but it had never been like he'd pictured as a kid – it wasn't soaring like a bird – it was like driving a big, heavy truck – tons of weight going at high-speed.

The thought of taking that up to super-sonic – and then only a couple feet apart?

It was flat beyond his ability – he was simply a lower-grade model.

Neither did he particularly aspire to be any kind of hero – certainly, he had spent the last decade hiding himself away – he'd gotten unacknowledged communications from his ex-wife that said so.

Although, as it turned out, that *had* saved his life.

Living well was the best revenge – or in this case, just living.

He almost smiled before remembering how literal that was, and felt a little ashamed.

Jonah hadn't spoken to his wife in years, but he knew her phone number, e-mail, where she worked, and where she lived.

Now he wondered if she was still alive.

Naomi, in that regard, was of remarkably little help – when he'd mentioned his divorce, she expressed theatrical shock that any woman might leave all *this*.

Jonah reminded himself they were only in proximity through circumstances.

It was ironic – his time with Naomi actually left him feeling lonelier than he ever had living alone. It was like being lab-partner with the popular-girl in high-school – with her embarrassed and chaffing under the forced contact.

Basically, if he was the second-to-last guy on Earth, she was STILL out of his league.

In fact, at dawn on day fifteen, Naomi informed him she was leaving.

He woke to find her dressed, packed, and ready to go.

"I hope you don't mind," she said, "I took a few supplies."

Jonah, who had been sleeping on his own couch, feet extended over one arm, had looked up blearily.

"What are you talking about?"

She made as if to check her watch.

"I told you, he's late," she said. "He always said he'd be in touch – he promised me he'd perform miracles. Said he'd move Heaven and Earth. But it's been two weeks and I haven't heard word-one."

She hiked her pack.

"That means, I'm going to have to go and find *him*."

She shook her head grimly. "And then, *God* help him."

Jonah was still wiping sleep out of his eyes.

"Hold on. Where exactly do you think you're going to go? You heard the last reports – everything's gone. Hell, the reports are gone."

Jonah had a regional map posted along one wall and Naomi pointed to Arcata Bay, bordering the town of Eureka, on the northern coast of California – maybe a hundred and fifty miles as the crow-flies, two-hundred or more by land.

"This is where we always said we'd meet," Naomi said. "If anything major went down."

"Why? There's nothing there."

"That's why. It's not likely to be a deliberate target – but it's a hubcap for military travel – by air and sea. You can usually count on at least one destroyer anchored offshore."

She tapped her dead cell-phone. "They've also got a new communications tower."

"Okay," Jonah said, "that's a couple hundred miles. How were you planning on getting there?"

"Well," she said, her hands on her hips, "I notice you have a plane. *And* a helicopter. But I'll walk if I have to."

She turned for the door as if ready to leave that very minute, tossing her hair impatiently over her shoulder.

"You are under no obligation to follow," she said.

Jonah muttered under his breath as he dressed. He pulled the keys to the chopper off the nail on the wall.

Naomi was already standing in front of the plane, studying it, and shaking her head disapprovingly.

Maybe he should try and claim repair issues, Jonah thought – stall another few days.

It *would* at least be sensible to do a maintenance once-over on the chopper – both air-craft were looking a bit like a mower that hadn't been ridden in a couple seasons.

But Naomi was eyeing him – poised to simply turn and walk back down the mountain without him.

Within the hour, they were in the air.

CHAPTER 13

To be fair, it was not a long flight – even in Jonah's taped-up little pod-fighter, they should safely make the distance inside a couple of hours.

He'd actually done the route semi-regularly in the past. The military comings and goings also made Eureka a hub for maintenance folk – both boat and air-men throughout the surrounding region took their engines there.

So there could be worse destinations, Jonah thought. Eureka also had air-parks and fuel stations – and Naomi was perfectly right about it being out of the way. It was actually not a bad spot for a predetermined rendezvous. Jonah was just glad her fighter-pilot hadn't told her to meet him in L.A.

They had taken his chopper instead of the plane – something Jonah knew by the numbers to be inherently more dangerous – a chopper was basically in a constant state of near-crashing – but when he was flying it, he could feel the wind – it wasn't like driving a big truck in the sky. The chopper was also easier to land in rough spots.

And besides, planes scared him. He'd never gotten used to driving the big trucks either, even though he'd done that for ten years too – he'd had a Budweiser-delivery truck on two-wheels once – he'd been eighteen at the time, and you just should have *seen* the guy's face in the convertible next to him.

As a pilot – *and* as a river-guide – his philosophy was, when possible, go by boat.

Naomi, for her part, seemed none-too-confident either, glancing nervously at Jonah at every sudden dip or lurch. She gripped her seat as they came down low for a look at the shattered landscape.

A closer view was no help.

"It looks like a fleet of tornadoes went through down there," Jonah said.

He could see where large swatches of the forest looked to have been mowed over. It had been like this for miles. Once they'd gotten out of the mountains, it was worse.

They were still in remote forest land, but it looked like a giant army had passed through. While there were wide areas that were largely untouched, whatever had fallen along the path was simply wiped away.

And scattered among the wrecked foliage, was the odd carcass of something giant.

These were mostly bones – pulled apart and spread across the forest floor. But they were BIG.

"How much further?" Naomi asked, looking just a touch green as the chopper again dipped suddenly in mid-air.

"We're about halfway," Jonah said. "I'm trying to take it easy on gas, just in case we have to make it back without refueling."

He glanced out the window.

"This is all a lot worse than I expected," he said. "I had a couple of fueling spots in mind down off Arcata Bay – I mean something I could maybe access, even if it was abandoned. But... well, if it's all like this..."

He trailed off, shaking his head.

"How far can we make it?" Naomi asked.

"We can get there," he said. "But if anything goes south, we could wind up having to put down in the middle of nowhere – on foot – with nothing for a hundred miles.

"So," Jonah said mildly, "thanks for thinking of this."

Naomi's eyes narrowed and she let out an irritated breath with practiced patience.

"*Just* the sort of thing my husband would say."

Sprawled across the river below them, was yet another massive carcass – more intact than the others – enough to recognize as a giant sauropod.

The length of its body seemed to stretch out on the valley floor forever.

Even more remarkable was the extent to which it had been utterly cannibalized, with just bits and pieces clinging to the giant bones. The carcass had also largely been abandoned, except for what looked like birds pecking away at the last hard-to-get spots.

They had heard reports of the giants before the radio cut out, but the littered carcasses were the first evidence they'd seen first-hand.

Although, now that Jonah thought about it, there HAD been that rex-sized sickle-claw back in Siskiyou Pass – the one with glowing green eyes.

As they flew overhead, the winged scavengers reacted to their presence, flocking away from the rotting meat like flies.

Then they spread out into flight, and Jonah could see the bat-like wings.

Not birds – pterosaurs.

Some of them were over thirty-feet across.

And now, Jonah realized, they were coming after *them*.

"Jonah...!" Naomi began.

"I see them!" he said, banking hard, but the flock had overtaken them in a cloud.

Some of them had beaks, others had teeth – they began to bite and claw at the chopper, and the first of them dipped into the rotating propellers.

There was the sound of chopping meat and a heron-squawk. The chopper jerked, splattering their windows with blood, as the rear rotor was broken away.

Jonah cursed. Naomi gripped her seat, pressing her feet into the floor as if trying to brake.

The chopper began to spin.

Jonah struggled to keep them level, but their bat-winged attackers weren't done.

In apparently mindless, instinctual aggression – the territorial equivalent of a gang-mugging – the flock of them kept coming, and now one of the large ones tipped a wing into the main-rotors.

The light-boned limb chopped right off, but so did part of one of the blades.

Their straggling spin, began to deteriorate into a rolling tumble. The terrain below was all trees and rocks.

"Ohhhh SHIT!" Jonah strained, struggling with the controls. "I wanted to stay at the goddamn cabin."

Naomi belted him in the arm, turning his shoulder instantly numb. "*Do something!*"

"I'm trying! This isn't exactly a glider!"

Jonah felt the chopper spinning fully out of control – their only chance was to get as near to the ground as he could before the rotors cut completely.

But this time, one of the pterosaurs attacked from above. Jonah could see it coming – a dive-bomb attack.

As it drew close, he could see its eyes – they were glowing green.

The bird-thing hit the top rotor, suicidally chopping itself to pieces.

But it was enough – the rotor broke loose and went spinning.

They were in free fall, plummeting to Earth.

Jonah shut his eyes, feeling Naomi's nails digging into his shoulder.

"Hang on!" he shouted.

The chopper crashed into the trees.

CHAPTER 14

Lucas was ready to move.

He had allowed himself three days convalescence. At dawn on the fourth day, he simply stood up and said, "Time to go people."

As a group, they had slept fitfully, and Lucas was met with little enthusiasm.

Lucas slapped his hands. "Seriously, folks. You all are civilians in a war-zone. That means it's my job to get you to safety. It'd sure make my job easier if you came along."

Rosa pointed at his still-swollen purple leg. "You still can't even walk."

Lucas tossed a dismissive wave. "I could always walk on it. I was just waiting until I could run."

He smiled, looking around at the circle of unhappy faces.

"What? No laugh?"

Rosa shut her eyes. She'd been expecting this – he'd been setting them all up for the last couple of days. She had watched him go to work on each of them – never for a moment stepping from behind the hard-boiled persona – and his methods were not subtle.

He had actually started with timid little Jamie, who, just like Julie, looked at him in awe, yet was also terrified of him. His first night in the garage, he had sat down next to her, coaxing her over like she once would have coaxed her little lost cat.

"Listen, honey," he had sad. "You don't gotta be afraid anymore. You just stick close."

Simple as that. Her face streaked with dirt and tears, Jamie looked up at him and nodded.

Lucas had tapped his busted foot. "Just need a day or two, myself. So right now it's sort of a rescue in slow-motion. Think you can follow me out of here?"

Jamie had smiled timidly for the first time since it all began.

Rosa had likewise watched him hobble down next to Bud and Allison – similarly direct and succinct, indicating Allison's barely-showing belly.

He eyed Bud meaningfully. "You've got a situation, here," he said.

Bud nodded.

"You're looking after her, right?"

Bud glanced at Allison. "I am," he said.

`Lucas clapped his shoulder agreeably. "I'm going to count on that."

Jeremy had been a bit put-out that his position as guard dog seemed to have been usurped – yet he was also in awe of this apparently authentic American hero.

Lucas had flicked his finger on Jeremy's security badge.

"What's this part-time bullshit? Why not the real thing?"

Jeremy glanced to see if Julie was in earshot, before replying in a low voice.

"I tried being a cop. I wasn't good enough."

"Wasn't good enough because you got the job and blew it, or because they wouldn't let you try?"

Before Jeremy could answer, Lucas stepped up eye-to-eye, like with a fresh recruit.

"Well," he said, tapping his name-tag again, "Jeremy. Here's your chance to be judged on your character instead of a checklist."

Jeremy looked uncertain.

"How you going to judge yourself, son?"

The younger man again glanced in the direction of Nurse Julie.

Lucas smiled, grabbing Jeremy's chin, and turned him in the other direction, where coffee-girl, Jamie sat alone.

"Trust me," he said, "try your luck over there, instead."

Rosa wasn't sure what was more galling – the deliberate nature of the manipulation or the fact that it worked.

Besides squaring the young man's shoulders, within the hour, Jeremy was sitting next to Jamie and the two of them had paired off like a couple of ducks.

"Smooth, isn't he?" Rosa had commented to Julie.

Julie had batted her eyes dreamily. *"Yeah*, he is."

Rosa suppressed a tired sigh.

She had also noticed the Lieutenant had made no effort to beguile *her*.

His methods now became clear.

Now that Lucas had spent two days psyching them all up, they would turn to Rosa to make the call. Seeing the set-up, Rosa attempted to abdicate by simply walking away – at least as far as the garage would allow. Lucas solved that by following her.

"Time to go, Doctor Holland."

"You've got everybody ready to charge over the hill, don't you?" Rosa said. She nodded at the others. "These people are refugees, not recruits."

Lucas nodded agreeably. "Still, if you're going to do something dangerous..."

He let the point hang.

"What if you end up getting everybody killed?" Rosa said.

Lucas sighed. "Honey, look around you. Things are not going to get better." He tapped a finger on his own forehead. "Don't you get it? I AM the rescue. There isn't anyone else that's going to come."

He took her shoulder and turned her so she had to meet his eyes.

"Doctor Holland. If you want out of here, you're going to have to walk out. Or you're going to die here. It's just that simple."

For a moment, the unrelenting bravado faded and he looked down at her with genuine sympathy.

"You're afraid. I understand the urge to hide," he said. "But you can't let yourself freeze up." He shook his head. "You *know* you can't just stay here indefinitely."

Rosa said nothing. She knew that perfectly well.

"Look," Lucas said. "I can see you've been taking care of these people. You probably feel responsible for them. Natural enough. You're a doctor. But that means I need *you* to help *me*."

Now he turned her towards the others, who were looking over expectantly – a simple, deliberate, obvious gesture.

"They're scared," he said. "But if you come with me, they'll follow."

He let her have a moment for the thought to sink in.

"The other option," he said, "is that I just throw you over my shoulder and carry you out of here caveman-style."

He tapped his watch again.

"Don't mean to be impatient," he said, "but we're running low on options."

Rosa would never admit it, but the caveman-thing actually helped. It took a little pressure off of her, realizing she wasn't really being offered a choice.

She shut her eyes.

"Okay," she said. "Let's go."

CHAPTER 15

As she followed him up the stairwell, Rosa knew that Lucas had been right – she *was* afraid.

The air actually seemed to grow heavier the closer they got to the surface. She stopped, catching her breath. Lucas stopped with her, as if ready to grab her if she should try and run. She eyed hem warily.

"You weren't really going to physically drag me out of here against my will, were you?"

Lucas smiled sincerely and patted her comfortingly on her head.

"Aw, honey," he said. "Of *course* I was."

"So, at this point, I'm really more your hostage, then?"

Lucas tilted his head, considering, but did not disagree.

He hiked his pack. "Whatever happens," he said, "you and Julie stay close to me. You're *my* watch."

"What?"

Lucas nodded at the others. "I've got Bud on Allison. Jeremy on Jamie. That means I've got to watch you two."

Rosa paused. "*Watch* us?" She said, "like we're the helpless females?"

She glanced over at Julie and was all the more irritated as the young nurse practically fluttered at the thought.

"That," Rosa said, "might be the most condescendingly chauvinistic thing I've ever heard."

"I *do* get that," Lucas allowed. "You really would like my wife."

But he remained nonplussed. "Still," he said, "survival is about pragmatism, and human-nature is human-nature."

Glancing back over his shoulder, he spoke loudly and openly, to all of them at once.

"Men are guard dogs," he said. "It's what we're good for." He turned an appraising eye on Rosa. "Wouldn't you expect your husband to take a bullet for you?"

"I'm not married," Rosa said.

Lucas snapped his fingers. "*That's* right. I forgot."

Beside her, Julie tittered. Rosa spared her a glare.

They had reached street-level, and before he poked his head experimentally into the open air, Lucas gave one last meaningful look to Rosa. "In all seriousness, Doctor Holland. Stick close."

It was still early morning – the beginning of another sunny San Francisco day.

In procession, they let themselves back up into the light.

Lucas made his way up the ridge of rubble that used to be the hospital – the vantage to the rest of the city.

Rosa and the others started to follow, but Lucas motioned for them to stay low. He pulled out his binoculars, and scanned what was left behind.

Rosa followed a few steps more until she could see.

The city was gone – nothing left but rubble – even the dust had settled.

Likewise, very little remained of the giant carcasses – the bones had been pulled apart and scattered, blending in with the rest of the debris.

What had Lucas said that first night?

This. Everywhere.

Lucas packed his binoculars, motioning the others back down the slope.

"You all stay put," he said. "I'm going to do a quick circle. I spotted a couple of vehicles." He turned to Rosa for emphasis, pointing her back down to the street.

"Wait *here*," he said.

With that, he hopped up and over the broken pilings.

After a moment – perhaps feeling a bit defiant – Rosa followed him up to the top – just far enough to watch him hit the street and dogtrot out of sight around the first demolished city block.

"Doctor Holland," Julie called softly, behind her. "The Lieutenant said to wait down here."

Rosa glanced irritably over her shoulder.

"I'm not going anywhere," she called back, "I just want to see."

She turned to the view of the city, and promptly slipped on the loose rubble.

The concrete beneath her feet shifted, and before she knew it, she was riding a mini-avalanche all the way down to the street.

She had been standing on a buried girder, or she might have actually been hurt quite badly – the scraps and mortar beneath her feet weighed in the tons – makeshift boulders, some the size of cars.

As it was, she was good and battered by the time she tumbled the forty feet to a rough landing on the road below.

She coughed in the fresh cloud of dust, and her eyes teared. When she wiped with her hands, they came away bloody.

Julie's head popped up over the top of the remaining pilings.

"Oh, my God! Doctor Holland, are you alright?"

Julie carefully began climbing down the slope, picking her way over the larger, more stable-looking slabs. Rosa was dusting herself off, counting her bruises, as Julie kneeled down beside her, helping her to her feet, immediately fussing over her abrasions.

Rosa patted her hands down, looking at Julie earnestly.

"We aren't going to be telling the Lieutenant about this," she said. "Are we agreed?"

Julie looked doubtful, as she dabbed at a bit of running blood on Rosa's forehead.

"He might ask," she said.

Rosa pushed Julie away, and turned back towards the ravaged skyline.

They had lost their vantage, and Rosa began to circle her way back towards the high-ground.

"Where are you going?" Julie asked, a frantic tone creeping into her voice, like a kid afraid of getting caught after curfew.

"For crying out loud," Rosa said, "I just want to get a look at the city."

Reluctantly, Julie followed the half-a-block to where the hilltop looked down into the main downtown area.

They stood for a moment, taking it all in.

The city maintained that same dead silence. Beyond general geography, it was hard even to tell what roads had been where.

Rosa found herself thinking, of all things, about her canceled date – a man she had never even met. He had lived right downtown.

He had sent her that one last text – 'Have a nice life,' it had said.

Was he out there right now? Crushed in the rubble – cannibalized by some scaly, pint-sized lizard?

Or what about her friend, Suzy, who lived downstate in L.A.?

Lucas had said they had *lost* in L.A.

Suzy also lived right downtown. She would have been right in the middle of it.

Rosa wondered if there was anything even physically left of her, let alone alive.

Beside her, Julie choked just a little bit.

Rosa found she didn't want to see anymore. She turned away from the ruined skyline...

... just as a voice behind them spoke practically into her ear.

"Well, honey – where did you come from?"

The voice was followed by the sound of rifle bolts sliding back.

CHAPTER 16

Three men separated from the surrounding rubble – all three with rifles – one of them looked like an AR.

The giants had been gone for days, Rosa thought belatedly – there hadn't been any looting in the city because no one was left alive.

These weren't city folk – at a glance, not much above transients – bumpkins living in the hills, come down into town to see what was salvageable.

Rosa and Julie both raised their hands.

"No need for guns," Rosa said. "We're no threat."

The man who had spoken nodded mildly. "Hear that, boys? They're no threat."

The other two men laughed. None of them lowered their guns.

Rosa could now safely assume their intentions.

The first man was looking Rosa up and down. "You didn't survive all this by yourself," he said. "You've got people with you." He held up the barrel of his rifle. "Where are they?"

Rosa said nothing.

The man smiled grimly. Then he turned his rifle and pressed it against Julie's head.

"One more time," he said, looking at Rosa meaningfully.

"Aw c'mon, Leroy," one of the others said. "She's hot. Don't waste her. Just shoot her in the leg or something."

Julie's breath had stopped, her eyes turned wide and frightened to Rosa.

"Don't," Rosa said, holding her hands up. "Please. Don't hurt her. There's just six of us. We've been trapped."

'Leroy' pushed Julie over next to Rosa and held his gun on them both.

"Where?" he said.

"Just around the corner."

Leroy nodded. "Then lead the way, ladies. Don't do anything stupid."

"Why are you doing this?" Rosa said, her voice rising in outrage. "For God's sake! Can't we just help each other?"

Leroy paused, considering. Then he reached out a beefy mitt and backhanded Rosa across the face.

The blow was nearly powerful enough to knock her out. She staggered into Julie's steadying hands. She felt her cheek, where a large, swelling knot had joined her already assorted bruises.

Leroy was staring at them both seriously. He held up his rifle.

Rosa knew the type. Some people bought guns for defense – some for hunting. Some because they wanted to kill somebody.

It was more common than you might think – not the psycho-serial-killer – more the alpha-wannabe – the guy who secretly hopes for the burglar to break in.

"Move," he said.

The pile of rubble that had been the hospital was still shifting, so Rosa and Julie led them around on the street. Thus they came upon their little group from behind, still huddled by the stairwell.

Jeremy was the first to look over his shoulder and see them.

"Oh, what the *hell*?"

Bud was on his feet in a moment, but Leroy and the other two men quickly fanned out to either side, their rifles already up and aimed.

"Stay right where you are, folks."

Bud didn't move, standing in front of Allison – Lucas' caveman psychology working as if programmed.

One of the other men was giving Jamie an approving once-over, and Jeremy immediately stepped between them – only to be met with a rifle butt across the face, knocking him to the ground.

When Jeremy looked up, Leroy had his gun on him.

"You're gonna be trouble, aren't ya, boy? Just can't wait to be a hero, can ya?"

He brought the barrel up to Jeremy's head.

Rosa stepped forward quickly, but Leroy's rifle quickly turned on her instead.

She stopped, looking up into his eyes, trying to see if he would really do it.

Before she could decide, a shot rang in her ears.

Rosa blinked – she'd actually felt the displacement of the bullet past her ear.

Leroy dropped to his knees, holding his shoulder, his rifle clattering on the pavement.

Lucas was standing atop the ridge of concrete, pistol out and aimed.

The other two men, both with high-caliber weapons, looked indecisive.

Lucas was smiling. "Hey fellas. You may have noticed I shot your buddy in the shoulder. They say never to do that. There's no point – it can kill you anyway – so they tell you just to aim for center of mass and be done with it." He shook his head. "Damn me and my insubordination."

He cocked back the hammer on his pistol.

"So," he said, "you fellas wanna be refugees, or casualties?"

While they were thinking it over, Allison took the opportunity to draw her own pistol – empty of bullets – stepping up behind the second man, and cocking the hammer right behind his ear.

The two men exchanged glances and raised their hands.

Lucas nodded approvingly. "Very good," he said, ambling leisurely down the embankment. "Jeremy? Would you and Mr. Adams be so kind as to relieve these gentlemen of their firearms?"

Bud and Jeremy, pulled the rifles off the two men's shoulders and then patted them down, coming away with assorted pistols and clips.

One was a 9 mm – which Bud handed to Allison, who tossed her old empty pistol aside.

Jeremy hefted one of the rifles – a 30.06.

"There you go," Lucas said as he walked up, his pistol held casually at his side, yet never straying from any of the three men. "Now you've got yourself a real gun."

Jeremy pulled the bolt back experimentally – then leveled the rifle at the man who'd just handed it to him – the one who had butted him with it across the face.

It was Bud who casually turned the barrel away, patting Jeremy on the shoulder.

"That's it," Lucas said, his easy smile never changing. "We're all friends, now, right?"

Now he turned to Rosa.

"You know, Doctor Holland," he said, "I asked you to stay put." He shook his head. "I swear, I know you're a smart girl – but at this point, it's faith that lets me know that."

Rosa started to object, but Lucas held up a placating hand.

"I get it," he said. "You've got a stubborn streak." He took a deep breath. "You'd *really* like my wife."

With that, Lucas squatted down next to where Leroy still sat holding his shoulder. He quickly and efficiently rifled any remaining weapons or shells from the wounded man's pockets, and then pulled him up off the ground and sat him on a flat slab of concrete.

"Doctor Holland," he said, "would you please look at this man's arm?"

As he gave the order – and it felt very much like an 'order' – particularly since Rosa promptly obeyed – Lucas moved back up the slope, resuming his vantage over the surrounding blocks.

He nodded urgently to Rosa. "Just a quick look please," he said. "He ought to be able to walk. That's why I didn't shoot him in the leg."

And then with a little slap in the air, as if he were swatting her tush, "And can we hurry, please?"

Pursing her lips, Rosa knelt down beside Leroy, who was looking doubtfully up at Lucas.

With her best professional smile, she asked, "So, Leroy, what are your friend's names?"

Leroy shrugged, turning to his companions. The tall one, who had hit Jeremy with the rifle butt waved nervously.

"Uh, I'm Daryl," he said.

"Bob," said the other.

Rosa pulled the shirt away from Leroy's wound – noting the precision of the shot – almost straight through the muscle. No doubt a second shot would have been just as precise through the eye.

Which, of course, as Rosa now knew, would be another broken rule – you were supposed to aim for center of mass.

Using the torn shirt, Rosa begin to clean the wound, prompting a squawk from Leroy.

Lucas was tapping his watch. "Uh, Doctor Holland. Can we put on make-up later? I just want to make sure he's not going to bleed to death in the next hour. So can you save the bed-side manner?"

Rosa stared back angrily. "Lieutenant Walker, you have just *shot* this man."

"I'll shoot him again if it'll get us moving. It's not a good idea to linger."

Rosa turned to where Leroy was trying to rise.

"I can walk," he said.

Rosa put her hands on his shoulders, pushing him to sit.

Leroy's eyes were wide. "That guy ain't gonna kill me, is he?"

Standing on the crest, Lucas sighed.

"No. But THEY might."

On the far side of the lot – just over the rise of wreckage opposite the hospital – sniffing at the rubble, following their noses – a pack of sickle-claws had appeared – big ones, leopard-sized or better.

Focused on the scent – they hadn't spotted them yet.

Lucas' voice was low and flat. "I found a rig," he said. "It's just down the way."

He nodded down the path behind them, where the rubble spilled into the street.

"Quietly," he said. "Everybody move."

He held back, waving everybody on. He had taken up Leroy's confiscated AR.

Rosa glanced back after him.

As she did so, her foot kicked up a rock.

On the ridge, one of the creatures turned.

And in the manner of an excited monkey, it began to hop up and down, hooting excitedly.

The other sickle-claws all turned. And as a flock, they came darting down the pilings, claws flexing back, coiling to leap.

Lucas let out a slow sigh, sparing Rosa a raised eyebrow, before putting his rifle to his shoulder and picking off the front row of the charging pack.

More of them, however, were poking their heads over the ridge. Lucas barked over his shoulder. "Go!"

But even as he turned, he saw that route was now cut off as well – the spindly creatures had flanked them, and they seemed to be materializing from the cracks in all directions.

Rosa knew it was undoubtedly their gunfire that had attracted the attention, but she couldn't help see the image – they were like packs of attack-dogs in brutal ancient wars – rooting out survivors – primitive and barbaric search-and-destroy missions.

She knew that was silly, of course – anthropomorphic projection – they were simply predators eating carrion and targeting easy prey.

Although, she thought, that was a distinction without a practical difference.

Either way, they were trapped.

Lucas cursed, stopping to pop a new clip into his rifle, glancing back at the others.

"Mr. Adams?" he said, "Jeremy? Would you please give me a hand shooting these goddamn things?"

And with that, he opened fire, picking off the advancing sickle-claws methodically, one at a time. He was joined by Bud, and then, after a moment of fiddling with his rifle, by Jeremy.

After the first barrage of gunfire, the advancing pack broke to either side of the street, moving into stalk mode, even as more of them continued to materialize out of the surrounding rubble.

Lucas placed his shots patiently, letting the near-random fire of the other two men keep the creatures scattered and off-balance.

In-between shots, he called over to Daryl and Bob.

"Gentlemen," he said, "would you two be so kind as to pull up that manhole?"

The two exchanged glances, hesitating – something that, in the heat of the moment, Lucas was not prepared to tolerate.

"Let's *go*!" he barked. "Right now, Goddamnit! Or I'll shoot you!"

In a single motion, the both of them reached down and started straining at the round metal plate. There was the loud scraping of iron on pavement, and a clattering as they tossed the heavy lid aside.

"Go!" Lucas shouted. "You two first – make sure it's clear." And then, when they again hesitated, "I swear, I will cap you *both*!"

Clearly not doubting him, Bob clambered down into the dark hole, followed quickly by Daryl.

Without waiting, Lucas motioned the others to follow. Looking fretful, Jamie nevertheless, slid herself down into the tunnel. Julie followed after.

Rosa, however, was helping Leroy with his injured arm. Looking impatient, Allison moved to help.

The sickle-claws, however, had discovered a new avenue of attack – a number of them had found a perch where the wreckage of a highway overpass crossed almost directly over their heads.

Rosa looked up just as three of them came leaping down, seemingly right out of the sky.

They first targeted the wounded Leroy, and he was yanked bodily out of Rosa's hands.

This was followed by a wet ripping sound, and Leroy began to scream.

Rosa gasped as she felt the second creature's claws latch onto her shoulders – not digging – just grabbing – pulling her back in to that disemboweling sickle.

A gunshot rang almost directly in her ear as Allison shot the creature between the eyes, before turning to the third, even as it landed almost on top of her.

Lucas, however, took that one out with a single shot.

Bud drew a bead on the remaining creature, even as it dug into Leroy's still-kicking body. Bud pumped five shots into its chest, blowing the creature off its feet.

Rosa blinked, as the dead sickle-claw twitched at her feet.

Lucas shouted again. "Go! They're still coming!"

From the broken overpass, more lizard-heads were peering down.

Allison clambered down into the manhole, followed by Jeremy and Bud.

Rosa, however, was bent over Leroy's torn, bleeding body.

She looked up. "He's still alive."

"No he isn't," Lucas said, and shot Leroy once in the forehead. Leroy's leg kicked once and went stiff.

Rosa gasped, stumbling back, staring up at Lucas in horror.

Lucas shook his head. "Didn't like him anyway," he said. "Get in the hole, Doctor."

Rosa stared back at him, speechless.

Above them, the sickle-claws were lined up along the overpass like crows, and several were poised to leap. Lucas picked off the cheekiest of them, and it dropped limply to the street.

This time however, the others did not retreat.

"DOCTOR..." Lucas began.

Rosa scrambled down into the tunnel.

A second later, Lucas was behind her, dragging the metal plate back over the top.

CHAPTER 17

"Well," Lucas said, "THAT didn't go as planned."

The sewer was dim, but the bits of broken light leaking in from the gratings was enough to see that they weren't the first who had tried to escape underground.

It was also clear why there weren't that many bodies left out on the street – they had been dragged down here.

Actually, there weren't bodies, so much as bones – gnawed clean.

There was a rustle of movement. But it was no skittering rat – it was one of those little sickle-clawed scavengers.

Its lips were bloody as it screeched at them – and the sound was so much like a human scream.

Lucas took a shot at it, and its head disappeared in a splatter. As the body went spinning, Rosa saw several more scurry for the corners. Lucas took a moment to pot shot as many as he could before they disappeared down the tunnel.

"I HATE those little bastards," he said.

He turned to the others. "Stick close," he said. Popping out a small but surprisingly bright flashlight, he led the way down the tunnel.

They all fell into procession. Julie was hugging close in Lucas' footsteps – not even consciously – just gravitating where she felt safe. Jeremy had Jamie under one protective arm, and Allison and Bud likewise huddled close. Bob and Daryl dutifully brought up the rear.

Rosa, herself, walked alone. She still had Leroy's blood and brain matter on her hands.

Lucas seemed utterly unconcerned, as if it were long past.

Rosa wondered how many people he had killed – he was a soldier, after all.

She wondered at the fact that she still seemed willing to follow him, even though he'd just shot someone literally right out of her hands.

Although, she was at least willing to admit that, if he hadn't, she would very likely be dead now – maybe both of them.

In point of fact, she thought, glancing back to where Allison walked behind her, she was lucky not to be dead several times over – but for the actions of others, who she had actually put at risk.

She slowed down in step next to Allison.

Allison never met her eye. Rosa had instinctively disliked her from the beginning – trashy and knocked-up – but Allison had twice saved her life.

It was true her type was tough in a crisis – but Rosa also knew that no one ever becomes tough on-purpose.

She, herself, was currently feeling rather helpless and foolish.

Allison didn't look up at her. Rosa tried anyway.

"Thanks for what you did up there," she said, and was rewarded with a quick furtive glance and an acknowledging nod.

Bud eyed Rosa warily – the protective guard dog, debating whether to tolerate a stranger. Clearly, she was encroaching.

"Some rough stuff happened to you," Rosa said.

Allison's lips twitched in a very small, ironic smile. She didn't answer.

"I've seen a lot of that kind of thing," Rosa ventured and now Allison sighed, looking over at her directly, perhaps for the first time.

"You know," she said, "it occurs to me. I can have a secret again."

Rosa blinked. "Pardon?"

Allison gestured around her. "All *this*." She rooted in her pocket for her dead cell-phone. "It's all gone. No one can search my name and find out all about me."

She shrugged. "See?" she said. "There's a good side to everything. Even the end of the world."

Rosa wasn't sure if she was serious or not – at best a tasteless joke. Rosa had intended to express gratitude, but instead she felt that instinctive dislike bubbling up again.

That wasn't helped when Allison, as if she'd only been holding it down all along, turned and was noisily sick.

Her morning sickness had been getting worse, Rosa thought, and moved forward to help, but then she felt Bud's restraining hand on her shoulder. He called up to Lucas in the lead. "Hold up!"

Lucas paused, looking back.

"Take five people," he said.

The group of them faded back, giving Allison a modicum of privacy.

"Doctor Holland," Bud said quietly, "I know you mean well, but I'm going to have to ask you to leave her alone."

"What happened to her?" Rosa asked.

"When you first saw her," Bud asked, "what kind of things did you think might have happened to her?"

Rosa sighed. "All the usual, I guess."

And boy was *that* cynical, she thought. She had to be careful what she tossed off as 'usual'. She was, after all, in a unique position to see ALL the human wreckage that other people missed. All the usual? Drugs? Domestic violence? *Street* violence? Gangs? Drugs again? Prostitution? Strip-bar, for *sure*.

Allison, Rosa thought, telling the truth to shame the Devil, just screamed ALL those things. You didn't get more counter-culture than your piercing and body-art crowd. Allison practically wore a uniform.

Rosa knew that story too – 'she-got-in-with-the-wrong-crowd'.

Of course, you had to be in the strip bar in the first place.

Rosa wondered if that was how Bud had met her.

Bud eyed her, as if anticipating her thought.

"I was a newspaper guy. Let's say I sort of stumbled into it."

"L.A.," he said. "'City of Fallen Angels. See, there's a reason a darker element goes with all this counter-culture – it's always where you get the sleaziest sort of exploitation. Trafficking, slavery, drugs – and all the crime and corruption that goes with it.

"But once you're in," he said, "that life doesn't let you go easy. Turns out some of the people she worked with were a little more serious than your average. You get a lot of people up too late on Crystal Meth, they get some funny ideas."

"What did they do to her?" Rosa asked, bracing for ugliness.

"What did they *do* to her? Name it. All the sorts of things that go on when a human being is considered an exchange of capital. Let's just say, there's a reason she carries a gun."

Bud glanced grimly over his shoulder, keeping his voice low.

"And part of it's *my* fault," he said.

He frowned bitterly. "When you stumble onto something bad, you can have naive moments of self-righteous idealism." He smiled cynically. "You might even think you can make a difference.

"It turned out, I was just letting a lot of really nasty people know someone was talking about them."

Bud eyed Rosa directly. "She hasn't been safe ever since. That's why it's my job to look after her."

In the corner, Allison's nausea seemed to have subsided, and she stood slowly, turning back to the group.

"Sorry," she said.

Bud handed her a small bottle of water. "Keep your fluids up," he said.

Lucas allowed them all another ten minutes before heaving himself back on his own broken foot. "Okay people, back to it."

All the little tin-soldiers fell into formation. Bud took Allison by the arm as if to help her, but she deliberately pulled away, determined to walk on her own.

Rosa said nothing more to her. If there was a kindness to be done, she decided, it was to just let her be.

So instead, she caught up to where Lucas ambled through the ankle-deep sewage as if he were on a parade march – purposeful, a slight smile, squared shoulders – as if there was nowhere else he'd rather be.

He had Julie prancing next to him like a puppy, teasing her with casually flirtatious barbs.

"You aren't a stripper, are you?" he was asking. "A lot of nurses I know are strippers – like one out of three. One out of two for the ones that are hot enough."

Rosa wondered if Lucas had overheard her talking to Bud.

Julie was blushing furiously, repressing a giggle, helplessly pleased.

It couldn't be just an act, Rosa thought. Just programmed?

She stepped up beside them, turning a stern, meaningful eye at Julie, who stopped in mid-titter and fell discreetly back out of ear-shot.

Lucas glanced at her, mildly. "Something on your mind, Doctor?"

"How do you do it?" Rosa asked.

"What's that, Doctor Holland?"

"How can you do what you do?"

He smiled. "It's a gift."

"Killing that man was nothing to you."

"Oh, it was something," Lucas said. "It was the difference between you living and dying. He was torn to shit. Didn't have five minutes left in him. But you would've dragged him that full five minutes, wouldn't you?"

"But you kill people," Rosa said. "You're a pilot. You kill people on a large scale. That's reality."

Lucas considered. Then he did the most amazing thing – he shrugged.

"There's a disconnect," he said. "When you're out there..." he nodded up to the sky, "... it's just a larger scale."

He glanced down at her. "But the 'reality' is that the job has to be done. *Someone* has to do it. And not very many people *can*."

"Therefore," he said, "I'm kind of obligated."

Rosa absorbed this quietly. She had called it 'programming' – but now she found herself comparing it to the specific discipline it had taken her to earn her own doctorate. At least part of it was training yourself to be aloof among the very people you were sworn to help... or in his case, protect – or blow to bits.

Living from such a perspective, Rosa could see how a man might start looking at those people as 'statistics' – and how he might become impatient with all the petty, bleeding-heart sensibilities that he was forced to live outside – yet to be held to on a dime.

To his credit, he seemed to be honestly considering his answer. He consistently did not try to bullshit her, as he had all the rest.

Of course, she thought, archly, maybe that was *how* he was bullshitting her. She had to admit, he *was* smooth.

"You want to know what it's like?" he said. "I'll try to tell you. You are what you do. When you behave according to your training, you're a soldier – and you get soldier results.

"It's like you," he said, "when you're cutting someone open, you disassociate. The open chest-cavity is just a workplace, and the scalpel is just a tool."

Now he nodded, as if saying it out-loud for the first time.

"You know how I do it? I look at the world two ways. When I'm out there..."

He paused, instinctively reaching for his wallet, and the worn snapshot kept protectively within. He touched his pocket briefly, like a talisman.

"...and when I'm with *her*," he finished.

He shrugged.

"That's it," he said. "That's what grounds me. That's what I'm fighting for. Every time."

Rosa glanced up, picturing the ruined city above their heads.

"Your wife," she began doubtfully. "Is she..., I mean... where is she?"

"Well," Lucas said, "we live up in the hills just north of the California border, up in Oregon. Or, I guess *she* does."

He paused, and for the slightest moment, the cocksure smile faltered just a little bit. Just for a second, Rosa could see past the shield.

"I do worry sometimes," he said. "I'm gone a lot. It's one thing to be gone a year – and then another year... but after about ten of those strung together..."

He stopped, hunting for the right words. "Well, I guess you kinda start to not know each other anymore. It's like remembering somebody they used to be."

Lucas fell silent a moment.

"You know," he said, "before all this, I was going to take some time off. Look at my options." He smiled regretfully. "Maybe come home for a while. Or maybe for good."

He sighed.

"But it seems like there's always one more thing to do."

Rosa hesitated, but asked the question anyway. "What I meant was... well, have you heard from her?"

Lucas smiled confidently.

"Oh, she pulled through, alright," he said. "She wouldn't have been near any of the epicenters. She'll be holed up, somewhere. And when she doesn't hear from me, she'll know where to meet up. We planned ALL this."

He shook his head, tapping his watch again. "And like I told you, she's going to be pissed if I'm late."

There was no doubt in his voice whatsoever – she was fine. All he had to do was get there.

No doubt in his mind.

He turned a furrowed eye down at Rosa. "What about you, Doctor Holland? You're easy on the eyes. Why haven't you got yourself a fella?"

"Well," Rosa said, "I guess I'm not exactly Suzy-homemaker."

'Hmm," Lucas said, considering. "Funny. I actually had you pegged as a Stepford-wife."

Rosa blinked. "I beg your pardon?"

"Oh, yeah," he said. "Cooking, cleaning, sexy lingerie. The trick with gals like you, is to make sure you think it's all your idea." He grinned. "It worked on my wife."

Rosa found herself struggling for a response.

"Boy," he continued. "I shouldn't have told you that. Now, if you ever meet her, I'll have to shoot you."

Rosa, with blood still splattered on her clothes, did not find that remark as flip as he probably meant it.

They had been walking for nearly an hour, and now Lucas stopped, listening.

Off in the distance, they could hear skittering – more of those little scavengers – probably following them.

Lucas started hunting around for the nearest access route back up to the street.

"There's probably a lot of those little bastards scurrying around," he said. "I'm sure not going to sleep down here."

He found a ladder and began to climb.

With a grunt, Lucas shoved the manhole at the top aside, popping his head up like a gopher, before climbing up onto the open street. Rosa could see him shoulder his rifle, scanning the area, before snapping his fingers, for everyone to follow.

Rosa was chagrined to find herself, along with all the others, responding like a troop of trained dogs. Programming, it seemed, worked even when you were aware of it – even in the short term. Rosa would never say Lieutenant Walker was not good at his job.

Neither did she make a fuss about keeping to his side, just like Julie, as he led them into the street

To Daryl and Bob, he each handed back one of the pistols he'd taken only a little over an hour before, along with clips.

"You're part of the group, now," he told them. "If you fuck us, I'll kill you."

"Yessir," they said together, and dutifully took point on either side.

Lucas had also taken a moment to check on Allison.

"We might have a walk," he said. "Are you up for it?"

Allison nodded.

Lucas eyed her. "Don't bullshit me to be tough. I need to know what's real. You're pregnant. That's draining. I need to know how far your legs are going to take you."

"All the way," Allison said – being tough.

Lucas glanced at Bud, who nodded. "We'll holler out if we need a break," he said.

Jamie had been hovering under Jeremy's wing, but now Lucas stepped up to her directly.

"You ready, soldier?"

She smiled furtively, all wide-eyes and trembling lip.

Lucas produced a nine-millimeter and handed it to Jeremy – empty with a clip.

"Here," he said, "show her how to use this."

Rosa had to hand it to him – boot-camp in five-minutes or less.

They had come out of the sewers near the north bay – they would still have to make their way nearly across the entire city.

"Boy," Lucas said, "you should have seen the rig I found back at the old spot. Four-by – eight-seater, air-conditioning, good CD collection – sure wish someone hadn't wandered off and fucked *that* all up."

Rosa breathed out steadily.

Okay, maybe she deserved that one.

Lucas led them first to the high-ground, finding a vantage point – another broken overpass – where he could take the lay of the land.

Motioning to keep low, he waved the others forward, to where they could all see.

On the not-far-off horizon, it seemed the giants had not gone after all.

Rosa recognized the giant Carcharodont from before – its stuporous, zombie-like daze was now joined by others – carnosaurs, ceratopsians, sauropods – they all seemed to be moving in a loose pack – a slow, lumbering gait that was taking them outside the city.

Like a flock, Rosa wondered? She'd heard dinosaurs were related to birds.

Of course, there was also that glowing in the eyes, and Rosa wondered instead if it was more likely simply another stage of the mental deterioration – indeed, the giant beasts almost seemed to sway.

She had seen a rabid dog once – it had been in the later stages of the disease – gasping, snarling, spitting, stumbling – barely able to walk.

These beasts were not yet there, but they were getting there.

This was the most dangerous stage – while they were still physically firing on all cylinders.

Yet, they didn't seem to be reacting to each other – and, in fact, seemed to be moving as one accord.

Lucas scanned the procession, focusing in on the big Carcharodont in the lead.

"Looks like they're leaving," he said.

He zoomed in on the leader.

"And look who's catching a free ride," he said, handing the binoculars to Rosa.

Rosa looked to where he was pointing and saw the big Carcharodont was packing a load of those little scavenger lizards – just as she had seen before – only a lot more of them this time. Apparently, when they ran out of human corpses, they ate bugs and maggots out of the skin of their still-living cousins.

She handed the binoculars back. "So," she said, "what now?"

Lucas pulled out his hat and set it backwards on his head, turning back towards the others.

"We follow," he said.

CHAPTER 18

Jonah had been drifting in and out of bleary semi-consciousness for a while now.

Trapped in the immobility of a dream, he thought he could hear sounds – the screech of flying dragons – maybe even the roar of approaching beasts.

These sounds were mildly worrisome, and he had been idly thinking he should get up soon and do something about it – maybe even open his eyes a little – just not quite yet.

He must have faded back out again, because now he started awake.

Something had tickled his nose, and he heard a voice say, "Yeah. This guy's comin' around. He's alive."

Jonah opened his eyes to find a shotgun tapping him gently on the face.

He snapped fully awake, but froze stone-still as the barrel now pressed against his cheek.

"You just keep still," the man holding the gun said.

Jonah looked around, blinking the crusted blood out of his eyes.

The first thing he was aware of was the Manson-style, hippie-van pulled up to the crash site – evidently, the property of the three men holding guns on them. The one who had spoken had his shotgun aimed through the chopper's broken window.

The other two had their guns on Naomi. She had apparently already crawled free – or perhaps been thrown clear of the crashed chopper. *And* apparently right into a hold-up.

Jonah remembered the chopper catching on one of the big trees as they had crashed – that was his last recollection – but as he looked around, he realized the tree itself had been taken down, along with two others, stretched out across an old mountain road.

The van had just happened along – opportunistic scavengers.

The shotgun tapped his nose again. "Step out slowly, mister."

One of the other men kicked at the wreck of the helicopter, laughing to the man with the gun on Jonah.

"Hey, Terry, these two tried to fly a chopper out."

'Terry' was shaking his head.

"Damned fools, aren't ya?" he said. "Don't you know it's damned dangerous to fly around these parts? I must have seen a dozen choppers go down. Those bloody-damn flying lizards'll swarm all over ya."

He nodded at the downed aircraft. "Planes are harder to catch," he said. "But, boy they go after choppers."

Naomi shot Jonah a look – he had personally sold her on taking the chopper.

The third man prodded her with his rifle.

"Hands up lady."

Slowly, looking at him like a maggot she'd just discovered on a garbage can lid, Naomi raised her hands.

As she did so, the gun-holster on her hip became visible.

The man nodded. "I'm gonna be needing that gun."

Naomi's head tilted mildly. "You aren't going to get it," she said.

Jonah had managed to extricate himself from the mangled chopper, and was running his hands over every bone, looking for potential breaks. He actually couldn't believe he wasn't hurt worse. The windshield glass had shattered, but tree-limbs had caught the scattered shrapnel of the propellers – and the collapsing evergreens had broken their fall. It was near-miraculous that they were alive.

And now *these* three assholes...

Naomi wasn't helping.

The man with the gun blustered. "I ain't kidding, lady."

Naomi smiled sweetly. Her reply involved his mother, farm animals, and a whorehouse.

At that point, Jonah started to interject – not sure yet what he might say after *that* – but then a sudden bellow echoed through the canyon.

Along with it, came an answering tremor in the ground.

Of course, a rumble in the ground was nothing new – it was a volcanic region, after all – Jonah was always hearing reports about how the Cascades could blow at any time – just like L.A. and the long-promised 'Big One' they kept saying was practically guaranteed, courtesy of the San Andres Fault.

But of course, this was no earthquake. Jonah could tell perfectly well what they were.

They were footsteps.

They'd heard about the giants. But they hadn't seen one alive yet – not in the sticks. Just those carcasses along the trail.

But now, something was coming – something BIG – just over the other side of the hilltop.

The three robbers exchanged nervous looks. Terry put his gun in Jonah's face.

"Enough," he said, looking at Naomi. "Tell your old lady to give up the gun, or I'll shoot you."

Jonah and Naomi both blurted at once, "We're not together!"

Terry took note of the worried look on Jonah's face, but decided to play the card anyway.

He pulled the hammer back. "I'm not kidding, lady."

Naomi made no move.

Another tremor struck – heavier than before, accompanied by another echoing bellow that shook the remaining glass loose from the broken chopper.

From over the ridge, towering over the tallest trees, the first of the giants appeared, silhouetted against the stars.

Its shadow blotted out the rising moon.

A sauropod – they had not seen many plant eaters – this was the first they'd encountered alive.

It was a monolith, taking up the whole horizon, its giraffe-like neck reaching more than a thousand feet high.

Jonah craned his neck up, looking for the tell-tale glowing green eyes, but found them absent.

After a moment, he realized why.

The beast had no head.

The tip of the two-hundred meter neck was tattered – the comparatively tiny skull had been torn completely away.

Jonah had seen chickens running around after decapitation – he'd heard of a hen that had survived seventeen days without its head, expiring only when its windpipe healed over and it suffocated.

The monster on the hill was far and away from that – and in the meantime, a truly mindless, utterly unstoppable juggernaut.

"You know," Jonah said tiredly, "I had supplies at the cabin that would have lasted us for *months*."

Naomi glared. "And if I'd come alone, I wouldn't have just crashed in a goddamn helicopter."

The three robbers exchanged glances, with Terry actually sparing Jonah a sympathetic man-nod.

Naomi promptly took advantage of the distraction to step forward and jam two fingers into the eyes of the man holding her at gunpoint. This was followed by a palm strike on the nose.

Everyone else blinked, startled, Jonah included.

For someone who didn't seem to see much of a hero in him, she sure seemed to *expect* it – apparently, just trusting him to up and take-out the other two armed men on his own.

Given no choice, Jonah did his level best.

As the two of them reflexively turned towards where Naomi was beating-up their friend, Jonah simply charged, shoving them both into each other, and then throwing a haymaker – maybe Terry would have a glass jaw.

Nope, he thought, as pain racked his knuckles – solid granite. But the blow staggered him, so Jonah slugged him again, and he went down.

Naomi was wrestling her man for his rifle – he was blinded and bleeding, but he still had the presence of mind to cling to his gun. He was also big, and starting to overpower her, so Naomi simply let go, stepping back and kicking him hard in the groin – a good, athletic soccer-style kick.

Caught completely off-guard, the man sucked a gasping breath, and dropped to one knee. Naomi wrenched the rifle from his hands, and then turned it butt-first into his forehead. The man dropped bonelessly to the ground.

Jonah tackled the second guy just as he was regaining his feet and bringing his own gun around again. But Jonah caught the barrel, and then, taking Naomi's example, turned the stock hard into his opponent's chin – this time knocking his man down and out.

Reaching for the loose rifle, Jonah was actually thinking he'd done alright, when behind him, the side-panel door of the van slid open and a woman popped out, pumping a shotgun, and pressing both barrels against the back of his head.

Terry was just picking himself up, reaching for his own shotgun, when Naomi stepped forward, and pressed her purloined rifle against *his* head.

The two women regarded each other.

"Put your gun down or I'll shoot him," Naomi said.

The hippie-chick in the van snorted derisive laughter.

"I don't give a shit, I can get another one of *him*." She poked the barrel into the back of Jonah's head. "You like *this* guy?"

Naomi returned the favor, with a poke to Terry's head.

Jonah and Terry exchanged nervous glances.

"Listen, Ariel," Terry began.

"You just shut your trap," Ariel responded curtly. "Gutless wonder."

On the ridge, the headless sauropod had started moving down the slope.

Its trajectory seemed to more or less be in their general direction.

Jonah cleared his voice. "Um. Ladies, do we really want to do this right now?"

Naomi and Ariel eyed each other warily, but then Ariel pulled her gun back.

"Okay," she said. "Get in."

Naomi likewise lowered her rifle. Terry looked at her warily, and then turned, knuckles up, and started to swing on Jonah one more time.

Ariel interrupted with a wide-open palm-slap, smacking Terry dead in the face. Terry staggered, grabbing his nose. "OWWW! Bitch!"

"Are you KIDDING?" Ariel shouted. "Get in the van!"

The sauropod had now been joined on the hillside.

A massive rex with bloody jaws towered high above the hundred-foot evergreens.

Jonah guessed they could stop wondering what had happened to the sauropod's missing head.

It wasn't alone, either. The rex was followed by nearly a dozen others, and together they began tearing massive chunks out of the shuffling, mindless beast – amputated of its ability to even react, as it was eaten alive on its feet.

The gang of them thundered down the hillside.

Like scampering mice, the tiny little humans piled into the van.

But as Jonah slid into the back, he was greeted by a parrot-like screech directly in his face.

There was a flash of lizard-like teeth and he realized they had one of those little sickle-clawed scavengers in a bird cage. The thing hissed at him like a snake.

"What the hell is *that*?"

"Oh, that's Otto," Terry said.

"You keep it as a pet?"

Terry twirled a finger around his temple. "The old lady's a bit loony."

The little lizard stared back at Jonah balefully. Then, with a squawk to clear its throat, repeated back in an eerie duplicate of his own voice: "What the hell is *that*?"

Great, Jonah thought. A myna-lizard.

Ariel gunned the van to life.

But then Jonah remembered the other two men, still lying unconscious in the clearing – he slapped Terry on the shoulder and pointed. Naomi shot him a disapproving look, but Terry rattled the back of Ariel's seat.

"Wait! We gotta get Brett and Rudy!" He started out the side-door.

Ariel, however, had taken a look at the avalanche of monsters cascading down on top of them, and decided to hell with Brett and Rudy. She floored the gas, nearly tumbling Terry out the door, if not for Jonah grabbing and pulling him back.

They tore out of the clearing not twenty seconds before the first of the giants touched down.

One of the men left behind – Jonah didn't know if it was Brett or Rudy – seemed to be recovering. He sat up, shaking his head, confused, and looking after the retreating van.

A moment later, a massive sauropod foot came crashing down, obliterating the clearing, the chopper – pulping whatever was left of Brett and Rudy into nothing.

It was joined a moment later by the lead rex.

Jonah crooked his head, trying to see.

Beside him, the little lizard in the cage let loose another shrill, warbling shriek.

The rex's head cocked, and then poised as if scenting the air.

Then it turned and stared down at them with those glowing green eyes.

Jonah had read that *T. rex* had a highly sensitive nose – comparable to a turkey vulture – like a shark that could follow a trail of blood for miles.

Had it spotted them? Or more properly, had it *smelled* them?

They were so small – it seemed ridiculous that they would represent prey.

Beside him, 'Otto' squawked again – in Terry's voice this time, learned through obvious repetition. "Ohhhh *shit*."

And even as the rest of the tyrannosaur-pack descended down from the mountain, tearing the dying sauropod apart in giant, gluteous mouthfuls, the lead rex turned away from the feast.

"Is that thing following us?" Naomi said, looking out the rear window.

Without waiting for confirmation, Ariel stomped the gas.

Behind them, in that false, avalanche-slow-motion, the rex was indeed coming after them.

It's stride covered forty meters in a step, crushing its way through hundred-foot trees in a headlong straight line.

A quarter mile ahead, was a tunnel where the highway led right through the base of the mountain. Jonah knew the route – it emptied you out west of the coastal range on the far side.

But behind them, the rex was gaining.

And for whatever reason, perhaps just following the leader, the rest of the pack seemed to have joined in.

The rumble of the earth threatened to simply shake them right off the road.

A *T. rex* charged teeth-first – the view coming up from behind was a dozen or more open, gaping jaws – yawning, STRAINING after them.

Ahead, the tunnel was dark – no power to the lights – pitch black beyond the entrance.

Ariel sailed them Hail-Mary over the threshold even as the rex's jaws crashed into the rocks behind them.

The impact shook the entrance loose and the tunnel began to collapse.

"Oh, *Ariel*," Terry began, but she cut him off, swearing.

"I said shut-up, asshole!"

"Asshole!" Otto repeated.

Terry glared at the little lizard.

There was another tremendous impact from behind and above.

Rocks were beginning to fall from the ceiling.

"The roof is collapsing," Naomi said. "How long is this tunnel?"

"Oh," Terry said, looking out the window unhappily, "almost half-a-mile."

There was utter blackness beyond the reach of the van's high-beams – in the dark of night, they couldn't even see the exit.

Another blow shook the rocks above, as if the rex was actually attacking the mountain itself. And now it felt as if the rest of the pack had joined the assault.

The rubble started falling faster, striking their roof, cracking the windshield.

Ariel simply gunned the accelerator, on blind faith that the road ahead was clear.

The tunnel seemed to groan.

A second later, it began to fall in upon itself.

Ariel shot the van out the other side, just as the collapsing rock filled the tunnel behind them.

The road almost immediately veered into a tight turn and the van squirreled the corner. Ariel wrestled for control.

Dust belched from the ruined mouth of the tunnel.

And echoing from over the peak, the bellows of the angry beasts raged like thunder – a living tsunami checked and stymied by the mountain.

And lest even the mountain not be enough to stop it, Ariel didn't slow, following the winding road as it led back up into the highlands.

CHAPTER 19

It was nineteen days in, when Major Tom finally received communication from below – as if some back-up system somewhere, had finally come on-line.

A shrill, piercing whine had sounded in his ear as a hundred frequencies suddenly battled all at once. Wincing, Tom had grabbed for the volume.

Oddly, he couldn't pinpoint the location of the active station – at first, he'd thought it was Eureka, but his instruments showed that still dark.

He had actually given up trying – either communications were down for good, or no one living remembered or cared if he was up there.

The digital age, he thought – there was so much there to be lost – technology – history – all it took was turning out the lights and it just no longer existed. There would be no ancient scrolls for future explorers to ponder – it would all just be deleted.

And down planet-side, the Food of the Gods was 'blooming' again.

Tom had picked up the expression from one of the last surviving broadcasts – the kids in Japan, who had managed to establish a brief network of their own – connecting with other scattered survivors, sending in messages and video – a lot of it in English, now, as they started making contacts – all broadcast right from one of their dorm rooms.

Smart kids – in a bizarre way, they actually seemed to be enjoying the opportunity to exploit their talents in a crisis.

They had also been the first to report the incoming second wave.

Tom hadn't heard from them since. That had been a week.

Likewise, Kristi-in-Alaska's broadcasts had become more intermittent.

She had also stopped talking to the camera – most of her new clips were nighttime, using the bright camera beam to scan her yard – always with darting shadows just at the edge of sight – growing ever-more bold.

Most new data he had been receiving came from remote sources – security cameras and stoplights – pieces of automation that somehow survived and simply droned on, mindlessly recording what was in front of them.

Tom *had* at least managed a little progress on his own front – accessing a number of satellites, and for the first time, he was able to collate images from the entire globe, recorded during the entire event – he was even able to focus telescopes on specific areas of the planet's surface.

He ran all the images together – chronologically documenting the Apocalypse.

Even from space, Tom could see that it was not over.

The beasts were on the move – particularly the giants, which seemed to be traveling in large packs.

Tom also noted that the warring-factions held.

Along the North American west coast, for example, tyrannosaurs had consolidated in the north – the carnosaurs in the south.

And from what Tom could gather, that was a contested situation that was likely going to be decided soon.

Tom had gotten some good clear views of infected Carcharodonts – code named: 'Shark Tooth' – marching in tandem, moving up from San Francisco.

The satellite image provided no sound, but Tom could only imagine the thunder of footsteps.

Besides the giant Carcharodonts, there were other flesh-eaters – other carnosaurs and megalosaurs – and even a number of herbivores – in fact, a rather large number of ceratopsians and several large sauropods.

And while the majority of the exodus were giants, the other end of the spectrum was represented too, with swarms of sickle-claws – from infected giants, to 'normals', that darted between their ankles like biting dogs – all the way down to those odd sickle-clawed scavengers he could see riding the giants' backs like birds on a hippo.

Tom had hunted up files on these little guys as well.

Sickle-claws in general were a bit of a departure from the theme of gigantism – apparently there had been some effort to breed for intelligence.

As it turned out, however, sickle-claws really weren't that smart.

In particular, this little guy – code-named: 'Otto' – displayed none of the predicted higher-functions – with the literature suggesting that some cognitive functions were simply not available on what was basically still a primitive, proto-avian/reptilian model.

Otto's base genome was a creature called a 'Toodon' – which Tom remembered had once invoked speculation that its relatively large brain-case might have eventually developed real intelligence – scientists had even fashioned a speculative 'dino-man' model that had received wide-circulation at the time.

Otto, himself, however, was described in the literature as a bit of a dud – although he *did* demonstrate remarkable vocalizations as well as a parrot-like talent for mimicry.

And while Otto might have torpedoed the idea that sickle-claws were smart, from what Tom could gather, he had become kind of a project mascot – there were pictures of members of the science team with the little lizard perched on their shoulders – often more than one.

But near as Tom could tell, 'Otto's' function in the new ecology was as a ghoul.

And uniquely, this also meant they were never affected by the Food of the Gods, because they didn't touch the giant carrion – they ate the dead *people*.

Almost as if it was their preference.

Tom wondered if that had been bred into them too.

Even from space, Tom felt a twinge of revulsion. Disgusting creatures.

The way they skittered across the giants' scales; Tom wondered if they itched like fleas.

On the other hand, some of the big sauropods would have approached two-hundred feet in length *before* the Food of the Gods – he'd seen direct evidence they wouldn't even notice a gunshot. Once they were infected, munitions-fire barely bothered them.

And the blooms were starting up again.

The infected areas were also no longer sequestered around the cities – it simply erupted wherever infected beasts died.

It was an unavoidable, inexorable pattern – soon every beast in the area would be infected – repeating the cycle of destruction – a traveling doomsday that just kept on going.

Tom found himself imagining ever-more disastrous scenarios – he wondered if the infection could be spread by mosquitoes.

Of course, he reminded himself, non-engineered organisms couldn't contain the chemical – a mosquito that fed on an infected giant would likely just *pop*.

Unless, it was an engineered mosquito.

He shut his eyes – now, why did he even have to even go and *think* that?

Because, he sighed, that was one of the things that was really bothering him.

This and other things that fit into the category of 'non-random'.

Cell-towers, for example, had been taken out in nearly every major city. Even given the totality of the destruction – and especially considering the pointedly out-of-the-way locations a tower was likely to be built – sheer odds should have left at least a *few* standing – but that few was very few.

Had this been an invading army of aliens, it would have seemed like a strategic hit.

In the immediacy of it, the impossibility of ALL of it, made it easy to overlook the impossibility of the *randomness* of it.

The beasts were just suddenly *there*.

Even granting the accidental release of the Food of the Gods, that meant they had to have *been* there – and been there for a while. How could they possibly have not revealed themselves?

But as he thought about it, the only possible answer presented itself.

They WERE there.

Rumors, after all, had persisted for years.

And to dismiss the possibility of random-event, by definition, that meant on-purpose.

Tom thought of all the marijuana grow-operations busted over the years – industrial sized fields, safely set-up in the protected areas of federal lands – they could operate indefinitely, undisturbed. They were also guarded zealously, which made them damn dangerous to stumble into on a hike.

On impulse, Tom brought up a search of 'protected government lands'.

Statistic: over eighty percent of United States landmass was uninhabited.

And many of the largest protected areas were not just bordering, but actually surrounding almost every populated area in the country.

Well, Tom thought, there's your breeding ground. Private – off-limits.

And Tom was willing to bet they were damn dangerous to stumble into on a hike.

He was further willing to bet anyone that wandered onto *that* grow-operation would be a story that would never get told. It wasn't like such wanderers would ever be found.

Having a pretty good idea what he was going to find, Tom correlated the protected land graphics with the first wave of the Food of the Gods, city by city.

It was the same graph.

There it was. They'd been out there all along. For years, at least – perhaps decades.

Waiting all this time, for some secret, silent alarm, to trigger them off.

Tom looked over at the blank screen he kept tuned to Kristi's frequency.

She hadn't posted since last night when she had turned the camera on, tracking a skulking shadow, before firing a single shot into the darkness.

Tom noticed she was becoming more sparing with her ammunition.

He had pin-pointed her general location, and had actually spent time trying to find her with a satellite-scope – so far unsuccessfully.

He also played back some of her earlier images. She had grown progressively more gaunt – the circles growing under her eyes.

Soon it would again be dark in her part of the world. And perhaps another one of her broadcasts would flicker to life – but eventually one of them would be the last.

'Nothing', he had told the pretty young reporterette, when she'd asked him what he missed about the Earth.

That seemed so arrogant now – even shameful.

It was almost as if he deserved this specific, unique punishment.

Tom shut his eyes.

He nearly shouted out-loud when the first shrill whine of static nearly blasted out his eardrum, sending him spinning in the constant floating free-fall.

Recovering quickly, he pulled himself back to his station.

On his console, a light was blinking – top-level communication from down below.

The BIG phone.

Tom hit the switch and suddenly a voice spoke over the speakers, loud and commanding.

"Goddamnit! Are we up and running? This is General Nathan Rhodes, acting Commander of the United States Armed Forces. Anyone reading this signal, report back immediately."

Tom blinked, hardly daring to believe.

"Sir," he said, speaking aloud for the first time in days, his voice cracking, "This is Major Tom Corbett. You've got the Eye in the Sky, sir."

CHAPTER 20

The Fort Hunter Base lay just ahead.

It had taken them four days and two vehicles, and they had left the last one almost ten miles back.

Four days, Rosa thought – not so long ago, that was a two-hour drive.

But Lucas had got them there. Never once had he broken stride, and never once had he allowed any one of *them* to break stride either.

She knew that single-minded focus well – long-hours, surgery, even disaster-aid sites – where there were no 'hours' – you just went on auto-pilot, acting out your function.

Lucas operated under two simple goals – keep the morale up, and keep them moving. Rosa's analytical mind couldn't help but see it, even as it worked on her all the same. He made sure you were empowered – then he propped you up to act like it.

During times they traveled on foot, he scavenged the demolished urban landscape like a woodsman living off the land. By the end of the first day, he'd had everyone armed – shotguns, pistols, rifles – it was amazing what people kept right in their cars.

For the moment, however, the fates seemed to smile on them – the exodus of beasts served to work in their favor. They had few encounters once they escaped the city.

Lucas, of course, played it discreet. The one band of roving sickle-claws they'd spotted, he'd steered them well-clear of. It had only been four of them, but Rosa noted the Lieutenant held back – even though she had now grown confident he could have dropped the group of them in short order.

But there was no sense drawing the attention of others.

That had, however, been the last contact outside the city. They had seen none of the larger carnosaurs.

And while Rosa was happy enough for the respite, she was also learning not to trust such inexplicable good fortune.

And even if their contact with the beasts was minimal, that still left a hundred miles of hard travel. On the first day's long march, Jamie had started lagging, her fair skin beginning to burn in the California sun. Lucas had not waited for her to complain, but instead stopped the group, confronting her face-to-face, his head tilted analytically.

"Here," he said, "that's probably heavy," and switched out her hand-held pistol for Jeremy's shoulder-strapped rifle. Then he nodded to Allison, who still carried her purse – rifling through, he pulled out a small cosmetics kit and slopped a glob of dark-make-up under both of the startled coffee-girl's eyes. Then he pulled a bandanna out of his own pocket and wrapped it around her head.

It was a remarkable transformation, Rosa thought. In less than two minutes, he had turned a timid parking-lot brewista into a wild-looking Rambo-groupie.

But it worked. The balance of the rifle mimicked her own lost purse, a weight she was accustomed to – the cloth and war-paint across her face kept her temperature down.

And again, most importantly, her posture had changed – Rambette was now acting out the part.

From her own assigned position at Lucas' flank, having also now been provided with a pistol of her own, Rosa found herself constantly amazed at his ability to pull it off.

In point of fact, she realized that somewhere in the middle, she had started to depend on him. Worse, to *believe* in him.

Her own third-person perspective always understood intellectually the concepts of military training, but she'd never experienced the psychology at work.

Part of her had always been rather contemptuous of the 'props' – the bluster and bravado. From a civilian perspective, she had always been cynically amused the way military jargon sounded like a coach revving up a football team to charge across a painted line. It seemed so trivial. Worse, it was like mind-control, because the emotions they evoked were all-too real. She'd doctored many a high-school player who had broken an arm or leg 'for the team."

Marching along in Lucas' path, however, in a rather thunderstruck '*duh*' moment, she realized that was backwards – historically, sports *were* training for war – *that* was where the jargon came from.

Rosa, of course, was always adamantly opposed to war, *anywhere* – she had stood in numerous protest lines, and she never believed in the 'good guys and the bad guys'. Her educated perspective necessitated a view of moral-relativity, and simple-minded military-code did not translate to her intellectual level.

She realized now, however, it was her own perspective that was limiting. These simple-minded 'coach's tricks' were actually complex behavior training that had endured for thousands of years.

And as currently being executed by a professional, these techniques were also what had kept them all alive.

Like Patton – lead 'em through hell and make 'em love ya.

And on an even deeper level, Rosa realized that it was just like Lucas himself had said – human-nature was human-nature.

She would be utterly lying to herself if she didn't admit – privately to herself, under threat of torture – that she felt comforted and safe under his wing – following the head caveman, just like his primary 'she'. It didn't even bother her that Julie was there – the symbolic position of handmaiden in waiting.

But even *that* was an illusion created by training and circumstance.

They *weren't* the lead caveman's females – they were his 'assignment'.

Lucas' cavewoman was somewhere else.

Now, as their journey was growing short, that assignment was nearly over, and he would be off to find *her*.

And in the same manner, with the efficiency of necessity, he would professionally hand-off his albatross to the system – dismissed with the same trained emotion that she would cut away loose tissue from a wound – to be numbed and stitched and never thought of again.

After their last rig had run out of gas, ten miles and almost four-hours ago, Lucas had stepped out, stomping his lame foot, as if for no other reason than to make the pain come.

"I feel like a hike," he said. "Almost there, folks."

And again, just like that, he had his people ready to charge that final hill – their goal at last in sight.

In fact, Rosa was only now realizing how much he had turned her own psychology around that simple goal – just getting there – and now she realized she hadn't given much thought to what happened next.

That finally brought it home – penetrating through weeks of survivalist-shock. If the world really *had* ended, she wondered what waited just over the rise. Some refugee camp? It wasn't like there was any chopper ride back home.

As they crested that final slope, she was overcome with an overwhelming sense of loneliness.

Lucas caught her expression almost right away.

"Hey," he said, "you okay?"

Rosa felt the momentary sting of tears – absolutely forbidden in her world – and she bit them back with the same professional face she wore when she told a patient or family member there was no hope.

"I'm fine," she said.

Lucas raised a skeptical eyebrow. "I've had more than one woman in my life tell me she was fine." He shook his head. "Never once was it true."

Rosa stayed stubbornly silent.

Lucas sighed. "Just like my wife," he said.

Ahead, the curve of the coastal highway gave them the first view of Fort Hunter.

The first thing they could see was the ocean beyond – filled like a parking lot with the entire pacific fleet – aircraft carriers seemed to have formed a new chain of islands.

And on the coast, surrounding the inland bay, Fort Hunter itself bustled – its sparse lodgings now joined by a make-shift shanty-town of temporary shelters – Rosa was reminded of a camp-out before a Dead-show.

Lucas turned to the others. "You're not officially survivors until you get there alive," he said.

He pulled a flare-gun from his pack and fired four blasts in succession over the top of the base. Lucas smiled. "I don't really feel like walking anymore."

Within minutes, there was the sound of vehicles approaching.

CHAPTER 21

Lucas waved down the first jeep as the small envoy trundled up along Highway 101 to meet them.

It was a well-fortified entourage, Rosa thought – three vehicles, all with armed men riding on back – overkill for simply answering an SOS flare, and perhaps suggestive of what the troops had been conditioned to expect.

Apparently sensing the same thing, as the procession rolled to a stop, Lucas nodded back to Rosa and the rest. "Be careful where you point your guns," he said. "The boys might be a little bit jumpy."

Lucas stepped up to the first jeep, introducing himself with a salute.

"Lieutenant Lucas Walker," he said. "Reporting in with hostages." He glanced over his shoulder, at Rosa. "Sorry – 'refugees'. Keep getting that one mixed up."

Rosa glared.

The leader actually looked rather surprised to see them. He introduced himself as Sergeant Farrell, and raised his brows when Lucas told him they'd just come down from San Francisco.

"San Fran was bad," Farrell said. "The General's going to want to talk to *you*, sir."

"Disarm them, sir?" one of the troops asked.

Farrell glanced at the rag tag lot and after a meaningful nod from Lucas, shook his head.

"Let's just get everybody back to base," he said. He nodded to Lucas. "Lieutenant, you ride with me."

Rosa looked at her fellow survivors – officially 'survivors', now that they'd got where they were going – and remembered that less than a few short weeks ago, they had been normal people – simply going about their anonymous lives in a bustling city.

Now they looked at the beckoning soldiers with furtive, feral hesitation – only moving when Lucas finally clapped his hands. "Let's go people."

Allison and Bud joined Daryl and Bob in the first jeep; Julie, Jamie and Jeremy in the second.

Rosa made sure to accompany Lucas in the third with Sergeant Farrell.

Farrell radioed ahead. "Sergeant Farrell. Bringing in eight civilian refugees, and one American Naval officer. Please advise General Rhodes, they came down out of San Francisco."

Their little envoy led them all the way up to the docks, providing them a little tour.

Rosa was reminded of downtown, whenever the fleets came in – except the scale of it was off the charts.

She realized, however, that was likely because this represented the sum total of armed forces on this side of the continent.

Destroyers were lined like a parking garage, right at the docks – the carriers in similar rows, two and three miles offshore.

Rosa tried to remember what other military installations existed along the west coast – outside California, there was a naval base in northern Washington State – nothing along the entire coast of Oregon.

As impressive as the forces before her might appear, taken all at once, in greater context, Rosa realized how far the mighty had fallen.

Sergeant Farrell turned the lead jeep off towards the docks as, behind them, the other two continued on.

"They're headed to the infirmary," Farrell explained. "They'll want to give your friends a quick medical once-over. Get them some food."

He nodded to Lucas. "But the General wants to talk to you first."

Farrell took them all the way to the end of the dock, where a man in combat fatigues was preparing to board a large PT boat.

When he saw them coming, he signaled the boat to wait, and he turned, straight and formal, as Farrell pulled the jeep up beside.

Rosa found herself rather intimidated by the man's direct stare as he appraised her briefly, up and down. Beside her, Lucas, clambered out of the jeep, giving a formal salute – the perfect soldier.

"Lieutenant Lucas Walker, sir," he said. "Reporting for duty."

Rosa stepped nervously beside Lucas as the man extended his hand.

"General Nathan Rhodes, Lieutenant. Pleased to meet you, son." He shook Lucas' hand briskly.

Rhodes turned to Rosa, who extended her own hand timidly. As opposed to the rough clench he had afforded Lucas, Rhodes shook her hand gingerly. Rosa could feel his hard, calloused grip held in check.

He met Rosa's eyes once – simultaneous acknowledgment and then dismissal, as he turned back to Lucas.

"Your people will be taken care of," he said.

"What's the refugee situation, sir?" Lucas asked.

Rhodes glanced at Rosa. "Well, son," he said, "there really hasn't *been* one. You're the first. California got hit hard, all the way down the coast. Near as we can tell, no one survived in any numbers." He shrugged. "We've got reports of more survivors back east – but around here, it's the cities and then the desert. Most of the people lived at ground zero.

"You," he said, "are the first we've seen come out of one of the epicenters still living. At least in California."

Rosa blinked. It had been how many weeks? And they were the FIRST?

"I'd like to talk to you, Lieutenant," Rhodes said, "about what you saw in San Fran," he said, "when we can get a moment alone." He nodded to Rosa. "Perhaps you could see to the lady, and meet me on board in one hour."

Rhodes started to turn, but Lucas spoke out.

"Sir? I've got a wife. She would have reported in up north at Eureka – right where they put up that new tower."

Rhodes stopped, letting out a slow breath, turning back slowly.

His face was solemn.

"You've been a little out of touch."

Rhodes met Lucas' eye levelly. "Eureka has been destroyed, Lieutenant. The area is a hotbed. And it's blooming."

For a heartbeat, Lucas was stone silent.

When he spoke, his voice was absolutely flat.

"How far?"

"Immediate region," Rhodes said. "You've seen it. Within the perimeter, destruction is total. Where there are buildings, they stomp them flat. Where they don't got buildings, they stomp the trees. It's like they're attacking the ground they walk on."

Lucas was shaking his head.

"But why? There's nothing there. That's why we picked it." He cleared his voice. "That's why I sent her there... that's... why..."

He stopped.

Rhodes put his heavy, calloused hand on Lucas' shoulder.

"I'm sorry, son," he said. He nodded again to Rosa. "See to your civilians, and report back."

"Yes, sir."

Rhodes waved back to his boat, but before he climbed aboard, he stopped, looking over his shoulder.

"If it's any consolation, son," he said, "we're about to start fighting back."

The PT pulled away from the dock, turning towards the waiting fleet.

Lucas stood on the dock, looking down at the water, saying nothing.

Rosa turned to where Sergeant Farrell stood attentively.

"Could you please give us a minute," she said.

Farrell nodded, stepping discreetly back, waiting by the jeep.

Rosa touched a tentative hand to Lucas' shoulder.

"You don't know she was there," she said.

Lucas turned slowly. And for just that moment, Rosa saw the ashen expression – a man utterly gut-kicked.

Then he deliberately cracked into the easy, wry smile.

"She better not be," he said. "Or else, I'm REALLY in trouble. I'll never hear the end of it. Eureka was my idea.

"No," he said, shaking his head affirmatively, "if she saw things going south, she'd have skedaddled right out of there."

The ashen-face was gone – there was no doubt in his mind.

"Yeah, she'll be holed-up somewhere," he said. "Just got to trust her to look after herself a little while longer."

Now the smile faded, but the determined, stoic soldier remained. "Always seems like there's something more to do."

Rosa wondered how much he was even talking to her rather than himself.

"Where are they taking you?" she asked.

Lucas pointed off-shore, out to the largest of the carriers, surrounded by the others – the flagship of the fleet.

"Right there," he said. "See? Not so far."

Now he was falling into his reassuring role. But this time Rosa wasn't even sure he was aware of it.

"You'll be alright," he said, nodding to the jeep. "The boys'll set you up."

"Just handing us off?" Rosa said.

He held up his hands. "I've got a job to do."

"So, that's all it is? Doing your job?"

"Well," he said, "you do *choose* the job. Don't you 'Doctor' Holland."

Rosa realized she'd heard this conversation before too – the grateful parent or spouse of someone she *had* saved. She always responded just like this – professional, polite – not overly accepting of praise – just doing her job.

Because you had to inoculate yourself from *all* of it. You couldn't accept the good either because that awakened deliberately cauterized emotions.

Today she was on the other end – and those emotions were not as cauterized as she had believed.

She looked up at Lucas and realized she may very well never see him again.

"I don't know what I'd have done without you," she said.

And then, abruptly – ridiculously – for the first time she'd known him – for the first time in this entire crisis... or even since she could actually remember – Rosa broke into tears.

She buried her face in her hands, utterly humiliated by her own sobs.

"I'm scared," she said. "I don't think I can handle this."

Then she felt his hands on her shoulders, and she looked up through blurry eyes to see him frowning at her scornfully.

"You know," he said, "that's the dumbest thing a smart woman ever said to me. And my wife says some pretty stupid shit." Lucas shook his head in wonder. "I always try to tell her, too. Just pisses her off. You'd think she'd want to know."

And despite his flip tone, he looked at her seriously.

"Doctor Holland. You are one of the toughest people I've ever met."

He smiled. "I even still have faith that you're smart. I mean, I still haven't seen any evidence of it yet, but I do have faith."

Amazingly, with tears still wet on her cheeks, Rosa felt the impulse to punch him right in his wise-ass mouth. Clearly as he intended.

And so instead, she pulled him close, and she kissed him.

It was her first kiss in *how* long? And a married man, no less.

The genteel knight took her in his arms, and she felt him kiss her back – an experienced kisser, for sure – letting her finish on her own, until she finally pulled back, looking up at him, breathless, with blinking eyes.

"A man could do no better than you, Doctor Holland," he said, smiling gently.

He set his hands on her shoulders.

"But my lady's still out there somewhere," he said. "And I can't go around making-out with hot doctors."

Rosa blushed.

"She's not stupid," he said. "She would have gone to ground."

Rosa saw him telling himself that – self-hypnosis.

It would be a long time before he would let himself believe otherwise.

Still, she couldn't help herself.

"Don't forget us," she said. And then whispered. "I'M here too."

His hand dropped from her shoulder to her hands.

"That's another reason why I've got to go," he said. "If I don't, there won't be anything left at all." He shrugged. "This is what I *do*."

Rosa nodded, tears still running down her cheeks, as he turned to walk her back where Sergeant Farrell waited by the jeep.

She squeezed his hands.

"Just don't get killed," she said.

CHAPTER 22

Jonah and Naomi had not yet, in fact, arrived in Eureka, but they were making good time.

Lured by the possibility of food and lodging, and having no better destination, Ariel had agreed to drive. Jonah wouldn't have figured it, but Naomi seemed to hit it off with the hippie-chick.

Of course, that also gave her the front passenger seat, while he was stuck in the back with the belligerent and somewhat over-ripe Terry – not to mention a scaly, talking parrot-lizard.

At least Terry's black-eye was beginning to fade, and Jonah could feel the anthropoid-male beginning to relax in his presence – just another guy on the road. Hooray for short-term memory.

Ariel and Terry apparently had barely known the two men who died – they had literally just picked them up on the road right at the onset – just two people running like everybody else.

"But *us* you decided to rob?" Jonah had asked.

"Well, we hadn't robbed you, yet," Terry responded. "We were just checking you out."

As far as Terry was concerned, that resolved it. Jonah decided to let it go.

They were taking the long route to the coast – despite cajoling by Naomi, Ariel kept them as high in the mountains as she could.

"The beasts," Ariel told her, "they don't like the mountains. They stick to the valleys." She tossed a finger back the direction they'd come. "I mean, they'll wander the hills around *here*, so long as there's lots of basins and flatlands – but they stay clear of the peaks."

Terry nodded. "Everybody that didn't figure that out early, is gone. We were just down looking for supplies."

Jonah thought about it, and it actually made sense – the Mesozoic Era was thick with high concentrations of oxygen. It stood to reason creatures adapted to that environment would shun the thin air up in the mountains – sticking to sea-level and valleys – where most major cities were built.

After being force-fed a lot of Terry's bullshit in the last several days, *that* one was worth knowing.

Terry and Ariel had survived on the road right from the beginning – and as they'd traveled with a CB, and had passed through a number of different radio ranges, they were able to fill in a few gaps.

Jonah and Naomi had known the cities had been hit, but they hadn't appreciated the sheer *extent* of it all.

But according to Ariel and Terry, the real war was lost in the towns.

"It was the little guys," he said, "coming right of the woods."

"Little like a *T. rex*?" Jonah said.

Terry nodded. "Everything going on in the cities – the 'mega-beasts', was what the news started calling them, just before all the stations went out – but it sure kept the soldier-boys busy. I guess, when you got skyscrapers getting knocked down, a regular old *T. rex* just ain't getting their attention.

"But that's where they gutted us," he said. "The towns. Where everybody ran to. Where everybody lived."

The 'bedroom communities', Jonah thought. Shock-and-awe in the cities – while meanwhile, they plundered the nest.

Like raptors.

Funny how instinctive behavior mimicked intelligence. And vice-versa.

There was a bit of a squiggly line there sometimes.

"We got out of Portland," Ariel said, "after the giants hit, but when we drove out into the country, they just came right out of the woods."

Ariel paused, and Jonah could see the too-recent memory in her eyes.

"It was almost worse in the towns," she said. "You could *see* it. It was more... personal."

Jonah understood. It was the difference between being crushed in an avalanche and being torn limb-from-limb – or bitten in half.

"We were in the country," he said. "We escaped into the mountains."

"That's why you're alive," Terry said. "That's why *we're* still alive."

Outside, it was beginning to get dark. Ariel pulled over to the roadside, finding a secluded spot between the trees.

As they did so, the little lizard – 'Otto' – started squawking.

"Terry, will you feed him?" Ariel called back from the front.

Grumbling, Terry peeled the tin off a can of cat-food and slipped it into the cage. The little lizard started pecking at it like a chicken.

"Why do you call it 'Otto'?" Jonah asked.

Terry shrugged. "It's what he calls himself." He tapped the cage. "Here, you little rat, tell him your name."

And in a clear, human voice – as polished as any ventriloquist – the little creature answered back, "My name is Otto."

Terry tapped the cage again. "Otto want a cracker?"

And in an uncanny mimicry, the lizard repeated back in Terry's own voice, "Otto want a cracker?"

Jonah watched the little lizard as it cocked its head expectantly. It had repeated the words exactly, in the same questioning tone – but with clear understanding that what it had just said meant 'give me food'.

Terry tossed a couple of saltines into the cage. Otto pushed aside the already-empty tin of cat-food and gobbled the crackers down.

Jonah wondered who had named him – whose voice he had spoken in.

"You think he was made in a lab, or something?" Terry asked.

Jonah didn't answer, but yes, he did.

Ariel had shut off the engine and now she climbed into the back, pushing Terry aside, and started fussing over the little lizard in its cage.

She made kissy-sounds as she fed it more crackers.

Otto repeated the kissy smacks back, this time in Ariel's voice, its head cocked in that cuckoo-bird stare.

That, Jonah decided, was maybe the creepiest thing he had ever seen.

They were making camp for the night – he slid the side-door open, stretching his legs and stepping out onto the road. Once the daylight faded, they would build a fire.

Jonah wasn't sure if the fire was smart or stupid – it was possible firelight at night could attract unwanted attention. On the other hand, if the caveman in him wanted a fire, that was old survival instinct at work. Ignore that at your peril.

Terry joined him, as he began to gather wood.

"So," he said, "that Naomi-chick. What's the deal with you two? Is she yours?"

Jonah shook his head. "She's married."

"So," Terry said, for clarification, "she's not yours? She's available?"

Jonah gave him a look. "No, she's not..." he stopped, indicating Ariel back in the van, "aren't you with *her*?"

Terry shrugged. "She's there," he said. "It's not like we're married. If you hadn't noticed, she's a little cuckoo."

Jonah HAD noticed – and he was anxious to defuse the entire subject.

"Look," he said, "she's married. *Very* married. And a couple phase-shifts out of my league even if she wasn't."

"Ah," Terry nodded wisely. "She's a queen. 'Treat the queens like whores and the whores like queens.' Works every time."

"So what would that make Ariel?"

Terry shrugged. "I told you. She's a loon."

Jonah was beginning to get impatient.

'You know what?" he said. "Just leave Naomi alone. She packs a gun, and she can get kind of pissy."

With that, he turned to stand face-to-face.

"And frankly, so can I."

Terry stared back a moment, debating the challenge.

But perhaps having not actually intended offense, he backed off.

"No need to get testy," he said. But before he moseyed his way back to the van, he gave Jonah a knowing man-nod to where Naomi was climbing out, stretching her own legs.

"It's the end of the world," Terry said. "Can't think of a better reason than that."

He nodded to Naomi as he climbed back in the van. Naomi looked at him, irritably, before marching over to Jonah.

"You know we could both hear you," she said. "It's the mountains. Your voice carries."

Behind her, there was a brief ruckus in the van and Ariel's voice – "A LOON? You asshole!" – followed by a load smack and a yelp from Terry: "Owww, BITCH!"

And then Otto: "Owww, BITCH!"

Jonah smiled a little, but it faded at Naomi's stern glare.

"I don't need you fighting my battles for me," she said.

"What battles? I told the guy to back off."

Naomi's eyes narrowed. "I am not YOURS to protect. Understand? I don't even know you. We are two people traveling together in a disaster."

Jonah was taken aback – and found himself a little bit angry.

"Fine," he said. "I will remember that."

And with that, he tossed the firewood he'd been gathering aside, brushing his hands, and simply stalked back to the van.

After a moment, Naomi picked up the loose branches and began gathering the wood herself.

Jonah kicked over a loose stump and sat down, staring after her as she meandered down the road.

He was actually mad at himself – he'd been stupid enough to let her drag him out into the middle of nowhere. He could be safe in his cabin right now – minus TV and Internet, he wouldn't be living demonstrably different than he had the last ten years.

And then to get THIS bullshit?

He was beginning to think he really didn't *like* Mrs. Naomi Kathryn Anderson-Walker all that damn much.

In fact, as he thought about it, his temper began to boil over.

Maybe it was just time to tell the queen about herself.

He found himself on his feet and moving after her.

The dumb bitch had wandered out of sight – which was stupid enough anyway – oh, but SHE could take care of herself.

Jonah followed the road around the first turn and saw her sitting down on a road-side log.

She had her dead phone out in her lap. Her head was in her hands and she was crying.

Jonah felt his temper fizzle.

A woman's tears, he thought – it was like a voodoo-hex.

And apparently because he really was just that stupid, he actually felt the momentary impulse to go and try and comfort her.

In other words, impose himself.

But he stopped, realizing that was clearly not what she wanted. So instead, he simply stood out of sight, watching the path until she was done.

Only then did he step loudly onto the road, calling over, "Hey! You got the firewood, yet?"

Naomi stood quickly, wiping her eyes. "Keep your shirt on," she hollered back.

Jonah turned back, hearing her muttering under her breath – nothing complimentary.

Back at camp, Terry and Ariel had apparently already made-up – again, hooray for short-term memory – and they were digging a pit for the fire.

And even though he'd been stuck in the back of the van all day, Jonah crawled wearily back inside, like a tired badger into its hole.

With a deep sigh, he lay his head down on his pack.

Above him, the bird-cage dangled. Inside, Otto cackled down in Terry's voice.

"So, she's not yours? She's available?"
Jonah spared the little lizard a dire eye.
"I hate that little bastard," he muttered.
Otto chittered.

CHAPTER 23

Lucas left his meeting with General Rhodes, ready for the fight.

He was a good soldier. He had his mission, and he knew as much as he needed, which was just enough to get it done.

Rudimentary communications had apparently been reestablished – with secrecy no longer a priority, basic contact was enough.

According to General Rhodes, some tower, somewhere, had kicked back on-line – perhaps through automation – and had reestablished contact with the EITS station, and with the back-up database in its computer system, the digital age had been reactivated – a half-life that had allowed direct communication with surviving overseas forces – holed up in bunkers in Europe, Russia, and China – and by extension, access to a world-wide nuclear arsenal that had never been released – because really, what use would it have been to nuke their own cities?

It was ironic – the cities failed, but the nuclear weapons designed to destroy them survived. The very last blurb of technology preserved, put back in human hands the power to make the destruction total.

Damn, he thought, that sounded like Doctor Holland.

Lucas had been quickly brought up to speed. They knew quite a bit more than when his plane had gone down just ten days before.

Most significantly, they knew about the Food of the Gods.

The EITS satellite had filled in a lot of the gaps – especially once Rhodes had provided his own clearance.

They knew about the 'blooms'.

The answer was going to be a tactical global nuclear assault.

It had to be burned away – otherwise the waves of destruction would keep on coming until there was nothing left.

Collateral damage was no longer a consideration.

Rhodes had also assured Lucas that would still be *far* from the end of it. *Then* there would be the guerrilla war waiting outside the cities.

The new Mother Nature taking over, as the song once said.

"We're making this up as we go," Rhodes had told him. "It's not like we studied this shit at West Point."

And once again, Lucas would be point man – the tip of the knife – the edge of the spear – death from above – that was HIS job. He was the one who *could*.

He had flown nuclear drills so many times before, he used to joke about just *once* he'd like to pull the trigger.

Funny how words come back to bite you.

Now he was going to get his chance – and at the end of his mission, an area approximately ten square miles would be utterly destroyed.

Doctor Holland – Rosa – had been right. He'd killed people. A lot of people. He knew it, for sure – he'd seen the buildings crumble.

When she had asked him about it, he had answered honestly enough – he was separate from it. It was a larger scale.

This time, however, there was one pesky little detail.

Rhodes had come to him personally and told him what his target would be.

The assault was to come from several venues. Wherever possible, remote silos would fire at long-range targets – they had even managed to access overseas facilities – they had accessed codes to European and even Russian nukes. Lucas was uncertain if these codes had been hacked, or simply turned over.

Then there would also be several squadrons carrying direct payloads – the remaining forces coordinated off of both coasts – the Pacific fleet would target sites within the continental United States, while the Atlantic faction covered Central America.

Lucas' own assigned target would be the infected region surrounding the demolished town of Eureka.

"Whatever hit that site," Rhodes said, "it attracted a party. Because we've got a bloom growing there. A big one. The EITS confirmed it from satellite."

Lucas had taken a look at the report himself. In point of fact, it was a bit different than the other blooms.

It was actually more of an exodus – the report detailed large numbers of big Carcharodonts and carnosaurs moving up from the southern California cities.

He recognized what it was. He had seen them.

It wasn't a 'bloom' so much as an incursion – because north was *T. rex* territory.

Based on what he saw now, Lucas had the feeling there was going to be a BIG fight to decide all that.

With ground-zero seeming to be right where he'd sent his wife.

And now he was supposed to drop a nuke on it.

Lucas pulled out his picture of Mrs. Naomi Walker.

Rosa had commented that he'd never called her by name – always 'my wife'.

Yeah, he'd responded. He liked saying that.

He knew she would have made her way to the base if she could.

Or she could have stayed in the mountains where it was safe.

She could have.

Never mind that he'd told her a hundred times where he would meet her. He'd move Heaven and Earth, he'd said.

That's assuming she'd survived at all.

"You're holding out hope for your lady, son," Rhodes had said. "You can stop. There's dead silence in that whole region. Wherever those beasts go, nothing stays alive. If your wife survived, she's nowhere near there. If not..."

Rhodes had stopped, looking Lucas directly in the eye.

"There's a reason I gave you this mission," he said. "I thought you might want a little payback.

"And," he said, "because this is a fresh bloom. We need this done, and you're the best we've got."

Then he had straightened his shoulders.

"But I'll reassign you, if you want. No shame."

But Lucas was a good soldier. He had accepted his mission.

Not for payback, however.

If it was going to be done, he would not have it done by someone else.

And when the time came, maybe he'd just make up his own mind.

"We need you on this one, son," Rhodes said, before he had choppered out.

"Yes sir," Lucas replied, with a formal salute.

Now he stood on the edge of the carrier, looking back to shore.

He wondered about his little band of refugees. They would have been ferreted off to some barracks by now. He wondered what the conditions were like. He'd left without even asking.

And why should he? His responsibility was finished. He'd saved their lives. It wasn't like he was supposed to babysit them forever.

Lucas found himself wondering about Rosa – she'd despised him almost from the start – although, he *had* seemed to have won her over right there near the end – right before he'd left her behind as well.

He wondered what she'd say about his mission today. He actually wished he could ask her.

He was not, however, being given time.

His plane was being prepped at that very moment, its lethal cargo loaded.

Death from above.

CHAPTER 24

Sergeant Farrell drove Rosa to meet the others at the infirmary. She identified herself as a doctor to the on-staff medics – offering her services.

The head nurse, a young woman – younger than Jamie – had smiled indulgently.

"Let's just get you checked out first, ma'am."

Beyond a few bruises and a little dehydration, most of the group checked out remarkably fine – a point of wonder the young nurse emphasized repeatedly – evidently, not quite able to believe it, especially after hearing their story.

"I'll want to meet this Lieutenant Walker," the young nurse said.

Now Rosa and her fellow refugee/survivors found themselves sequestered in their own tent – likely a hastily re-purposed storage shelter with cots – in the rear with the gear, not a hundred yards from the back gate where they'd first come in.

"You got in just under the wire," the nurse explained. "They're gearing up for a big operation."

"There haven't been any other survivors?" Rosa asked.

The nurse shook her head slowly. "It's been bad, ma'am," she said.

Behind her, the small group of them stared at each other with new awareness.

They were a lot closer to the last people on Earth than they had even thought.

"Where's Lieutenant Walker?" Jamie asked.

Rosa shrugged. "He's gone back to work," she said.

"So," Jeremy said, "what are *we* supposed to do?"

Rosa shook her head. "I don't think they've given that much thought yet. For the moment, I think they'd rather we just stay out of the way."

"Well," Daryl said, hovering at the back, "I'm fine with that."

Bud was more interested in what 'operations' the military had planned.

"What did you hear?" he asked.

"Nothing except that they were going to 'start fighting back.'"

Rosa sighed.

"That," she said, "and that the town where Lieutenant Walker was looking to find his wife apparently has been hit. Up in Eureka."

As one, the group of them fell silent.

"Lieutenant Walker," Julie said, "is he...? Is he alright?"

Rosa thought for a second how to answer truthfully.

"Lieutenant Walker," she said, "is Lieutenant Walker."

Somber eyes looked back at her, uncomforted.

Rosa was feeling rather uncomforted herself.

She turned, pushing back the flap of their tent to find two armed soldiers standing guard.

The first, a young man whose badge identified him as Private Jones, stepped to meet her.

"Sorry ma'am," he said. "We've got operations going on. Civilians are going to have to lay low, for the time being."

Rosa frowned. "Are we prisoners?"

Private Jones shook his head. "No, ma'am. It's for your safety."

Julie pushed her way out of the tent beside her. "What's going on?"

The second guard – Private Barnes – stepped forward. "Please, ma'am. Just stay inside the tent."

Rosa looked down at the guns, but remained where she was, exchanging direct eye-contact with both young soldiers before turning her attention out onto the docks. Their position, stashed unobtrusively at the back entrance of the compound, just where the land started to slope back up towards the highway, gave them a slightly elevated vantage – and she could definitely see activity – choppers were circling the carriers – and even from the distance, she could see the squadrons firing up.

Lucas was in one of them, she knew – and undoubtedly would be in the lead.

The last fight had nearly killed him. He had crashed and burned.

In point of fact, that was the one time Rosa had saved *him*.

She wondered what he had waiting for him out there now.

Beside her, Julie was watching the buzzing choppers – preparation for war.

All-out last-ditch war, Rosa realized.

Even after the last three weeks, that was still dawning on her.

Julie had started crying.

"He's out there, isn't he?"

Rosa looked at the young nurse, with very little to say in the way of comfort.

As a doctor, she realized she was sadly lacking in that regard. It wasn't what she did – she *fixed* people – and did so emotionlessly and mechanically. She *had* to. Just like Lucas said. It was the nature of the job. And you do *choose* the job.

She put her hand on Julie's shoulder – a young woman who had left her family behind to come to the University and learn her field – a corn-fed Kansas-girl, granted academic scholarship. She had left a high-school sweetheart – an on-again/off-again distance romance that was now off-again forever.

Lucas hadn't just been their rescuer – he'd played surrogate for all that.

Rosa was just beginning to realize the weight he had carried just getting them here.

"We're never going to see him again, are we?" Julie said.

Rosa shut her eyes, pushing the thought away – denying the possibility.

She'd learned *that* much from him at least.

"He looked out for all eight of us at once," Rosa said. "Now all he's got to do is look after himself."

She nodded, believing it.

"And now he's going to go fight. That's his job."

Rosa turned and looked at Julie seriously – and it was as much for herself. "Don't lose heart," she said.

Over the dull roar of the surf, came the sound of jet-engines coming alive. Whatever was happening, Rosa thought, was happening soon.

"Don't lose heart," she whispered.

CHAPTER 25

The human race took its first counter-strike against the Apocalypse at 1800 hours, Pacific-time – two hours short of twenty days after the first bloom hit New York City.

Major Tom was the first to realize that it was not going to go as planned.

Tom was only just beginning to absorb certain realities he had known for weeks, but it had taken his first contact to make it real.

General Rhodes had offered the cold comfort of duty – he had put him right to work – locking in satellites – networking silos. Tom had found he could pick up on the accelerated energy signature of the infected giants, and thus track them – especially when they moved en-masse.

But in the nearly forty-eight hours since first regaining contact, a lot also got swept aside.

It turned out for example, that Rhodes *had*, in fact, been broadcasting all along – out to space and everywhere – and while Tom had been analyzing radio feeds from Kansas, he had somehow missed apparently twenty-four-hour-a-day efforts to specifically raise *him*.

It was as if the EITS had been frequency-blind across the entire military band.

There was also no good explanation as for why communication had kicked in again now.

Notwithstanding *those* particularly nagging concerns, there was also one consideration he had actually been avoiding bringing up – primarily because he already knew the only possible answer.

And when Tom, in the midst of brisk exchange of orders and information, had finally asked about the possibility of getting him down out of orbit, Rhodes had given it to him right between the eyes.

"We're going to have to worry about that later," the General said. "At the moment, we're damn lucky we got you there. Once we've saved the goddamned planet, we'll do whatever we can for you."

Tom had wondered if Rhodes would leave it at that, and not say out-loud what they both already knew.

But General Nathan Rhodes was nothing if not a realist – and he made sure *you* were a realist too.

"Having said that, you realize that dying for your country is in the job description, right?"

"Yes sir," Tom had replied.

"We're in this for the species, Major. I'm not going to lie to you. And I can't kick your ass from here. So instead, I'll simply ask. Are you ready to do your job? Whatever it takes?"

"Yes sir," Tom said again.

He didn't say the next thing – that it was one thing to die, but it was another to be left up here alone, forever.

But the General was right. That was for later. For now, they had to save the world.

Still, there was one more thing.

The last signal from Kristi in Alaska had come in just that morning. Her first direct address to the camera in days.

She was running low on ammo and was debating whether she should just hole up, or try to make it cross-country while she still had bullets.

Tom had pinpointed where she lived. Now with contact – if there was anyone who was in the area...

"Sir?" he said, "I've been picking up distress signals from all over, sir. I've got people trapped. Is it possible we could get someone to them?"

There had been a long silence from Rhodes.

"You understand how thinly we're stretched, don't you, son?"

Tom shut his eyes, not looking at Kristi's blank screen.

"I understand, sir."

In the time since, he had simply followed orders. He had isolated blooms, set up coordinates, extrapolated damage.

And he began counting down the launch – the biggest nuclear exchange in history.

He was well aware, as he made his preparations, of the potential ramifications of an engagement of this magnitude – he might get to test that EMP scenario after all.

The silos would be activated simultaneously with the launch of the fighters and their direct payloads – all set up within forty-eight hours of re-establishing contact with the EITS station.

Tom realized he was enabling an awful lot by just following orders.

And while he well-recognized the necessity to cut away the cancer, he wondered whether the cure might kill the patient anyway.

He also realized it was within his power to stop it – at least the remote launch.

Tom was not the bombardier, but he *was* its eyes.

The countdown had begun and, faced with the reality on the ground, Tom still wasn't sure what he would do when those final seconds came.

The codes for launch would be sent through the station out to the satellites – on General Rhodes' clearance. But it was still Tom sitting there holding the switch.

Or so he thought.

In the descending minutes before final launch, even as below, the jet-engines thundered to life on the carrier's runways, communication from below abruptly blinked out.

For several seconds, every screen on his console went black.

Tom sat there in the dark.

"Ummmm..."

He ran his fingers over the unresponsive keyboard.

Then the screens blinked back to life again, this time accompanied by the whine of static, as well as General Rhodes' voice struggling to filter through.

The words came in choppy bits: "...dammit... this is General Nathan Rhodes..." – followed by a burst of heavy interference – ".... repeating... clearance codes as follows..."

"Sir?" Tom said, tapping his speaker. "I'm barely reading you, sir."

"Send... while... still can," Rhodes' voice said into his ear.

Tom looked at the screen. Rhodes was trying to verify coordinates.

But even as Tom brought them up, the data simply scrambled.

It was as if that unknown tower that had come on-line was now blinking back off again.

The signal was still there, but only incrementally – and now he realized it seemed to be coming from the Eureka site after all.

Had that been it all along? Rhodes had told him the area had been hit – satellite imagery confirmed it – but the tower was built off-shore – had it somehow been missed? Or perhaps only partially damaged?

But then it was gone again.

Across the board, the coordinates for the launch had effectively been erased.

The launch countdown, however, continued.

General Rhodes' clearance codes had passed through. The order had been given.

Tom looked blankly at the screens even as they continued to blink like strobe lights.

"Oh my God," he breathed, as the full import struck.

The silos were firing blind – two dozen tactical nukes.

And at the moment, he couldn't even watch.

The countdown ticked off at ten minutes and counting.

CHAPTER 26

The Pacific Fleet stretched out for miles – every surviving carrier on the west coast. In between the fortress-sized ships, the destroyers patrolled.

There was a rumble in the air as squadrons of fighter jets roared to life – readying for war – a battle for ownership of the planet.

The creature that circled below had once ruled these waters – absolutely, and in number.

Hidden at the twilight where visibility faded into the dark depths, it could see the usurpers – massive shadows gathered on the surface.

For the moment, it waited.

Megalodon – code-name: 'Big Tooth' – was at once an extremely complex and extremely primitive creature. Intelligent like a smart-missile, it responded to programming – rather than conscious will, it acted on instinct.

But when those instincts were activated, there was no arguing.

It didn't know *why* it and others of its kind had congregated here – other than the basic impulse to follow a scent.

Beyond that, it was a simple matter of targeting surface prey.

And now a shadow crossed directly above – much like whales that had once cruised these waters – stalked from below the way modern white sharks targeted seals.

The Meg did not know the circumstances of its own existence – it was unaware its kind had been absent from these oceans for upwards of four-million years – just as it was unaware of the green glow that now highlighted the once-ebony blackness of its unblinking eyes.

It was a simple creature. And just like white sharks sometimes mistook kayaks for seals – activating a simple sight-and-strike mechanism – so did similar stimuli, a comparable shadow on the surface, activate the Meg.

It did not know, as it turned towards the surface, that it was no longer a 'normal' version of its own species – it had no idea of the scale as it locked on its target.

Over six-hundred feet from nose to tail – and unguessable weight – it rose to the surface like a force of nature.

CHAPTER 27

Sitting in the cockpit of his F-16, waiting on the launch order, Lucas knew things were already going to hell.

Well-begun is half-done, as his father used to say.

By that standard, they were already screwed.

But battle was an extremely fluid environment – Lucas waited on his orders – because either way, this was crunch time.

The first thing that happened, with ten-minutes and counting, was General Rhodes breaking in on all channels and informing them they had lost contact with the EITS.

"Communications are completely down," Rhodes told them all at once. "That means the silos are forfeit."

Rhodes had left them perhaps ten seconds to absorb that information.

It was skillful, Lucas noted – he waited until just the moment where you'd waited too long and then he said, "Gentlemen. This means it's up to you."

Amazing, Lucas thought, how the psychology worked, even when you were *trained* in it.

He understood as much as he needed to – their prospects had gone from dim to ebon.

But he could feel Rhodes' words activating his own grim resolve – a psychological response – almost instinctual.

It was not so different from the beasts themselves. Maybe it was even what was necessary to fight them on their own level.

The countdown to launch continued.

He turned his eye to the coast, where he'd left Rosa behind. He never even knew where on the base she and the others had been stationed – probably sequestered together.

He wondered if Rosa had volunteered at the infirmary yet.

Lucas smiled a little. There, he thought, something else to fight for.

Today, for the first time in his life, 'up there' and 'down here' were the same thing. The balm of separation was gone.

'Lieutenant Walker' was now 'Lucas'. And he was emotionally involved.

To serve and protect. Death from above.

Kick a little ass.

"Command order," Rhodes said in his ear, "Fighters wave one. Launch."

Lucas felt his anchor-cable fall away and he fired his engines.

The explosion of power was beyond what God ever intended in the hands of any one human being – that's why He made so few pilots.

That was not to mention the nuclear death he carried on its wings.

Lucas roared down the runway.

And even as he did, he felt the impact from below.

As if hit by a giant rocket, the entire carrier lifted in the water.

Lucas felt his wheels twist, and for a moment his nose dipped – if he touched on the tarmac, he would roll and explode.

Instead, he jerked the flaps down and launched the fighter into the air.

He arced into a near-vertical climb. As he did so, he looked back over his shoulder.

The entire carrier had been knocked bodily from the water.

Cresting in mid-air – an impossible weight pausing almost in flight – the carrier's stern was locked in the jaws of a gigantic shark.

The carrier itself ignited into flame, as nearly a hundred thousand tons of steel crashed back down into the water.

In the next moment, the entire ocean seemed to explode.

The carriers were hit from below – ALL of them – across the entire chain of artificial iron islands.

Megalodon, Lucas thought – Big Tooth. It had been on his list.

He had seen footage of Great Whites hitting seals – carrying them their full body-length into the air – the impact utterly destroying its target. He'd even seen speculative reconstructions of Megalodons hitting whales.

This was an entirely new dimension.

It had taken the *Titanic* three-hours to sink after hitting that iceberg.

The biggest aircraft-carriers went almost half-again the size of *Titanic,* and were taken out in a single strike.

Some of them exploded on contact, others broke and took water. But every one was hit and every one destroyed.

There was a buzz of flying wasps as a handful of fighters managed to escape the sudden conflagration.

Static blasted in Lucas' ear as General Rhodes shouted into the radio.

"Report! Anyone! Goddamnit, is anyone *alive* out there?"

Lucas veered back towards the other circling jets, who were falling into formation together.

Below him, the sea boiled.

And then, Lucas thought, 'the skies fell'.

As he looked towards the coast, he realized the sky had darkened.

Dark clouds, coming from the east, over the mountains. A dark, living cloud.

Pterosaurs. Flying dragons. Winged dreadnoughts that blotted out the sky.

Lucas looked down at the demolished fleet.

There was no way not to see it – this was coordination.

Where the hell was THAT coming from?

He veered in to join the formation of surviving fighters, shouting out his call-sign.

"Skywalker, here, sir," he said. "And I've got a bad feeling about this."

Chapter 28

Rosa could see it all from shore. In the space of minutes, the entire Pacific Fleet had been obliterated.

The eruption from below was like a fleet of submarines breaking surface – fired with the impact of a torpedo – giant torpedoes with teeth.

Rosa heard Julie gasp, holding up her hands to hide the sight. Privates Barnes and Jones stared slack-jawed.

All at once, the Pacific was simultaneously on fire, even as the ocean itself seemed to rise up in a deluge.

In the air above, Rosa could see the fighters that escaped, circling.

And soaring in from overhead, she also saw the cloud of flying dragons.

They moved after the fighters like bats after insects – feeding on the wing.

Humanity's counter-offensive was bare-minutes old and it had already been decimated.

Rosa, however, realized that there was a more immediate danger.

"Everybody get out here!" she shouted suddenly into the tent. "Everybody! Now!"

Her tone was convincing. Jeremy was already on his feet with his gun, pulling Jamie along with him, nearly tripping over Bud and Allison. Bob and Daryl were likewise armed and ready, as they crowded through the tent-flaps.

For a split second, they all stood transfixed at the sight of the burning ocean.

But Rosa was shouting in their ears. "We've got to get out of here. *Now!*"

She was already moving towards the two parked jeeps, pulling Private Jones by the arm.

"We're at sea-level," she said, pointing at the beach.

The surf was pulling back.

How many *million* tons had just been detonated right off the coast?

The equal and opposite displacement of water was on its way.

Private Jones' eyes widened in realization. "Oh shit!"

As a group, they bolted for the jeeps.

"Hurry!" Rosa said, smacking Jones on the head, in good Lieutenant Walker style, even as the soldier fumbled for his keys.

Jones gunned the jeep's engine – behind him, Barnes revved the second – and both vehicles peeled out onto the dirt road.

Had they not been sequestered near the rear of the base, already up on the hill, it might have been different – they might have been caught in the confused uproar – people were still reacting to the erupting inferno out on the water – not to mention the incoming aerial assault of flying-dragons – and they hadn't yet realized the more imminent peril.

Rosa tried to shout out a warning.

"Tsunami!!" she screamed out the side, "Get to high-ground!"

Private Jones took her lead and started broadcasting over his speakers – his siren blaring. "Retreat to high-ground. Tsunami warning. Get to high-ground."

But as they passed overhead, Rosa saw the alarm was already too late – too many on foot, already crowding the make-shift roads.

She remembered the young tsunami-survivor she had treated – he'd said the wave had been on him in seconds.

Rosa shut her eyes, unable to watch.

The two jeeps were just cresting the hill when the incoming wave hit the beach.

It washed over the entire base in a matter of moments.

Rosa saw no other vehicles that made it out.

And the wave was closing on them fast – the wall of water came at them as if they weren't even moving, bearing down like a freight train.

The ramp up to the highway was just ahead.

Jones at the wheel sent them skidding around the final curves up the hillside – Rosa could feel the jeep leaning tantalizingly into the turn, ready to send them tumbling like dice. Private Barnes, hot on their tail, likewise tipped for one precarious moment, leaning over the drop-off.

Both rigs shot out onto the highway just as the wave broke on the cliff just below.

The surf crashed against rocks, tossing spray and foam over their windows, and both vehicles skidded to a stop, drenched and blinded.

For a moment, Rosa thought they were going to be pulled back anyway – just washed right back into the ocean.

But the wave broke against the rocks.

As quickly as it came, the water receded, pulling the wreckage of the base back with it, washing it all out to sea.

Her legs shaking, drenched and battered, Rosa pulled the door latch, nearly tripping out onto the street.

She looked down where the base had stood. She squinted her eyes, looking for any survivors.

Above them, there was the sound of guns and missile-fire as the aerial battle – one-sided as it was – was engaged.

Rosa had a strange doubling back as the small group of them stood, their eyes turning between the burning ocean below and the exploding skies above – another childhood memory – her family watching fireworks, camped high up on the hill.

Everywhere was fire. It was hypnotic. For long moments, nobody moved, nobody spoke.

The silence was finally broken by Jeremy, his shoulders squared in an unconscious parody of Lieutenant Walker.

"Well," he said, "*that* fucked us. What the hell do we do *now*?"

Rosa turned to Privates Jones and Barnes, who both shrugged. Jones pulled out his radio.

"Private Jones to anybody. Anybody out there at all?"

The answer back was static.

"Well," Jones said mildly, "*this* is getting close to as bad as it can get."

And as if in response, just over their shoulders, from the heavily-forested ridge above the highway, there came the sound of a creaking, collapsing tree – followed by a loud and belligerent, bellowing roar.

They all turned to the hillside behind them.

Pushing through the trees was an Allosaurus.

Rosa was getting better at naming her dinosaurs.

It was a 'normal' – probably three or four tons – absent the green glowing eyes.

And it was not alone.

Emerging from the forest, darting at its feet, were packs of sickle-claws.

And looming behind, were the ten-ton carcharodonts.

A whole LOT of them.

Rosa wondered what as yet, may still be waiting beyond the ridge.

As if answering some silent call-to-arms, the creatures' bellows suddenly rose together in an all-encompassing, ear-shattering thunder.

And as the tiny humans below watched helplessly, the beasts began to advance down the hill.

CHAPTER 29

The countdown had completed.

Powerless, Major Tom had watched the seconds tick down to zero.

His screens were still up – his power was on, but he was completely cut off from below – yet somehow enough of a signal had made it through to activate the launch.

It shouldn't have been possible.

And that was the frustrating thing – as a man of science, he *knew* there was no such thing as 'impossible' if it actually happened – it just meant you didn't understand how.

Again, Tom harkened back to the only thing he'd ruled out as truly impossible – the utter impossibility of random-event.

But for humanity, the 'why?' of it might be an academic matter.

It was done. The nukes were off.

And Tom had absolutely no idea where they were headed.

CHAPTER 30

The Eureka Base had been long-since destroyed when Jonah and Naomi finally arrived.

It wasn't really a 'base', actually, so much as a depot and the small town that surrounded it.

Regardless, it had been smashed into rubble.

They surveyed the ruins from the opposite shore. Ariel had had been following the highway down the coast, and now she pulled them over. Terry had let out a long slow whistle – mirrored a moment later by Otto.

Naomi had been increasingly anxious all morning – she'd fallen silent in the van, fidgeting with her dead cell-phone.

Today she had deigned to share the back with Jonah, granting Terry shotgun-seat privileges, allowing her to stretch her legs – but she couldn't relax. By now, Jonah knew enough to just leave her alone.

Too late – she caught his eye contact.

He braced for claws. But instead she held up her phone – an expensive I-pod that Jonah couldn't identify at gunpoint – its battery long-since dead, even if the networks somehow miraculously revived.

"I don't even have a picture of him," she said. "They were all in here."

Jonah said nothing – clearly it was a rhetorical remark.

He only had one picture in his own wallet – his wife. *Ex*-wife. He never pulled it out – he didn't now – but he always knew it was there.

He wondered if she ever thought about him.

That was the thing when your wife traded up – it wasn't *mutual* heartbreak.

Still, he kept her picture.

Naomi didn't show it – she remained stoic as ever – but there was a subtle wilt in her shoulders as the coastal highway finally led them down the north shore of Arcata Bay, just opposite the town of Eureka.

That was when they first *saw*.

The residential community that surrounded the bay had been broken down into kindling and had burned – even the paving on the roads had been crushed into kibble.

It was just like the swaths they had seen cut through the forest. In fact, their side of the water – the entire island-shoal that split the bay from the open ocean, was largely untouched – several small structures and boat-houses still lined piers on both sides – a number of boats remained tethered out on the water.

The only structure of any size, however, that remained standing, was mounted on a small atoll perhaps a half mile off the beach – that new communications tower.

But then Naomi pulled at his shoulder.

"Look," she said, pointing breathlessly out over the ocean.

The sun was cresting, just beginning its slow descent into afternoon, and the glare over the water had hidden a naval destroyer anchored just beyond the atoll – perhaps another mile out.

Naomi's fingers were digging into Jonah's skin – he repressed a yelp.

"We've got to get out there," she said, and actually started moving forward as if to head on down the hill on her own. Jonah was actually obliged to hold her back.

She turned on him quickly, her eyes feral, showing too much white. After weeks of rigidly denying despair, a desperate hope had now lit her up like a sugar burn.

Ariel joined Jonah, gently pulling her back.

"Come on, honey," Ariel said. "We've got this far. Don't go off half-cocked *now*."

Naomi allowed herself to be led back to the van, shaking her head, muttering, "He just better *be* there."

Ariel pulled them back out on to the road, taking the next exit down to the west docks.

As they left the highway, the same overhead glare that had hidden the surviving navy boat also blinded them to the massive shape that rose up over the ridge behind them.

Even at twenty-stories tall – even at twenty-thousand tons – the rex could move with surprising stealth when it chose to.

Its green glowing eyes found the taillights of the van as it descended down towards the docks.

Then it turned its gaze to where the destroyer waited a mile-and-a-half offshore.

CHAPTER 31

They found a working boat on the docks, where the west beach sported several boat-houses and even a small air-park.

Jonah selected a large out-board – still a bit small for the open ocean, but he figured he'd taken smaller boats over rougher water – and it would hold all of them.

Ariel clambered aboard, carrying Otto in his cage.

Terry frowned. "What the hell are you bringing *that* thing for?"

"I'm not leaving him. If they've got a shower and a bed on board, I'm not coming back."

Naomi posed on the bow, squinting out over the water.

The ship was too distant to tell if it had power – or any activity on board.

Jonah was basically a river-guy and as he steered them out into the open ocean, he was immediately aware of the difference in scale. It wasn't like the chop of the rapids – not even *big* rapids – he could feel the *power* of the water, as the sturdy craft rose and dipped like flotsom.

As they passed the tower, he stayed clear of the atoll and the jagged rocks that surrounded it, before the coast broke off into the deep water. The tower itself, actually looked out of place, simply by virtue that it was still standing – the one spot the tornado had missed.

Past the atoll, Jonah picked up speed. As they drew closer, Naomi stood up, shielding her eyes against the sun.

"I still can't see anything," she said. "It doesn't look like there's anything moving."

Jonah was about to tell her to sit – it wasn't safe – when the boat suddenly lurched.

Naomi stumbled, grabbing the railing, and glared back accusingly at Jonah.

Then the boat rose up in the water, as a large swell lifted them up – the outboard crested for one stomach-floating moment before dropping them back down again.

Rather like something large passing just beneath them.

"Did you feel that?" Ariel said.

Jonah definitely had.

"*No,*" he said.

Glancing nervously at the surrounding water, he leaned on the throttle a little more.

The destroyer lay just ahead. They could see lights. It seemed to have power.

But as they grew close, they realized Naomi had been right – there was nothing moving.

Jonah frowned. It seemed extremely unlikely under *any* circumstances that their approach on a naval vessel would be so completely unguarded. Yet, there was no activity at all.

Naomi's face was grim. "Pull up starboard," she said.

Jonah obliged, sidling them up alongside the main deck. Naomi stood again, hollering through her hands.

"HELLO! Anyone there?"

Her voice echoed.

The ship was a dead hulk in the water.

Naomi turned to the others. "We've got to get on board."

"Wait a minute," Terry said. "Are we sure that's a good idea? I mean, it's like a ghost-ship or something."

Naomi turned a dire eye in his direction, and Terry held up his hands, placatingly.

They circled until they found a boarding dock with a ladder that led up to the rear decks. Jonah pulled them up and tied them off.

The waves pushed their outboard roughly up against the steel hull – there was the sound of scraping metal.

Without waiting for the others, Naomi grabbed the ladder and begin to climb.

Ariel let out an exasperated breath. *"Girl,"* she said, but nevertheless, started up after her.

Terry glanced doubtfully at Jonah, but nevertheless, dutifully tossed his shotgun over his shoulder, and followed.

Jonah sighed, shouldering his own rifle, making sure the outboard was secure, before grabbing hold of the ladder himself.

Behind him, Otto squawked in Terry's voice: "Are we sure that's a good idea?"

Jonah paused a second, frowning at the little lizard, before he turned and began to climb.

CHAPTER 32

The ship appeared deserted.

The rear deck was empty – and dead silent.

"HELLO!" Naomi shouted again, nearly startling Jonah into dropping his rifle. Her voice bounced across the barren decks, but there was still no answer.

Jonah glanced at her sideways.

But the nervous light in her eye had receded as caution reasserted itself. She nodded, pulling out her pistol.

The upper decks were all empty.

It was not, however, as it turned out, a 'ghost-ship'.

They found the crew below decks.

The smell hit them first. Ariel turned and was noisily sick.

Not a ghost-ship. A DEATH ship.

Pieces of the crew lay in the halls – dismembered, cannibalized.

And crouched all over them, gnawing on bones, gorged, with bloody lips, were dozens of those little scavengers – Ottos – everywhere – feeding.

"Now *that*," Terry said, "is just a little too fucked-up."

He shouldered his shotgun and fired a blast at the nearest of them, splattering the little lizard across the wall – whereupon Terry proceeded to pump off five shots in a row, blasting as many of the little scavengers as he could before they scattered – buckshots ricocheted like shrapnel off the walls.

"Jesus!" Ariel said, swatting him.

Terry fired one last blast, shuddering in disgust. "I HATE those little bastards."

He turned to Ariel sternly. "That's it. When we get back to the boat, I am dropping that scaly little rat in the cage overboard."

They could hear the little lizards, skittering down the hall.

"We need to find the control tower," Naomi said. "If the ship's communications are operational, we can get in contact with somebody."

"Hold on," Terry said. "There might be more of those things. Where's the control tower?"

Naomi pointed down the hallway in the direction the Ottos had disappeared – smeared with charnel and bones, slippery in blood.

"Of course it is," Terry said.

Jonah had never been on a military ship before – the necessity of efficiency of any sea-going vessel was taken to a claustrophobic extreme – they weren't following a hallway, so much as a tunnel.

The overhead bulbs were motion-activated, clicking on as they entered each separate chamber – and the minimal lighting also allowed for a lot of shadows – nooks and crannies for skittering clawed feet. Jonah could hear minute chirps and squawks echoing through the corridor.

Along the metal floor were scattered bones, some with clinging meat, and the odd patch of clothing or hair.

They made their way past the crew's lodgings, following the stair-step ladders up to the next level into the infirmary, where the creepy-dark grime gave way to an antiseptic, back-lit white.

The corridor led past several long, aquarium-style windows, looking into what appeared to be surgery units.

Ariel made another observation.

"There are no bones," she said.

Terry peered through the aquarium glass – the lights inside were already on.

Jonah found himself wondering if they were motion-activated as well.

Which would suggest the room had been recently vacated.

He listened for scattering feet.

Jonah was reminded of the Mary Celeste – one of those old naval ghost-stories – a ship that had been found floating deserted – fully-supplied with all its cargo – purportedly with food on the table and the fire still burning in the furnace – just no crew. With no clear explanation, the story had naturally inspired legends of sea-monsters.

Of course, they didn't need 'legends' anymore, did they?

The med-unit was also absent of the general disarray below decks – it remained clean and orderly.

And as he looked closer, Jonah saw the counter along the back wall was stacked with vials of liquid, lined in rows, almost like an assembly line.

The liquid inside glowed emerald green.

"Now, what the hell are those?" Terry asked. "Plutonium-shooters?"

Jonah, however, couldn't help but make the obvious connection.

Glowing green eyes.

"You know," Ariel said, backing away from the window, "I'm kind of not wanting to be here anymore."

They all looked to Naomi.

She glanced up – the control tower was two decks ahead. She wasn't stopping now.

"You are under no obligation to follow," she told them.

Without waiting, she turned, climbing the stair-steps to the next deck.

Not wanting to be there anymore himself, Jonah, nevertheless, began climbing up after her. Ariel took a resigned breath before following.

Terry stood another moment at the window, frowning in at the green glowing vials, before turning to catch-up.

As in the infirmary below, there were lights already on in the radio room just ahead.

This time, they could hear voices.

One of them was broken by static and carried loudly down the hall – rising and desperate.

".... Sir..., this is Major Tom Corbett... In he Sky... repeat, please... come in..."

The door ahead was ajar – it looked as if it had been jury-rigged.

Upper control-decks on a Navy destroyer were not supposed to be easily accessible – that was why you couldn't get there from the main deck.

Naomi touched her hand on the door, pausing for just a second, summoning her nerve. She glanced quickly to Jonah, who was little help – he shrugged helplessly.

Terry and Ariel were no better – Ariel was shaking her head in a silent 'No'.

Naomi pushed open the door.

The radio-room was like the med-chamber – a functioning unit, fully powered.

Jonah could see radar blips, sonar, and every screen active.

That desperate voice burst in again over the radio.

"Sir! Please, come in!"

And standing on the desks and chairs – over a dozen of them, stationed at each receiver, and at every microphone – Otto spoke aloud in a barking, commanding voice:

"This is General Nathan Rhodes. Command override!"

The desperate, broken voice blared back. "Sir, the coordinates are wiped... must abort..."

As one, the Ottos turned to the intruders at the door.

And then they spoke – all in one voice together – like several speakers playing the same song all at once.

"Launch," the voice said.

The myna-bird, Jonah thought, didn't just mindlessly repeat sounds – they understood contextual meaning – that was why they asked for a cracker.

This was a bit more than just contextual understanding.

The Otto standing at the desk hissed aloud, flaring its claws. A moment later, the rest responded in tandem.

Naomi blinked, jerking her head as if catching a whiff of smelling salts. For a second, she wobbled on her feet. Jonah reached to steady her, even as Ariel seemed to stagger as well.

Jonah and Terry exchanged shrugs, feeling nothing.

The little lizards hissed.

Naomi blinked, as if having been slapped.

"Otto," Ariel said, her voice a whisper, shaking her head. "All along."

"Okay," Terry said, shrugging her off his shoulder, "Fuck this."

He kicked the door open and started shooting.

The shotgun blasts were explosions in the closed space. The first of the Ottos ducked under the desktop, while the others scattered.

But a moment later, they hopped back onto the counter.

The first – the one that had spoken into the microphone – was now holding what looked like a small pneumatic injector-needle – the sort of air-gun used to inject livestock when pressed against the animal's hide.

Like the vials in the med-unit, the loaded chamber was full of liquid that glowed emerald green.

The lizard turned to its fellow and pressed the needle up against its scaly, proto-feathered hide.

The second little beast squawked as the vial emptied its full contents into the little creature's bloodstream.

The other Ottos scattered as the injected animal *screamed.*

It was a horrible, lingering sound – worse than a shot rabbit – both Naomi and Ariel faded back, holding their hands to their ears.

The creature writhed and twisted off the desk, falling to the floor...

... even as it began to *grow.*

The warbling shriek reached a siren-pitch – whatever was happening, it looked like it hurt.

In the space of a few time-lapsed seconds, the cat-sized beast was now as large as a small dog.

By happenstance, the hooked sickle-claw was also now accordingly more formidable.

The first Otto injected a second dose into another of its fellows. And then another – each injection with a soft 'puft'.

Naomi was backing towards the stairs.

"We've got to get out of here."

The other two injected beasts toppled to the floor, their haranguing warbles rising in pitch.

But the first had gained its feet and stood, snarling up at them, its eyes already glowing green and mad.

Claws outstretched, it leaped to attack.

CHAPTER 33

The thing tore into Ariel like a rabid dog.

Ariel had her gun out and already aimed, yet it looked as if she hesitated – perhaps she was seeing her pet – even as the claws came for her throat and belly.

It wasn't even like a predator taking down prey – the thing flung itself at her, claws in her face, the disemboweling sickle digging at her guts.

She started to scream, but then her throat was gone, and all that came out were choking gasps. She fell over backwards with the thing still tearing at her with all four limbs and teeth.

It happened before any of them could react.

A second and forever too late, Terry pumped his shotgun and blew the creature off of Ariel's crumpled and twitching form.

Terry's voice was as ragged as if his own throat had been ripped.

"You BASTARDS!"

He continued firing – meat splattered off the dead creature's body with each blast, even as it spasmodically kicked and twitched.

In the radio room, the two other infected lizards had gained their feet and turned on them.

Jonah threw his weight against the door, pushing it shut, but the latch wouldn't catch – perhaps disabled. Two heavy blows struck from the other side.

He also distinctly heard the air-blasts of two more injections, and the following caterwaul.

The door bumped open – Jonah shoved it back shut.

Naomi pushed herself up next to him, even as one of the scaly faces tried to force its way through the gap. She placed her pistol against its muzzle and shot it twice.

Terry was bent over Ariel's gutted body, afraid to touch.

It didn't matter – she had likely been killed in the first few seconds.

"Terry," Naomi said, straining against the door. "We've got to go."

The blows from the other side were growing more frenzied.

Terry stood and turned slowly.

His jaw was set. Any tears had been put on hold.

"She was a bit of a loon," he said. "But who the hell else would be with *me*?"

Terry pushed Jonah and Naomi aside, setting his feet and putting his shoulder against the vibrating door.

He was a big guy – he shoved the door shut.

Jonah hadn't actually thought much of him – or his woman, really – their lives hadn't even been dramatically altered by the apocalypse – they were already living in a van down by the river.

But from his end, at least, Terry had never even considered living without her. He apparently still didn't.

"You guys go," Terry said. He nodded to Jonah. "You've got your own loon to take care of. Good luck with that."

Several heavy blows clanged against the metal door.

Naomi pulled at Jonah's arm. "Let's go," she said.

He turned to follow her down the spiraling stairs.

She was three steps ahead of him, and had just touched the metal floor below, when there was a loud, trilling screech.

Naomi instantly dropped and fired at something Jonah couldn't see. He heard another squawk, followed by two more shots. When he made it down beside her, there were three dead Ottos laying in the hall.

"Watch the corners," she said, "they're going for your eyes."

Behind them, the birdlike screech had dropped an octave, into a hooting bellow, as ever-heavier weight continued to pound against the radio-room's metal door. They could hear Terry cussing as he held the line.

Jonah paused, looking back. Were they really going to leave him behind – even if he chose it?

Naomi grabbed his shoulder, shaking her head.

They turned and ran down the corridor.

The Ottos *were* going for their eyes – one of them nearly caught Jonah on the third deck, leaping out of hiding almost directly into his face. If it had got hold of him, it probably could have slashed his throat. Instead, he used a trick that worked on yellow-jackets – just center their weight and smack them right out of the air. He caught the little lizard dead center with an open-handed blow, knocking it to the floor. Not wasting a bullet, he stomped it flat, feeling the thin-bones breaking like a bird's.

Naomi stomped it once for good measure.

Behind them, there was the sound of shotgun blasts.

Terry's cursing gave way to screams.

The creatures were out.

Above them, they could see daylight.

They could also hear the snarling beasts behind, and the echoing clatter of large, clawed feet on metal floor.

Naomi pushed open the hatch as they climbed out into the open air.

Jonah turned and slapped the hatch shut behind them. With a grunt, he twisted the latch.

A second later, something struck the door from behind.

The latch twitched.

Jonah took his own rifle and wedged it between the door-jam and the latch.

He shrugged at Naomi. "I guess you're going to have to do the shooting. You're better than I am, anyway."

More screeching sounded from over their heads, and they turned to see the Ottos lining the rooftops over the control tower – dozens of them, all blinking down.

The gaggle of lizards were poised to leap, ready to start flocking forward in a mob – but then, as a group, they paused.

Their oddly-birdlike heads cocked as if scenting the air.

Then the entire ship was shaken by massive impact.

The destroyer itself was picked up out of the water and the very air reverberated with a foghorn, gale-storm ROAR.

Jonah and Naomi grabbed the railing as the ship smashed back down into the water. The Ottos scattered from the rooftops.

Clamped onto the front hull, Jonah saw massive jaws shaking the entire craft like a gargantuan crocodile latched onto a buffalo.

A giant rex.

THE rex, Jonah wondered? The same from before?

Was it following them?

The beast reared up in the water, as if to clamber onboard, even as it began to tear the ship apart.

Naomi hiked her hips over the railing and simply jumped overboard, splashing down into the ocean, not ten feet from where they had tied-off their purloined outboard below.

Jonah looked back briefly over his shoulder before he turned and leaped over the side after her.

There was that weird dip in his stomach as he dropped nearly fifty-feet to the water – the stinging impact was immediately drowned by shocking cold.

He sputtered to the surface, looking tor Naomi.

But the weight of the massive ship dropping back down sent a rush of water, carrying them out into open ocean – in fact, probably saving their lives as nine-thousand tons of steel crashed into the surf.

Their little outboard was torn loose of its moorings and partly swamped. Jonah grabbed hold of its rail, while Naomi grabbed his other hand, and together, they managed to pull themselves on board, collapsing into the foot-deep water filling the craft's bottom.

Still sitting in his cage, Ariel's pet Otto screeched into their ears.

Naomi sat up, regarding the little lizard.

"You know what?" she said, "*Fuck* you."

She picked up the cage and dropped it overboard into the ocean.

The little lizard made one more small squawk, this time in Naomi's voice – "*Fuck* you!" – before it sunk into the depths, out of sight.

Behind them, the rex rocked the destroyer the way Jonah had seen bears roll a log.

On board, he could also see squads of Ottos flocking overboard like fleeing rats.

The rex actually seemed to take the time to go after them – smashing them like ants as they made a break for the water.

Is that what it was about, Jonah wondered? That big rex just didn't like those scaly little vermin?

Well, by all means, let it have them – Jonah didn't particularly like them either.

The ship was lifted up once again, pushing up another huge swell. Their tiny outboard was tossed.

Clinging to the rail, Naomi wiped water from her eyes. "Get us out of here, Jonah!"

Jonah turned to start the engine and had given it one good crank when suddenly the ocean simply up and exploded from below.

Now the rex itself, was knocked completely clear of the water, with the destroyer capsizing and rolling into the brine.

The eruption of water carried the rex right along with it, and through the deluge, Jonah could see the Tyrant King – King of the Dinosaurs – most terrible land-predator that ever lived – locked in the jaws of a giant shark.

The rex screamed.

The impact of the attack carried both beasts several hundred feet straight up, before finally cresting in mid-air.

Then they began to fall back towards the water.

The destroyer had already rolled – and that alone might have already been enough to send waves big enough to swamp the shore – but then the battling beasts tumbled down on top of it.

"Oh shit," Jonah said, forgetting the engine and grabbing the railing. "Hang on!"

Naomi cursed, shutting her eyes, latching onto the rail

The wave of impact hit a moment later, capsizing the outboard, and washed them both over the side.

CHAPTER 34

Jonah had fallen into rapids before, and he knew better than to fight the water. But this was something he'd never experienced – he was tossed bodily, like a leaf in the surf – he had no idea which way was the surface, or if he was ten feet or forty feet down.

The sheer torque of the water battered the wind from his lungs – it was like trying to hold your breath while falling out of a tree and hitting every branch on the way down.

He was quickly nearing exhaustion, and felt the stirrings of panic, when his head miraculously popped to the surface.

The destroyer had up-ended, buoyed by trapped air, but sinking fast, and Jonah could already feel the pull of the suction as it went down.

And behind the sinking ship, the rex churned the surface as it battled something unseen.

The massive jaws snapped into the foaming brine, and evidently found a target, as a pair of gargantuan fins and a slapping tail suddenly flapped and rolled in the water.

Floating debris from the destroyer's top decks were scattered – including several doughnut-ring life-preservers. Jonah grabbed one up, latching his arm around it, and took a moment to finally catch his wind. He looked around for Naomi, but the chop was too rough to see.

But then he spotted her – she was clinging to the wreckage of the outboard, latched like a barnacle onto the overturned hull. She hung limp, barely conscious.

Jonah started fighting his way towards her through the current.

Behind him, however, the furor of battle had momentarily abated, as the shark had apparently released its grip on the rex.

But the ocean was flooded in red. The rex kicked in a circle, clearly struggling.

If a shark could follow a drop of blood in a body of water the size of an Olympic swimming pool, what might an ocean full of pumping arterial fluid attract?

Taking advantage of what was likely only a momentary calm, Jonah caught up to Naomi, who groaned, dazed, as she felt his hands on her.

She'd taken a pretty good shot in the temple, and blood was running down her face. She reflexively resisted as Jonah pried her fingers loose from the upturned hull.

As he pulled her over to the life-preserver, she seemed to blink back to awareness, looking from him to the shore.

Jonah gauged the distance. A mile and a half.

Beneath their dangling feet, they felt the swell of something large passing below.

"Did you feel that?" Naomi said.

"No," Jonah responded. "Start swimming."

Just keep swimming, Jonah thought.

Behind them, for lack of a better target, the rex had actually started back after the sinking destroyer, ignoring the ghastly bite-wounds that continued to cloud the ocean in its blood, even as parts of the ship now started exploding in its face.

It was nothing if not a stubborn beast.

"*Jonah...*" Naomi whispered, stiffening suddenly in the water beside him.

Passing just to their right, not twenty yards away, was a giant fin – ever eighty feet high.

A swell lifted them on their tiny doughnut.

The fin passed leisurely by, and as Jonah looked around, he realized it was not alone – it had been joined by at least half-a-dozen others.

They began to circle.

The rex seemed to sense it, breaking off its assault on the crippled destroyer, letting the poor mangled hulk finally slip beneath the surface.

Jonah saw the first of the circling fins veer in its direction, and then drop out of sight.

A moment later, the rex was grabbed from below and pulled under.

CHAPTER 35

The rex felt itself being dragged down deep. Likewise, it was aware of the other circling shadows that prowled just beyond the range of visibility.

It responded in the way nature provided.

Megalodon had likely never before encountered jaws as formidable as its own – pound-for-pound, an even more damaging bite – two alpha-predators, both designed for the 'massively-destructive first strike' attack-strategy.

At this point in their battle, both combatants had landed more than one of those.

And while the shark had a demonstrable advantage in size, it nevertheless relented when the rex locked its own jaws just above its gills.

A little lower and it might have been a crippling bite. As it was, the Meg released its own grip and shook itself loose.

The rex started kicking for the surface, still pumping blood from its hip and leg.

None of the other encroaching shadows had quite yet dared get involved, although that was only a matter of time.

Just like modern Great Whites, the Megs circled – the big females hovered close, ready to take first dibs once the prey was safely incapacitated – with smaller individuals lurking at the perimeter.

In the simple manner that it understood things, the rex realized his peril – yet, its rudimentary emotional response was limited. All it knew was that it was being attacked – and that it was being challenged.

The rex also felt the rudimentary stirrings of anger – a goading pulse beyond simple instinctive response.

Then there was that growing buzzing in its head. The rex could not have isolated the catalyst that drove it on – it was not quite a scent, not quite a sensation – it was almost like a pheromone, or a chemical thing. Or perhaps even some form of mental dominance.

And *that* was really the key-word – 'dominance'.

As a side-effect, due to the extremity of its biological weaponry – where true inter-specific conflict was too-easily fatal – *T. rex* had also evolved an over-developed sense of hierarchy.

In ecological terms, the 'Tyrant King' didn't have a 'submission' mode.

A socio-biological perfect-storm, *T. rex* was the purest expression of a rogue.

The rex itself, of course, consciously knew none of this, and cared even less.

There was only the primal understanding that a blood-enemy was near – and whatever else it was that buzzed its senses, egging it onward – this attempt to dominate instead activated a single-minded resistance and an automatic attack instinct.

The Megalodon was just the current recipient of that instinct.

The Meg, itself, was an even simpler mind – responding to a few basic stimuli. Free will had not evolved sufficiently to be a factor.

It simply circled its prey like a smart missile, locking on its target.

For the rex's part, it recognized the larger predator – as well as its own inability to safely retreat.

But if the Meg got him, he would be going out with a piece of its ass in his teeth.

The Meg dropped below the surface.

The rex dropped below to meet it, face-to-face, its jaws open and ready.

Barely visible in the periphery, the other giant shapes circled patiently, waiting in the wings.

With a snap of its tail, the Meg attacked.

CHAPTER 36

The battle itself was probably what saved their lives, Jonah thought.

Besides providing distraction for whatever other nasty critters lurked below, the clashing beasts created an artificial high-tide, bustling them along towards shore.

But the water was still rough. Naomi was bleeding and probably concussed. Jonah did as much kicking for the both of them as he could, while making sure her hands stayed locked on the preserver.

She was conscious, but the battering had taken her stamina – she clung to the doughnut by sheer force of will.

They were still out over the coastal drop-off – the darkness below was endless and absolute.

Even as a kid, Jonah had never liked deep water, where you couldn't see the bottom.

Anything could come up at you out of that darkness.

As if to prove it, the ocean seemed to swell up, yet again – an unseen clash that still raged on beneath the surface – the rex was evidently making a fight of it.

But now, several other circling fins turned in all at once, ignoring the two tiny, struggling humans in favor of bigger prey.

Another of the towering dorsals sailed past – part of the body actually passed underneath them – first threatening to pull them along in its wake, and then nearly slapping them with a hundred-foot tail.

While he was no Navy pilot, Jonah was in good-shape for a man his age, and nature had also provided him with sufficient instinctive motivation of his own – 'fight or flight' pumped adrenaline like an overdose of amphetamines. He kicked until his legs burned, fighting against the dragging backwash of a six-hundred-foot living submarine with a mouthful of butcher's knives.

If he gave in to exhaustion, they were going to die.

It was going to be close.

He even felt part of his mind trying to give up.

It was the antelope that sat down after being run too hard by the cheetah – that just sits and waits for the claws.

After all, what was really waiting for him even if they made it to shore? The world *was* over, wasn't it?

Seriously, what kind of life was left to live? Why not just let it end?

It was actually scary how much sense that made.

Of course, it wasn't just *his* life.

Right now, Naomi was depending on him too – whether she liked it or not – and she had given every indication that *she* had something she wanted to live for.

He had to hand it to her – she had dragged them across air, land, and sea – and Jonah knew she *still* had not given up hope.

Jonah wondered what it was like to have someone love you that much.

Who was he to snuff that out, just by giving up?

Who the hell was he to let them both die?

And as long as he was giving fuel to the fire, he might as well admit she had been perfectly right, about him, all along – right from the moment she caught him checking her out at the store. He was smitten the first second he saw her. Of *course* he had been – just LOOK at her.

And so, just like pretty much everything else he'd done since the moment they met, he would do it for her – whether she liked it or not.

See, *that* was a survival mechanism too – a real basic one – and the simplest ones always worked best.

As his own strength began to fade, he needed to tap into all he could get.

Maybe he was no Navy pilot, but he'd gotten handed the assignment anyway.

He also knew now why she expected him to be a hero.

It was because she deserved one – that was why she had married one.

But the flip side of a hero is that he's out doing hero stuff – leaving her all alone.

So she made do with a surrogate – a dog to lay curled around at her feet – but if need be, it was there with its teeth.

If she didn't have a hero handy, she brought it out in *you*.

Really, that was its own kind of super-power.

Damn, he thought. He loved her after all.

Damn. Damn, damn, damn.

Worse, he loved her like Dopey loved Snow White – because *that* was his role – he was the seven dwarfs and it was up to him to get her safely home to Prince Charming – the happily-ever-after part was *that* guy's job.

Jonah had to stand-in just a while longer.

The current was pushing them north. They were in range of the Tower and Jonah was tempted to try for it, but that would only leave them stranded. One way or another, they had to make shore.

Behind them, the turmoil in the water seemed to have finally subsided.

Jonah still couldn't see over the rough chop, but whatever had gone on down below had apparently now been decided.

With the shore finally in sight, Naomi was beginning to fade.

But Jonah wouldn't let her quit either.

"Almost there," he said. "We can make it."

She didn't answer, didn't look at him, but she bent forwards and kicked harder.

Jonah had never met anyone who had made him want to be brave.

His own ex-wife basically made him want to run and hide.

Right about now, Jonah felt like fighting.

And then suddenly, amazingly, they were in standing water, not thirty yards from the beach.

Tantalizingly close. The ocean seemed to grasp at them and pull them back.

Struggling against the waves, they staggered the rest of the way to the shore, collapsing in the surf onto the sand.

They sat there for a moment, utterly exhausted.

Then they looked at each other.

Saying nothing, they simply hugged.

It was the first time she had voluntarily touched him since he'd known her.

He decided it was okay to be a dog at her feet. Just call me, 'Dopey'.

Jonah took her hand, helping her to her feet, and they stood together, turning to look back over the sea.

The water had calmed. The ocean was empty. The wreck of the destroyer had vanished beneath the waves.

But then, not two-hundred yards out, the surface broke once again.

Rising up out of the bay, rearing its full twenty-stories high, was the rex.

Its hide was savaged, with ugly, gaping wounds.

It also sported what looked like a mouthful of shark-meat – attached to a piece of tail.

As it pulled its massive weight out of the water, the rex seemed to falter for just a second – perhaps from exhaustion – perhaps from its injuries.

Then, slowly, obviously in pain, it began to move, striding through the surf, towards shore.

Jonah didn't know if it was after them, or just lumbering forward.

One more time, it didn't matter.

And despite the ugly bite-wounds, the green glow in its eyes actually seemed brighter – the energy burn of an accelerated heartbeat.

Jonah and Naomi turned and started running down the beach.

The coastline north of Eureka was shadowed by a ridge that led into the mountains – heavily forested, with redwoods that were sometimes over three-hundred feet tall.

Over the top crest of the south ridge, the tree line parted. There was a slow creak as a two-hundred-foot tree was broken and came tumbling down.

Jonah and Naomi stumbled to a stop.

Another giant was perched on the ridge – its eyes glowing green.

Not a rex this time.

Bigger. A Carcharodont.

At the sight of a rival, the rex paused as well.

Up on the hillside, more trees were pushed aside and toppled over, as the giant carnosaur was now joined by others.

Jonah couldn't tell how many – but it was a lot. The living mountains stared down into the basin.

And what might yet be lurking beyond the ridge?

Jonah looked around at the land-locked beach. The Apocalypse had finally found them, and they had nowhere left to go.

CHAPTER 37

The rex stepped up onto shore, facing the big Carcharodont as it reared up on the hillside.

It recognized the challenge of a rival predator, activating its own territorial instinct. But more than that, it understood on some more basic level, the conflict was larger than that.

The rex also recognized the skittering little rats crawling all over the big Carcharodont's back. He recognized them as a foulness – like sulfur – something just beyond scent – a psychic stench.

Although the rex had no words for it, he also understood the role of the little creatures in this conflict – despite appearances, they were not fleas or lice, or even Savannah birds cleaning up parasites off a giant's back.

They were steering.

The big carcharodont advanced down the hill. The moment it moved, the rest moved with it, and the Earth rumbled.

It was not just carnosaurs – the enemy had arrived in legion. The rex could see towering sauropods, as well as an entourage of all the most dangerous herd-beasts, adorned in spikes, horns, and armor.

The rex had no idea by how much it was out-numbered, although he knew it was a significant measure. Nor did it take into account its own already-ghastly, bleeding wounds.

Instead, it did the only thing it knew how – what evolution had bred into it. The rex stamped its feet, ready to meet the assault head-on.

It was only peripherally aware of the tiny apes on the beach, who were now running towards the north ridge.

But the tiny apes stopped again when the treeline of the northern hillside began toppling over as well.

Now it was the Carcharodonts who paused.

If the rex could have smiled, it would have at that moment.

The pack of tyrannosaurs lined up along the opposite horizon – eyes glowing green.

His *own* gang had arrived.

The rex-pack almost seemed to pose on the hill, as if letting the moment sink in.

Then they began to move.

Standing on the beach, the rex turned its eyes back to the lead Carcharodont, even as the big carnosaur now hung deliberately back, letting its foot-soldiers move forward to engage instead.

The two factions faced each other – all attracted by the same psychic stench.

For one faction – perhaps just a touch more primitive – that stench was just base stimuli – the impetus to move forward – to bite, to stomp. They couldn't even fairly be said to obey – they simply followed where they were led.

The other faction, however, was there to stamp that stench out like fire or stinging ants.

T. rex was the last of the dinosaurs to evolve – and could therefore be said to be somewhat more advanced – known to pair-bond – perhaps the bare-beginnings of the concepts of companionship and empathy.

Perhaps it even understood on some level, that this anomaly had made him and his kind a threat – that the enemy wanted them wiped-out. He was a 'resistance' that could not be tolerated.

Or maybe it was just stubborn – a by-product of its own long-evolved *T. rex* socio-biology – nothing more than that.

Either way, it was enough.

The rex didn't know what was happening in other regions, or other continents – or all over the planet. It didn't matter – he had his own fight right in front of him.

And on the hillside, as if in answer, the lead Carcharodont threw its head back and ROARED.

Its troops followed suit – and the bellowing thunder echoed through the mountains.

From the beach, the rex returned the challenge.

On the hill to the north, the rex-gang answered.

From the south ridge, the opposing army marched forward to meet them.

The big rex eyed the lead Carcharodont, which still stood back, allowing its fellows to charge past it down the hill.

The swarming little lizards crested on the big carnosaur's head and shoulders as if to watch – generals sending out their troops.

The first of the Carcharodonts hit the beach.

The rex attacked, with wide, gaping jaws.

CHAPTER 38

Circling in orbit, it was nearly thirty-minutes before the EITS station's screens clicked back on.

At this point, Major Tom had no clue why his systems were clicking in and out – it was like a cat was dancing on some unseen keyboard. He didn't know why the systems had gone down, he didn't know why they were up again. Before, it had been just the military frequencies that had been blocked – this was everything.

But during that thirty minutes in the dark, he could still see the planet's surface out the window.

He could see the nukes hit – he could see them popping like bulbs on a Christmas tree.

Asia and Africa seemed to get it the worst. Even from a distance, there was a strobing effect.

When the lights clicked back on, most of his screens had gone blank.

How many nukes had landed? At least a dozen. Probably some had not fired – it was impossible to tell.

Once his power kicked back on, Tom began linking back up with the surviving satellites, to see if he could get a telescope back up – maybe track some of the blasts through ambient radioactivity.

At least one missile had hit the North American continent – he had pinpointed the impact.

Southern California, fifty-miles east of Los Angeles.

Dead center of the San Andreas Fault.

CHAPTER 39

Lucas had been with the first wave in San Francisco. Besides himself, his entire squadron had been wiped out.

This was worse.

In most wars, even the losers had survivors.

Clearly, that was not the intended outcome here today. Once the 'warfare' was settled, priorities would shift to extermination.

In the smoking ocean beneath, the carriers were gone – down to the last ship – the floating wreckage leaked fuel that burned the water's surface like a forest fire.

A number of the smaller destroyers had survived the initial assault and had buzzed briefly about – accomplishing little besides prolonging the crewmen's lives a few minutes more.

Lucas saw several hit from below as the carriers had been. And that was before the ocean itself began to burn. It was difficult to tell if any had yet survived.

At least one of the nine-thousand-ton boats had also been taken by something that looked like a giant pair of crocodile jaws, grafted onto the body of a sea-lion – the jaws alone were over a hundred feet, and they had snapped the destroyer in half like kindling.

Lucas *had* taken note that the follow-up strikes on the destroyers had been in succession – not like the simultaneous first-strike.

It was as if, once activated, whatever guiding force that motivated these beasts, simply allowed their charges to act out as their instincts dictated – their simple nature and the Food of the Gods was enough.

And Lucas no longer doubted there was a guiding force.

The aerial assault alone was evidence enough. During that first-wave assault on San Fran, the sky dragons had been there – one of them had taken him out – but it hadn't been like *this*.

This was overwhelming force – intended to stamp them out once and for all.

The flying dreadnoughts filled the sky as far as Lucas could see.

And every damned one of them was a green-eyed, infected giant.

This against a few surviving F-16s.

When the carriers had been taken, most of the fighters had still been on the pad. Lucas estimated less than a dozen had survived the first strike.

He knew none of the pilots by name – only brief call-signs – 'Ballsy', O'Reilly, 'Gentle Ben', Wilson. He likewise had no idea how many had already been taken out.

Lucas had seen one pilot eject the moment before his fighter was hit, bare seconds before the craft exploded. Unfortunately, that still left him dangling in a parachute – a floating morsel with the chute itself practically advertising his position. He was snapped up within seconds.

The flying dragons also barely noticed their retaliatory machine-gun fire. Missiles were a little better – pterosaurs were, by design, lightweight – but these sky-beasts stretched wingspans over four-hundred feet, and your clip ran dry of missiles fast.

Then of course, Lucas thought, there was his payload.

It was really no different than any other flight – he just had a nuke on his wing. He'd done it all the time.

Theoretically, they wouldn't explode on impact – but Lucas wasn't quite prepared to trust *that* little bit of scientific folklore.

There was one particularly nasty pterosaur – one of the ones with teeth, hard-pressed on his tail – that seemed determined to put it to the test.

It was a fast one too. It also banked on a dime, cutting angles with its sheer size.

The critter that had taken him down in San Fran had clipped him with its wing when he'd tried to bank. But Lucas was wise to that trick this time, and instead, he shot straight up, aiming for the stratosphere.

The flying beast followed doggedly after him – literally until it passed out from oxygen starvation. The giant pterosaur fell slowly limp, cresting into a slow, probably fatal, tumble back to Earth.

As he arced in a plummeting dive back into the fight, Lucas wondered for the first time what was happening on shore.

As he re-entered the air-space, he veered off towards the beach.

That was when he saw that the base itself was gone – completely washed away.

The import took a moment to sink in.

Did that mean everybody was dead – all those people he'd promised to save?

That pretty young nurse, that poor little coffee girl? That stupid kid who wanted to be a hero?

Doctor Holland – Rosa – who he thought he'd won over right there near the end, and who turned out to be a pretty good kisser.

He'd led them all here to be killed.

But then he shook his head.

He'd spent several days in close contact with Doctor Rosa Holland, and he had come to know her enough to be impressed. She reminded him of his wife – and not *just* because she was a good kisser.

She would have found a way – she would have gotten them out of there. She would have done it just to show that she could. She had that stubborn streak.

So Lucas did a fly-by over the flooded base, right in the direction *he* would have taken – to the high-ground back up on the highway.

And sure enough, he spotted two vehicles – right on the road where the cliff broke away – the very bastion that had stopped the wave. And when he sailed over low, he saw the familiar faces, as they looked up to watch his jet pass.

Lucas smiled despite himself. You had to hand it to her.

But as he passed the ridge, he also saw what was coming for them out of the forests just beyond.

He flew low over the trees, taking it all in.

He had been right. *This* was the extermination part – the search-and-destroy mission, sent in to clean out the stragglers.

'Normals' this time – not the giants.

And assuming strategic consideration, a moment's thought suggested why – the giants would have shown up on the EITS station's scanners.

Now it only remained for the first of them to become infected.

The beasts were already moving down the ridge towards the shattered base.

Well, he thought, machine-gun fire may not bother the flying giants, but he could personally testify that the 'normals' didn't like the caliber of bullet that came out of an F-16.

Lucas began to circle back around where the small group of escapees was trapped on the highway.

But at that moment, his headphones burst alive with static, and General Rhodes' barking voice blared in his ear.

"All surviving aircraft, report in! Is anyone out there still alive?"

Lucas counted the replies of six call-signs – six survivors out of the entire fleet – before he called in his own.

"Skywalker here, sir," Lucas responded. "We have met the enemy and they are kicking our asses, sir."

"Lieutenant," Rhodes said, "I need you all to break away from this battle and deliver your payloads. Nothing has changed. Your targets are all the continental United States – THAT is our priority. THAT is what's at stake here, gentlemen."

"Sir," Lucas interjected, "we've got survivors on the hill."

Rhodes' voice was flat.

"Deliver your payload, son."

Lucas noticed the General made no effort to persuade him by telling him his survivors would be taken care of. Rhodes wasn't the type to lie.

He gave orders. He had higher priorities.

So that's how it was, Lucas thought. Destroy the town where he'd sent his wife, and abandon the woman who had saved his life.

Duty and honor.

Death from above.

Lucas realized at that moment, how much of the immediate future really was up to him.

"Lieutenant?" Rhodes said again.

"Yes, sir," Lucas responded.

He had a job to do. His job was to be the hero.

Somebody had to, right?

That meant he had to pull it ALL off.

Perform miracles. Move Heaven and Earth.

He turned off his radio. Rhodes had given his orders. Lucas would follow them.

But first he had a little something to do.

CHAPTER 40

Rosa thought again of the war-dogs. It was a more literal analogy than she thought.

It wasn't *like* that – it *was* that.

Rosa didn't know if the beasts had seen them yet, or were just charging mindlessly down the hill – the highway south was already cut-off, but they still had 101 North.

Although, she thought, as she watched the trees above them tumble, perhaps not for long.

The wolf-sized sickle-claws had outpaced their ten-ton carnosaur cousins and several darted out onto the road. And now, the first of them turned in their direction.

Daryl and Bob both opened fire, joined a moment later by Jeremy, and even barista-turned-gunslinger Jamie, who set her feet, firing her bolt-action rifle with strict, freshly-taught form.

Rosa grabbed Julie in one hand and Private Jones in the other and began running for the jeeps. Private Barnes followed, already fumbling with his keys, with Bud and Allison right behind him.

The wave, however, had saturated both vehicles – the engines choked and sputtered.

Several of the advancing sickle-claws went down before the barrage of gunfire, but the shots attracted the attention of the others.

There were *packs* of them. And the big carnosaurs were not far behind.

Private Jones finally gunned the engine to life.

"Come on!" Rosa shouted to the others.

But the sickle-claws were coming in too fast.

One of them closed on Jamie, dodging the coffee-girl's nervous, erratic shots, and leaped upon her. Jamie fell backward with a scream, even as the seven-inch foot-claw arced towards her throat.

Jeremy, helpless to shoot without hitting her, simply bodily tackled the thing, and the two of them went tumbling.

The creature's claws, however, turned dexterously inward, and Jeremy's voice rose in a strangled shriek as it gutted him.

Jamie, her arms clawed and bloody, let loose a scream of her own – an anguished howl of rage that Rosa could have never imagined from her.

And as Jeremy was disemboweled before her eyes, Jamie – cut-sleeves, bandanna and all – actually *charged* the thing, firing her rifle, screaming hysterically.

Gone were the tentative, careful shots – she blew the crouched sickle-claw off Jeremy's twitching corpse and continued to blast away, as it kicked and struggled on the ground.

Two more of them landed on her a moment later.

Jamie never had a chance to scream – one of the sickles found her throat, cutting off her voice, even as the other bore her to the ground.

Daryl and Bob both opened fire, dropping both creatures in their tracks – clearly too late. Daryl took half a step towards Jamie's torn and bloody body but stopped as the first of the big carnosaurs finally burst through the trees out onto the highway.

It was a big Allosaurus – probably close to forty feet long – at least five-tons.

Daryl and Bob exchanged glances, thn turned and ran for the jeeps.

Private Barns was still grinding his dead engine.

"Forget it," Rosa shouted again from the other jeep. "Come on!"

Barnes cursed, lurching out of the driver's seat. Bud pulled Allison out of the back and they all began to run.

The allosaur had caught Daryl – stamping him down with one clawed foot, trapping him, while the hand-claws shredded him from the abdomen out.

Rosa could actually see the creature's throat expanding like a snake as it swallowed Daryl in two pieces. Then it turned after them again.

Jones gunned the jeep, starting to pull away, even as Barnes and the others ran up alongside.

Rosa and Julie both reached out the rear-window for Private Barnes' hand as he pulled himself up and onto the back.

Two sickle-claws had caught Bob – he shrieked as they tore him into bloody rags.

Bud was cursing aloud, pacing the moving jeep, catching the door and practically flinging Allison inside. But then he tripped as he tried to pull himself in after her – his hand clinging to the door, he found himself being dragged.

The allosaur was back on their tail.

And not too far behind, more of the big carnosaurs had made the highway, pushing some of the smaller trees out into the road – the first of the big Carcharodonts.

One of the sickle-claws, hot on their tail, made a grab for Bud's dragging feet – he yanked them back precariously close to the spinning wheels. Both Julie and Rosa grabbed him by the arm, but the beast's reaching claws now latched onto his leg.

Allison pulled back.

Rosa had time to wonder – was this it? Was this where Allison – that *type* – at last threw the poor guy under the bus? But a moment later, she reappeared with her pistol and shot the thing in both eyes, sending it tumbling behind them on the road.

Then she grabbed Bud's other hand and the three women together hauled Bud on board like a grain sack.

The big allosaur, however, was coming up fast.

Private Barnes, hanging from the back by one hand, shouldered his rifle with the other, turned and started firing.

The allosaur didn't like it. It closed briefly with the jeep, snatching Barnes by the arm, yanking him off the back.

There was an explosion of gunfire as Barnes reflexively fired down the creature's gullet.

That turned out to be a vulnerable spot – the big carnosaur's throat was blasted open, and it staggered, Barnes still clamped in its mouth, before toppling over.

A final gesture for Barnes, as part of him fell away from the bladed jaws, bitten in half across the chest.

But just now, along the ridge above the northern highway, the tree line was parted yet again.

More carnosaurs – megalosaurs and ceratosaurs too – sauropods and ceratopsians.

They were going to cut them off before they could make the pass.

Private Jones stepped on it anyway.

Behind them, sprinting sickle-claws darted between the Carcharodonts' ankles as the army of marching monsters spilled out onto the highway.

They were trapped.

The bigger beasts were moving on them now. There was no way out this time. They would simply stomp their little truck into scrap.

Private Jones slowed to a stop.

They all looked at each other, drawing their guns – ready to fight – knowing it was already over.

Behind them, the first of the big Carcharodonts stopped, sniffing at the dead and still-twitching allosaur.

But in a manner very unlike predators, they turned away from the free meat, eyeing the retreating jeep instead.

War-dogs, Rosa thought again.

She could hear a rising roar...

... which she realized wasn't coming from the beasts at all.

The roar came from above.

War-dog meet war-bird.

They had seen a single fighter-jet pass above. Now it had apparently circled back, almost level with the tree line, unloading its guns on the advancing horde.

The machine gunfire tore into even the big Carcharodonts and the beasts *screamed*.

There was a blast of wind and a sonic-boom as the jet rocketed past overhead.

"Is that Lieutenant Walker?" Julie breathed, hardly daring to believe.

Rosa said nothing – of course there was no way to be sure.

But she knew. It was Lucas alright.

It was in the cock of the wing, as the pilot turned the craft back again for a second pass – this time targeting the beasts blocking the highway to the north – he had seen their escape route.

Now the jet let loose with missiles. The northern ridge erupted in fire and bestial screams.

The highway was broken in the blast, but the way through was clear.

Private Jones gunned the engine, jerking them forward, taking them up and over the pass. Once they reached the north highway, Jones floored it.

Above them, the jet circled back once more, as if seeing them off.

Then it turned and left them behind.

Rosa saw the jet bank abruptly, due north, and in moments, it was out of sight.

He'd given them a window – a fighting chance. But behind them, still more of the beasts perked up and over the hillside.

Jones wasn't taking any chances, he didn't slow. In fact, it felt almost as if he was losing control.

But then Rosa realized it wasn't just the rough, broken road – the ground beneath them was shaking.

It was not like that first day in the city – it wasn't the impact tremors of advancing giant footsteps.

This was the earth itself.

The tremors began to build.

Rosa had been barely two-years old when a 6.9 quake had hit San Francisco back in 1989 – she had actually been at the televised baseball game – and she remembered how the ground had just *kept* rumbling, kept getting worse – and as a toddler, it seemed it would never end.

Rosa had ridden out a lot of quakes since then. This was different.

Rocks began to tumble where the road had been cut into the cliff-side. Private Jones steered wildly to avoid them.

Then the ground REALLY began to shake.

The jeep skidded to one side, and Private Jones braked hard, even as a near-avalanche of beach-ball-sized boulders came tumbling down around them.

Then right next to her, Rosa heard Julie's voice – a small, hushed whisper. "Oh my God."

They all turned to look back the way they had come.

The coast highway – the cliffside itself – was crumbling away.

The coastline was breaking off into the ocean.

Rosa, of course, knew what it was – the good Catholic schoolgirl in her recognized it immediately, just as on that first day, she had recognized the Beast from the Pit.

She heard the verse in her head, rehearsed just like a nursery rhyme.

'There was a great earthquake; and the sun became black as sackcloth... and the whole moon became like blood.'

Also known, in California-folklore, as 'The Big One'.

The breaking fissure seemed to chase after them like a giant serpent – splitting open the ground, and then sending it crumbling off into the sea. The ocean frothed with countless tons of collapsing earth and rock.

Rosa could hear the screams of the beasts.

Today, nothing would be spared.

"Get us out of here," Rosa whispered, hitting Jones on the shoulder.

But even then, the very road, the highway itself, began to fall away beneath them.

Rosa shut her eyes as she felt the jeep begin to roll.

Then the avalanche caught them, as the cliffside broke away.

CHAPTER 41

It was quite a sight from his altitude, Tom thought, as the southwest coast of California dropped off into the ocean. He could see it with the naked eye from space.

The fault-line split away from the main landmass, just like they always said it would.

Tom focused as many satellite-scopes as were in range.

Numbly, he absorbed the devastation – no longer just the cities and towns, but even the land itself.

LA was gone. That had been the biggest chunk of it, right at first – the closest to ground zero. But even as Tom watched, the fault-line continued to grow, stretching north.

Watching a geological event in real-time was humbling.

When mountains crumbled, even the beasts were crushed into nonexistence – less than nothing before the tectonic forces of the Earth itself.

By that scale, it was really just the continent shifting its shoulders, shedding a layer.

For a thousand miles, by the humble measure of man, the destruction was absolute.

Tom had no idea how far north the collapse would eventually reach – at the very least, volcanic and seismic activity were likely to be activated up the entire west coast – they would probably be feeling tremors in Canada.

Or even Alaska, Tom thought, glancing at the empty screen where he'd last seen Kristi's face.

Tom shut his eyes – the watchman could stand to see no more.

The numbness threatened to break.

By sheer act of will, he forced his eyes open. Cold reality was his only friend.

'Courage' was not the word – he simply had no other option.

For whatever reason, this was the fate that had befallen him.

And so he would fill his role – he would correlate and collate – he would chronicle and compose.

When the aliens he had always wanted to meet finally arrived, at least there would be some record – a legacy.

Otherwise, the only remaining evidence of the human race would be a four-foot flag on the moon.

Tom sat before his screens, and waited for it to all end.

CHAPTER 42

The tyrannosaurs were out-numbered, but in close quarters, the advantage was theirs. They were the pit-bull model of theropod. While a big Carcharodont was longer, and might outweigh the average adult rex, it was a much more lightly-boned animal.

It was the nature of its prey – even a big Carcharodont didn't want to grapple with a giant sauropod – especially the gigantic titanosaurs. Employing a low-impact strategy similar to modern Komodo dragons, it would instead attack and retreat, falling back to let the slashing wounds fester, leaving the prey to weaken and die – providing a mountain of meat with little risk and little contact.

T. rex, on the other hand, was a Triceratops killer – a fast, dangerous prey, of equal size and reaction time – attack and retreat was not an option for an animal that could turn on a dime, with horns and shield. *T. rex* needed to kill at a stroke.

The first of the Carcharodonts felt the difference the moment the front-lines came together.

Down in L.A. and San Francisco, the tyrannosaurs had been driven out by sheer numbers. Here, that advantage was not as stark.

And in the close-quarters of the basin, a 'low-impact' attack strategy was not an advantage.

The big rex locked jaws with the first of the big Carcharodonts – a massive beast, even larger than the rex itself. At first, the greater weight of the carnosaur began to push the rex back.

But once the narrow saw-blades were pitted against the railroad spikes – a construct intended to carry a lot of weight lightly versus bio-mechanics designed to send a lot of weight against a target at high-velocity – the result was no contest.

Once the giant carnosaur's jaws had locked with the rex, it was trapped – and once the rex began to torque and bulldog its head back-and-forth, the Carcharodont's jaws were simply torn right off.

Spurting blood, the Carcharodont toppled, lifelessly, even as the rex turned to meet the next attacker.

The rex-gang joined, fangs-first, beside him, and the front line of carnosaurs were pushed back.

There *were*, however, also a number of two-thousand-foot sauropods – and of course a platoon of ceratopsians, specifically evolved to take on a rex.

The big dominant female was the first casualty on the rex's side – at the horns of a bull Triceratops.

Under almost no other circumstances would an adult rex approach one of the three-horned dreadnoughts face-to-face – the deadly horns were aimed unerringly at a rex's belly – just as the blade of its shield would chop at the face of any tyrannosaur foolish enough to go for a neck bite. Any *T. rex* that lived long enough to try it more than once, quickly learned that the way to attack a trike was from the rear – a one-shot, incapacitating bite to the hips and spine.

But circumstances were not normal, and on this day, with the hot-blood of battle, the big female charged the horns head-on.

The initial clash took the female's eye as one of the horns slid deep into its socket.

Pulling back with an outraged scream, the rex reared up – exposing her belly.

Its target wide-open, the trike charged forward, catching the tyrant-queen in the ribs with all three horns, piercing her heart.

The giant sauropods also did some damage – one big titanosaur nearly broke the rex front line – two adolescent males were crushed and trampled before the pack took the giant beast down at the legs, gigantic bites cleaving huge chunks out of both bone and muscle, as well as severing tendons.

All else being equal, the sheer number of the invaders, would seemingly, eventually *have* to finally prevail.

The narrow beach, however, congested the advancing horde – its own numbers kept the weight of its forces from being a factor.

At the forefront of the battle, the big rex – once a rogue, but now clearly acknowledged as pride-leader – scoured the ridge for the lead Carcharodont – the big one that had first appeared upon the hill – the one with all the Ottos crawling all over it.

He spotted the big carnosaur still hovering at the periphery on the ridge.

The beast itself seemed to have gone into a stupor – as if a button had just clicked dormant in it head.

But the rex could see the skittering little beasts on its back.

T. rex did not know strategic terms like 'command station', or 'home-base', but he instinctively recognized this particular target among all the others.

He found he really did not care about all these other beasts he found himself contending with this day. THOSE little bastards were what he wanted.

That psychic-stench. The rex was determined to stamp it out.

The scaly little rats had tried to dominate him. That was reason enough.

The rex began to fight his way up the slope.

On the hill above, the Carcharodont seemed to suddenly blink awake. Its head cocked, eyeing the rex's approach.

The Ottos on its back were hissing and screeching – a near-embolism pulse on the rex's tiny brain.

Focused on its goal, the rex paid no attention to another sound, coming from the south, as an F-16 appeared on the horizon.

CHAPTER 43

Jonah and Naomi ran down the beach – both ridges north and south were cut off, and straight ahead was sheer rock wall.

That left the narrow strip of coast that led down to the north bay, opposite the remains of Eureka.

The small grouping of buildings that surrounded the docks remained undisturbed – although likely would not much longer.

There were also the air and boat parks.

The war, however, was erupting literally right over their heads.

So far, the beasts were focused on each other. But they were all infected giants.

There was a mixed blessing there – two humans on foot were not enough to attract their attention. But the wall of walking mountains would crush them like ants – absence of malice or not.

They reached the dock even as the impact of first clash seemed to shake the entire coast.

The pier's main office was locked, and Jonah kicked the door open – a dock foreman usually kept spare keys to the crafts and vessels in his charge.

Jonah glanced down over the water at the handful of boats that remained.

Getting back out on the ocean wasn't exactly an attractive alternative either – not with six-hundred foot Megalodons patrolling the coast.

Options, however, were running extremely thin.

There was, however, the air-park too.

Jonah looked across the way to the fenced-off air-field.

A couple of crop-dusters – both with missing engines. A chopper that looked like it had been wrecked.

And at the end of the dock, tarped-up for the season, was a sea-plane.

Boy, Jonah thought, he *really* didn't like the looks of *that* contraption.

Naomi, however, had turned away, and Jonah saw her standing out on the dock, her head turned up to the sky.

Jonah turned, following her gaze to the south, and he spotted it.

But for the roar of the beasts, he would have heard it already – the drone of an approaching fighter jet.

A single plane.

And on its tail, was every horror out of hell – a swarm of infected flying dragons.

Even as Jonah watched, one of the beasts nearly closed, making a grab for the fighter with its giant beak. The pilot dodged the strike artfully, twisting into a spiraling spin, as the pterosaur's jaws snapped shut on its jet-wash.

Jonah heard Naomi suck an involuntary breath.

The fighter seemed to engage with them all at once, even as flying beasts swarmed – circling asteroids with wings and teeth.

"Naomi?" Jonah began, but she was not listening. She stood breathless, oblivious to his words – oblivious even to the conflagration of giants erupting just over her shoulder, less than the length of two football fields behind.

She glanced at Jonah, her eyes wide – Jonah didn't know if it was hope or tears.

Naomi would never be able to tell him – the words would choke in her throat – but she *knew* that particular spin move. It was *cocky*.

It was *just* like him.

And as the fighter made its first pass overhead, she recognized the payload as well.

She knew why he was here. His target was all around them.

The infected giants. They were going to burn it all out.

"We've got to get out of here," Naomi said.

She pushed past Jonah and reached for the keys to the sea-plane docked at the end of the pier, and pressed them firmly in Jonah's reluctant hand.

Jonah frowned but nodded.

The two of them ran for the end of the dock.

CHAPTER 44

Lucas made one fly-by over the ground-war below.

The exodus of the Carcharodont-led army filled in from the south through the little alleyway created by the ragged coastal highlands, funneling onto the beach.

A smaller force stood them off. The tyrannosaurs were holding ground. And even as the marching army ascended from the south, Lucas could see more of the rex-clan filling in the ranks over the ridge from the north.

For whatever reason, all the beasts in the region were congregating at once.

The General had been right – it was a big bloom, alright.

As he passed above, he could see both factions stretching for miles.

Behind him, the army of flying dragons cut his path off in every direction.

Lucas knew his mission – and he could clearly see the consequences of his failure.

And he could see that Eureka had been clearly destroyed.

The General had admonished him for holding out hope.

If she was alive, she was nowhere near here, Rhodes had said.

But what if he was wrong? What if she was down there somewhere right now, maybe even cussing him for being late – and for *damn* sure, cussing him for sending her to this monster-infested hell-hole.

What if she was out there right now? Maybe even looking up and seeing him, believing she was seeing the incoming cavalry?

It was doubtful – one in a million.

Just like Mrs. Naomi Walker.

The question was, could he do it anyway? Not knowing?

No one else could.

It was his duty.

Death from above.

The flying dragons had flanked him and he veered back towards the bay, but they were coming in too great of numbers.

One of the largest had locked onto his tail. It had tracked his trajectory, and was heading him off in midair. In another moment, it would be upon him.

He had to make his choice – do or die – right NOW.

Two things happened right then.

First he cooled his heart to ice – and the very same moment, it broke forever.

He begged God to forgive him.

Tears began to run from his eyes.

"Naomi...?" he choked. "Baby. Oh, God, I love you SO much."

Lucas fired his missiles.

Half-a-moment later, the teeth crashed through the fragile metal of the cockpit.

The last thing Lucas was aware of was a sense of impact, and a blast of cold air.

Then explosion and fire.

But the missiles were away.

CHAPTER 45

Jonah had flown exactly one sea-plane in his life – he'd had the idea it would be good for remote lakes without landing strips. That was before he'd made his first take-off with the bogged-down pontoons off of water instead of wheels and a nice-sturdy tarmac. Landing had been even worse.

He had bought the chopper shortly thereafter.

And that had been on a nice, easy-flowing river – hardly the conditions that met them today.

Naomi wasn't even looking at him, staring back over her shoulder as the F-16 was now circling back around.

The flying beasts were hard on its tail, and seemed to be congregating to cut off any avenue of retreat.

In another few moments, they might cut off their escape as well.

"Jonah..." Naomi began.

But Jonah had the key in the ignition, lighting the rusty propellers to life and firing-up a coughing engine.

Great, Jonah thought – a jalopy.

As he pulled away from the dock, out over the water, he wondered what might be prowling from below, attracted by the vibrations of the struggling motor.

But it was far past time to worry about the unseen.

Jonah took them up to speed and hit the flaps, launching them into the air, with lurching, wounded-sparrow hops.

He had no direction – just fired them straight up the coast over the northern ridge.

Naomi twisted in her seat, looking anxiously behind.

Jonah heard a breaking sob in her throat as one of the flying beasts finally closed on the F-16.

She saw the pilot drop his payload, even as the beast's jaws snapped shut over the fragile fuselage.

She hid her eyes as the fighter exploded.

But the missiles were true.

Jonah cranked the throttle, gaining distance, even as seconds evaporated away.

Looking back over his shoulder, he saw the basin disappear into light.

The mushroom cloud erupted on the horizon.

Then the blast-wave hit, and blew them out of the sky.

CHAPTER 46

The plane was blown sideways and Jonah could feel the wings strain, threatening to simply tear away. But instead, it was the pontoons that broke loose – first one, then the other – the abrupt back and forth of dropping ballasts jerked them nearly vertical.

Naomi was gripping her seat, her eyes squeezed shut.

Jonah had a pretty good idea who she had seen in that exploding F-16 – whether it really was or not.

Until that moment, that had been what had kept her going – a single-minded purpose.

That was over now. She was ready to die, and she didn't want to see it coming.

And that loss of faith almost did it for Jonah too.

His own focus had been getting her there. A moot point, now.

Jonah wondered what it must have been like for that fighter-pilot – just the moment before the dragons got him – staying focused – letting your last action on the mortal plane be an act of defiance – to spit past death at the Devil waiting behind.

A higher-grade model, Jonah thought.

For some reason, that set his teeth.

Well, he decided, you just have to work with what you've got.

They were in near free-fall, riding the blast in a near-vertical launch pose. Jonah flipped the flaps, knocking them forward.

The bulky aircraft immediately threatened to spin, but Jonah pulled hard, using their own momentum to stabilize them.

It was a little like ice-skating backwards – something he hadn't done since he was a kid. You had to lean in exactly the opposite direction it *felt* like you needed to go.

They were ajar, off-center, but were at least leveling out.

If they could maintain altitude, Jonah was just beginning to believe he could ride it out. Naomi opened her eyes warily – but that was when the motors quit – the propellers on both wings choked and died.

Almost immediately, they began to drop towards the Earth.

Naomi moaned aloud. *"Oh* my God."

Below was ocean and a narrow beach – bordered by sheer cliff.

They had no pontoons. There were no wheels. And even if they did, if they landed askew as they were coming in now, they would tumble anyway – rolling and breaking apart.

The blast wave was finally fading with distance. How far back had they left ground-zero? Ten miles? Maybe more?

Riding the blast was like back-draft in a burning building. Jonah wondered what the safe distance for radiation contamination might be – he was very doubtful this particular mission had been flown with over-much concern for collateral damage.

He struggled with the controls – they were coming in too low, too fast.

Naomi's low moan grew louder. Now her eyes were open wide – unable to look away.

"*Jonah...*"

At barely fifty-feet of altitude, Jonah jerked their nose straight, and as they finally touched down, he sailed them just out past the fast-approaching beach over where the rolling waves met the shore.

The beach was long and flat, extending out into the surf.

They landed not quite fifty-yards offshore. The sea-plane's concave base struck the water, like diving a boat into the rapids.

That, Jonah thought, was something he was actually good at.

For a second, he believed he was really going to pull it off.

But then the starboard wing broke off and they began to tumble anyway.

Naomi screamed aloud in his ear. Jonah finally shut his eyes, as the aircraft pitched and rolled.

The windshield smashed open and ocean water flooded in.

Three full rotations and the sea-plane at last tumbled to a stop.

They had planted nose-first into the surf, their tail sticking up like a flag.

Jonah opened his eyes. The waves rolled past – they had landed in less than three feet of water.

But they were alive.

They sat there for several minutes, as the roar of the nuclear wind faded, like the warm, charcoal-tasting after-breeze from a burning wildfire.

Then they climbed out of the wrecked sea-plane, into the surf, and made their way up to the beach.

They turned to the south where the radioactive incandescence out of the town of Eureka still shined.

The day had reached its late afternoon – and along the southward coast, a second, nuclear sun had joined Sol, and its fading glow colored the horizon.

As the minutes ticked past, the burning cinder began to fade.

Naomi sat down in the sand.

After a moment, Jonah sat down next to her.

Naomi nodded at the crashed sea-plane – pegged into the surf like a javelin.

"You know," she said, "you really aren't a very good pilot. I've flown with you twice and you've crashed both times."

And then abruptly, she broke down and began to cry.

It was the broken dam – the cracks Jonah had seen in that private moment he had allowed her back on the mountain, had finally given way.

This time he held her.

But the apocalypse left no allowance for grief.

Now it was the Earth itself that began to rumble beneath them.

Jonah knew in a moment that this was no impact tremor – no footstep of some approaching giant.

This was another level.

Mother Earth herself had joined the party.

Whether triggered by the blast, or perhaps just petulance or boredom, the volcanic range announced its presence beneath their feet.

With tears still drying on her cheeks, Naomi stood, looking around wide-eyed. Her voice was teary and angry – frustrated and helpless.

"What's *happening*!?" she screamed aloud.

Around them, rocks began to tumble down from the cliffs. The ground shook in ever-increasing tremors.

And while Jonah would never know it, his thoughts mirrored those of Doctor Rosa Holland – Earthquake: check – sun black as sackcloth: check – the moon as blood.

Had to admit, the description matched.

Jonah grabbed Naomi's hand and began to run up the beach, dragging her with him, ignoring her gasping breaths, yanking her along when she began to trip – simply fleeing blind, with no greater destination than away.

The avalanche seemed to follow right behind as the cliffside collapsed over the sand into the surf.

And somewhere in the middle, there was nothing left but to hide.

Below the highway, emptying out onto the beach, Jonah found a drainage pipe cut into the rock.

Four-feet wide – steel reinforced by concrete.

They scrambled inside, even as the rocks began to break away, tumbling down from the crumbling cliff wall.

The mouth of the pipe was quickly covered by falling debris. Jonah worried for perhaps half-a-second that their entrance would be buried – but as the tremors continued to build with each passing moment, he realized that was at best, a secondary priority.

It was already too late anyway.

They were trapped in the dark as the world destroyed itself around them.

Clinging to each other like the tiniest of mice, they hunkered down together to somehow wait it out until the end.

CHAPTER 47

In the wake of the blast, the rex lay on the hillside, Carcharodont-flesh still in its teeth.

The Tyrant King had finally found a power greater than itself.

It had not identified the approaching fighter-jet as a threat – but apparently Otto had, because at the sound of the war-bird's engine, the great Carcharodont that saddled them on its back, had suddenly turned and run.

The rex had no idea why – it simply saw its opponent retreat, prompting the instinctual reaction of pursuit.

And if it hadn't, the screaming caterwauling of the Ottos swarming over the retreating carnosaur's back would have been enough.

It was battery-acid on its senses – the physic poke of a needle – and in the mob of already-rampaging beasts, the warbling cry seemed to trigger a near-epileptic rage.

It was also gas on a fire – the muddying of the water – a smoke cloud to provide cover for a strategic retreat.

The big rex itself was actually staggered – the screeching pin-prick combining with its own deteriorating mental faculties induced momentary vertigo.

It blinked, refocusing on its target.

It pursued.

The Carcharodont's retreat was headlong. The rex made no connection with the F-16 flying over – nor did it give more than cursory notice when the fighter itself exploded in the jaws of one of the flying dragons, high above its head.

It paid no attention to the payload that had been released, that was even at that moment zeroing in on the battlefield behind.

All the rex knew, as it ran down the retreating Carcharodont, was that here, finally, it had caught that psychic-stench – that foulness – and would now stamp it out forever.

The big carnosaur turned to face the rex as it closed – the razor-toothed jaws spread wide.

And while a Carcharodont wasn't a bulldog like a rex, the big carnosaur's jaws were evolved to take out the largest prey animals that ever existed – a giant saw-blade that would cleave entire slabs of flesh off the sides of giant sauropods.

These bladed jaws slipped past the rex's charging strike, catching the tyrannosaur off-guard, slashing a long, deep wound across its torso and neck.

The rex bellowed in outrage and pain, snapping in retaliation, even as the carnosaur quickly withdrew. The Carcharodont circled, jaws agape, waiting for another opening.

For a moment, the rex staggered.

At this point, the sum total of its wounds was probably already fatal – even as its eyes glowed ever-brighter with the chemical that was already killing it.

But it was a rex, and so it stood in defiance.

And something in its posture activated a similar impulse in the Carcharodont.

The big carnosaur had fought tyrannosaurs before – *T. rex* was as vulnerable as a sauropod to a long, hemorrhaging bite – even more so, as the rex was much smaller. The Carcharodont had learned to treat the pugnacious tyrannosaurs no different than prey – to simply bite and retreat.

But the rex wanted to *fight*.

And for just a moment, in the face of the belligerent display, the Carcharodont did too. As an animal of instincts, instead of waiting for inattentive prey, it moved forward as if to attack a rival.

The big carnosaur likely never realized its mistake.

But Otto obviously did – as the monster's jaws locked, a flood of scaly little beasts began to scatter off the big Carcharodont's back – rats deserting the ship.

The rex, however, wasn't having it.

It had the Carcharodont in its grip now, but the big carnosaur didn't quite yet realize it, feeling only its own superior weight.

But after another moment, it realized its own jaws were simply being bitten *into* – just a moment before the rex began to thrash back and forth, torqueing the bigger carnosaur's slender neck, twisting and snapping the vertebra, even as it bore the larger beast to the ground.

The retreating Ottos made for the brush as the still-kicking carcass collapsed.

It wasn't even close. The rex stamped them out like ants.

With single-minded precision, guided by its unfailing nose, the big tyrannosaur stomped the foliage flat, until every last one of the scaly little rats was bloody-paste, smashed into the dirt beneath its feet.

And then, just beyond the ridge, partially blocked by the hillside, the payload hit.

The rex was aware of a blinding blast of light.

Then it was picked up and carried – thrown, as if by a category-10 tornado.

The battlefield behind was obliterated.

Debris and burning wreckage were blown past.

The rex felt itself burn.

And when it finally rolled and tumbled to a stop, part of its primitive mind remained conscious and aware.

Its body was shattered – although, as a rex, it simply wasn't conditioned to stop.

Its hip and back were broken – as well as both legs – yet, it struggled vainly to rise.

Then it felt the Earth itself begin to shake. Whatever balance its broken body retained, whatever coordination was left in its dying nervous system, finally fizzled out like a burnt fuse.

The rex collapsed.

The struggling chain-stokes breath choked to a stop. The green glow in its eyes faded.

It again felt the ground shaking beneath him – perhaps as homage to the passing of a king.

The rex stiffened and lay still.

Long live the king.

CHAPTER 48

World-wide, the battle would eventually wind down over a period of weeks.

Major Tom had programmed the satellites to focus in on the blooms wherever they sprouted.

He was also able to isolate where most of the nuke strikes had landed.

Besides the blast in Eureka – finally obliterating that damned tower once and for all – two other fighter-pilots had successfully dropped their payloads. None of the pilots, Tom was able to ascertain, had survived.

Not that he'd received communication of any kind from the ground. Whatever remained of global networking, had been fried in the EMP that followed multiple detonations all over the planet.

But continental North America, at least west of the Rockies, had been cleaned out – the blooms had been burned.

The rest of the world was not so lucky. The battle would run its course, as would the cycle of the Food of the Gods.

But eventually, even that began to burn itself out – the giants inevitably died – where the chemical didn't kill them, they killed each other.

Enough scorched Earth, and there was nothing left to grow.

Then there were those 'scrambled signals' – missiles fired from silos to 'random' locations.

Random like the San Andreas fFault?

As well as what was left of London, and Hong Kong – or pretty much any epicenter where humanity might cling to a foothold?

Practical extermination.

That had been the first thing the analyst in him had eliminated – the possibility of random event.

The world below had gone dark. His own eyes in the sky were partially blind. The EMP had knocked out a couple of satellites too, and his networking across the board was growing steadily more blinky.

Mostly, he had been looking for any remaining signal coming in from the planet below.

But there was nothing.

Tom sat there, floating weightless – almost like a ghost himself.

He felt like he should *want* to cry – yet, somehow he couldn't – perhaps it was a defense mechanism – as if that part of his mind had simply shut down.

It was possible that in that moment, his hair went a little bit gray.

Tom looked around at the one-hundred square yards where he would spend the rest of his life.

Two days before, he had found Kristi's cabin in Alaska.

It had actually been as simple as finding her last name in the database and mapping her associated address.

The property was boarded-up and looked abandoned.

She had evidently gone looking for help, braving the wilds, looking for some other sign of human habitation.

Which, near as Tom could tell, did not exist for several thousand miles in any direction.

Even if surviving military had regrouped, Tom didn't know where.

He wondered how long Kristi had waited before abandoning her home. Had she been desperate? Or perhaps she had gone out well-fortified, well-planned and ready?

Tom could not imagine a scenario where it could possibly matter.

He tried not to feel sorry for himself, for the fact that he would never know.

And then, just because he couldn't stand the silence any longer, he flicked his screens back on – bringing back repeating images of the recent past. Computer-simulations blinked to life, and began to shuffle and analyze, looking for new patterns in old re-runs.

As he floated up here forever.

Burning out his fuse up there alone.

What did he miss?

He had said 'nothing'.

Funny how words came back to bite you.

Tom buried his face in his hands.

CHAPTER 49

None of the pilots ever returned. The fleet and the base were gone. If the military had regrouped, it was nowhere near

Rosa sat out on the beach, looking out at the ocean. Beside her sat Allison and Bud. Behind them, was the wreck of the coastline, where the cliffside had crumbled away.

The jeep had tumbled with the rocks. It had been a crazy, rolling sensation – it was LOUD – with a sense of weight so immense – so CRUSHING – that it took your breath away before it even touched you.

If they had been buried, it would have been over, but they had tumbled with the rest of the rolling avalanche. The jeep itself was actually uniquely well-reinforced for this specific kind of trauma – the solid roll-bars keeping the crushing boulders at bay.

Rosa wasn't really aware of it at the time – it happened so fast – but what had really saved her was her seat-belt – a reflexive habit, she didn't even remember strapping across her waist. Bud had done likewise – his overprotective self – for both him and Allison.

The others had died.

Julie had been thrown out the window almost at once. Rosa heard one brief scream, and then she was gone. They never saw even a trace of her again.

Private Jones had clung to the overhead bar and his seat – bracing himself, his tendons stretching like wire – but he was, nevertheless, also pitched into the stampeding boulders.

Not that Rosa expected it to matter.

How many times, now, she thought? How many times had she gotten herself ready to die?

At this point, she almost wanted to just get it over with. She was simply too tired to fight it anymore.

The avalanche had continued down the beach into the ocean, even as the falling rubble filled the foam-splitting fissures.

Rosa remembered feeling the spray of the ocean, and then impact.

She lay in darkness. She didn't know how long.

But the next thing she remembered was being carried, and then sat down with care on a bed of hard rocks.

That had been three days ago. Since then, the tide had come and gone three times as well.

It was amazing, Rosa thought, how quickly it all washed away.

The collapsed coastal wall was a jagged quarry of smashed rock, but the passage of the surf had already begun to fill in the cracks with sand.

Their jeep still lay where it had landed, just at the surf-line, near the top of a dead-fall of boulders.

And now they waited to see if anyone was coming back.

Correction: Rosa was waiting to see if *Lucas* was coming back.

As a kindness, Bud and Allison had allowed her to wait.

But now, on the eve of the third day, as the tide washed the sand back into the cracks, Bud sat down next to her, in front of the little campfire they'd built among the rocks.

He said nothing right away, but Rosa knew what was on his mind.

Allison had wandered a ways up the beach, looking for driftwood. They had already salvaged what they could from the jeep – mostly a few matches, some kerosene, a first-aid kit.

Allison also found a little ammo for her 9 mm.

Rosa found herself again wondering about the woman's past. Based on what she knew, those circles under the eyes had been hard-won.

No doubt they were mirrored in her own eyes, just now.

No one gets tough on purpose.

Rosa glanced sideways at Bud.

"You're thinking it's time to move on," she said.

Bud nodded slowly, letting out a long sigh.

"We've been running for a long time," he said. "I think it's time we stopped."

Rosa looked off to where Allison walked alone on the beach, safely out of earshot.

'Fallen Woman', Rosa thought, her Catholic upbringing rearing its ugly head once again.

But Allison was also a survivor.

If God existed, if His Will had played any hand, that also meant she had been spared. Carrying a child, with her own Joseph to look after her.

"She saved *my* life, too," Bud said quietly. "She had a little love left to give, at a time when I needed it."

Now he smiled a little. "Just like now," he said. "Just like always."

They both fell silent, watching the incoming waves.

Allison ambled up with her load of kindling and dropped it on the fire, before sitting down next to Bud.

At the warmth of the fire, she felt her belly – just barely showing.

"When are you due?" Rosa asked.

"Six-and-a-half months," Allison said.

Rosa found herself wondering again – an unforgivable question that she would never ask – if Bud was the father.

Instead, she regarded the two of them together.

"So, what are your plans?"

Allison and Bud exchanged glances.

"Well," Bud began, "we were actually thinking of heading out pretty soon. Like maybe tomorrow." He nodded at the wrecked coastline. "Not much here to salvage."

"And go where?"

"North. Just follow the coast until we see landscape again. Find a place to try and live."

Rosa nodded silently.

"You're welcome to join us," Bud said and he patted Allison's belly. "We could use a doctor."

Rosa felt the sting of tears. How many times had these people saved her life?

"Have you got a name?" she asked.

Bud smiled. "How about 'Rosa', if it's a girl?"

Another sting. "And if it's a boy?"

This time it was Allison who answered, and as she spoke, her hard face became something almost gentle.

"If it's a boy," she said, "I'm going to call him 'Lucas'."

And with that, Rosa had given up the battle with her tears.

She cried for quite a long time. Bud and Allison had quietly stepped aside until she was done.

Now she sat alone on the beach looking out at the setting sun.

She knew the process well – she had seen it a hundred, a *thousand* times – and so, formally, professionally, she allowed herself to grieve.

Tomorrow, they would leave it all behind in search of a new life.

But she would allow herself tonight.

CHAPTER 50

It took the better part of two days for Jonah and Naomi to dig their way out.

The drainage pipe had been completely buried early on. Trapped there in the dark, it seemed like the violent upheaval would never end. The air was almost too clouded to breathe, and they had no recourse but to simply cover their faces, shut their eyes and wait.

Jonah had no idea how long it was before the tremors finally ended. It was even longer before they dared to even move.

The pipe had held, but now they were trapped in pure pitch dark, with the entrance buried underneath tons of rubble. That left no other option than to follow the pipe to its other end – which had once been the cliff-side above. Jonah wasn't sure – he hadn't exactly picked his landing strip – but he believed the road above was Highway 101.

It was actually the size of the boulders that made the difference – it had been the bedrock of the cliff itself that had collapsed and huge chunks of rock were braced against each other – it had, in point of fact, broken the pipe in half, as the cliff and the road above had fallen away. But larger chunks had also prevented the cracks from being filled in with smaller debris.

Jonah had a box of matches – habitually kept in a plastic bag in his jacket pocket – and with these alone, they had rationed enough light to dig steadily for two days, working their way up until they finally found daylight.

Neither of them had spoken – neither of them had tried to sleep. Jonah had resigned to dig until he dropped – it seemed ridiculous to die now – he was determined to at least make it to the surface.

He was beginning to think they wouldn't, when he felt the first gust of air breezing in.

It had still taken two more hours to see daylight.

But in the end, the two little mice finally crawled out from between the broken rocks.

Jonah felt the first hint of coastal mist as he pushed his way to the surface. After a moment, he pulled Naomi up beside him.

Where the highway had once been, there was now broken rubble.

Below, however, the tide was filling in the cracks with a brand-new beach – a brand-new coastline.

Bloodied, caked in dirt and granite, dehydrated and spent, they made their way down the shattered cliff to the sand.

Naomi walked to where the surf broke and sat down on a piece of driftwood.

Jonah sat down next to her, and for several minutes they simply sat there looking out at the Pacific Ocean as it crashed and bashed like it always had – utterly uncaring.

The sun had reached late afternoon and was beginning to set.

They looked up and down the coast and there was destruction as far as they could see.

For a long time, the only sound was the crash of the surf, and the squawk of seagulls.

It was finally Naomi who broke the silence.

"You know," she said, "you were safe in your cabin. If you'd just stayed where you were, you could have avoided ALL this."

Jonah sighed. "Well," he agreed, "I never have been very smart."

Naomi didn't smile. She glanced up at him briefly, uncharacteristically furtive, not quite willing to meet his eyes.

All of her tears had been cried out. But her pain was still quite fresh.

"You know why I couldn't stay, right?" she said. "Why I had to come?"

"Yes."

Now she turned and looked at him steadily.

"Why did *you*?"

Jonah honestly considered.

"I guess," he said finally, "because I was supposed to."

That seemed to satisfy her. She even smiled a little.

"So," she said, "what now?"

And with that, Jonah stood.

"Well," he said, "*Now*, it's about two-hundred miles northeast back to my cabin."

He made as if to check his watch. "Think we can make it?"

She looked up at him quizzically.

"*We*?" she said.

Jonah sighed.

Never giving an inch, he thought. He tried to imagine what it must be like to play in her league. It took a higher-grade model.

"Well," he said, "*I'm* going home."

Jonah turned, as if ready to start walking up the beach that very moment, pausing only to look back over his shoulder.

"You are under no obligation to follow," he said.

He started to walk, turning his back, leaving her still sitting there on her log.

He wondered what he would do if she didn't follow.

But he knew well enough. He stopped and waited.

And then she was standing beside him.

"Okay," she said. "Let's go."

Jonah found himself smiling – and it must have been a bit too smug, because she reached out and slugged him in the arm – right in that spot where the shoulder meets the bone.

Naomi tilted her head.

"That didn't *hurt*, did it?"

Jonah tossed a tear off his cheek. "Nah."

And now she smiled back.

The tide was coming in and the beach up ahead was growing narrow. Jonah wondered how far before they could find a path up into the hills – and then he wondered what the terrain might look like on the far side.

Two-hundred miles – and that was assuming his cabin was still there. No telling how far the seismic upheaval had traveled – or for that matter, if it was even all done.

Only one way to find out, he decided.

Naomi fell into step beside him.

Ahead of them, a new world waited. Jonah didn't know if that world had a place for them in it.

Time would tell.

CHAPTER 51

The rex lay where it had fallen.

After the blast, much of the surrounding forest had burned, spreading the damage far beyond the ten-mile blast-radius.

It had actually been the quake that had gone a long way towards smothering that fire – burying it. The air had gone black with smoke and floating bits of ash, from both volcanic and nuclear eruption.

But now the dust settled. The body of the rex was covered as if with a light layer of snow.

And finally, after three days, the first of the scavengers appeared at the edges.

Otto hopped out of the surrounding brush.

There were several of them, in fact. They scampered to the edge of the stream, chirping excitedly at the body of the fallen tyrant.

Things had gone badly in this region. The majority of their war-beasts had been taken out in the blast – and Otto himself – *them*selves – had been nearly wiped-out.

Not that it mattered, in the larger picture – there wasn't really ONE of them, anymore – they had been cloned so many times that none of them would have known the difference anyway.

Otto had been one of the first products of the 'Monster Island' project – judged an amusing failure, he/it/they had been around for a long time.

And they had been all over. They had been a mascot, after all.

And wherever a rat could be, so could Otto.

The military word for it was 'infiltration'.

And whatever communal, hive-mind that the little lizards shared, their organic memory banks had absorbed every command, every clearance code, mimicked every voice – as well as a working knowledge of every base, communication tower – every missile silo – as well as access to almost all the world's munitions.

That was not to mention other, not so conventional doomsday devices, that all the different governments kept coming up with – such as a super-virus to disable the entire worldwide web, all at once.

Not that the nuclear strikes hadn't been wildly successful – except locally, of course. But world-wide, the disgusting tailless apes that had infested the planet had been effectively cleansed away.

That left only the cleaning of its own house.

Besides straggling vestiges of two-legged apes in this particular region, there was the matter of the rex packs – curiously immune to their domination.

Time to fix that.

The Food of the Gods had run its cycle – by now most of the infected beasts would have died – and where they hadn't, the nukes had burned it out.

There still remained, however, the odd carcass – like that of the rex.

If Otto could have understood poetic irony, it might have appreciated the thought that the rex itself would be the vehicle to finally wipe out the pesky stubborn resistance of its kind once and for all.

The pack of Ottos began to screech and howl, and the call was more than vocal – it was that psychic stench that seemed to reek worse wherever they were in numbers.

There were still 'normals' stocked deep in the woods – all just waiting for their turn at the plate.

It was tyrannosaur territory, but the exodus had brought in killers of all kinds.

None of the big carnosaurs dared the area – not yet. But a few of the larger sickle-claws were already poking out from the brush, eyeing the massive carcass laid out in the basin.

It was a start.

Now they would simply begin again.

The little pack of Ottos hopped discreetly out of the way, as the first of their larger cousins cautiously approached the tantalizing mountain of free meat.

A few of them began to nibble experimentally, pulling at the tough flesh.

Otto watched. They would wait for them to feed.

Soon their eyes would begin to glow green.

And then they would have another rampaging army.

They would wipe out those last pockets of hairless apes once and for all. There would be little resistance this time.

More sickle-claws were venturing from the brush. The little pack of Ottos continued to squawk and howl.

So intent were they, however, that they failed to notice the shadow in the brush behind them.

The rex was a big rogue – nearly fourteen meters long and approaching nine tons. But it could still move with surprising stealth when it chose to.

It had learned to sneak up on these little scavengers – they with their psychic-stench.

He didn't even usually bother to eat them – just stomped them out like fire ants.

It was actually rather therapeutic – just like popping insulation bubbles.

The pack of Ottos screeched and fled, even as the rex's foot came down, smashing the pack of them flat.

Then it wiped its foot disgustedly on the forest floor.

It HATED those little bastards.

Now the rex turned its attention to the gargantuan carcass and the sickle-claws that were now staring doubtfully down from its back.

The rex let out a low, rumbling growl, and the sickle-claws scattered.

Satisfied, the big rogue settled down and began to feed.

At the edge of the forest, another small troop of Ottos emerged.

The little creatures stared up balefully. The rex eyed them right back – just like another pack of insulation bubbles.

The Ottos hissed and shrieked, and the rex felt that sense of static shock – that pepper-spray in the sinus.

The big rex snorted a brief sneeze of irritation.

Then it rose to its full height, growling dangerously – and now its eyes had begun to glow emerald green.

The little creatures turned and disappeared into the forest.

THE END

CHECK OUT OTHER GREAT DINOSAUR BOOKS

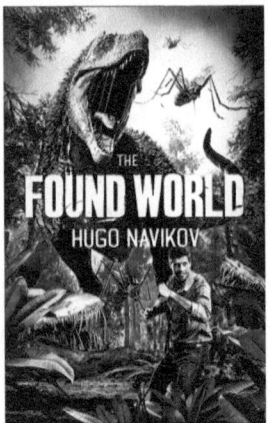

THE FOUND WORLD
by **Hugo Navikov**

A powerful global cabal wants adventurer Brett Russell to retrieve a superweapon stolen by the scientist who built it. To entice him to travel underneath one of the most dangerous volcanoes on Earth to find the scientist, this shadowy organization will pay him the only thing he cares about: information that will allow him to avenge his family's murder.

But before he can get paid, he and his team must enter an underground hellscape of killer plants, giant insects, terrifying dinosaurs, and an army of other predators never previously seen by man.

At the end of this journey awaits a revelation that could alter the fate of mankind ... if they can make it back from this horrifying found world.

HOUSE OF THE GODS
by **Davide Mana**

High above the steamy jungle of the Amazon basin, rise the flat plateaus known as the Tepui, the House of the Gods. Lost worlds of unknown beauty, a naturalistic wonder, each an ecology onto itself, shunned by the local tribes for centuries. The House of the Gods was not made for men.

But now, the crew and passengers of a small charter plane are about to find what was hidden for sixty million years.

Lost on an island in the clouds 10.000 feet above the jungle, surrounded by dinosaurs, hunted by mysterious mercenaries, the survivors of Sligo Air flight 001 will quickly learn the only rule of life on Earth: Extinction.

 SEVEREDPRESS

facebook.com/severedpress
twitter.com/severedpress

CHECK OUT OTHER GREAT DINOSAUR BOOKS

FLIPSIDE
by JAKE BIBLE

The year is 2046 and dinosaurs are real.

Time bubbles across the world, many as large as one hundred square miles, turn like clockwork, revealing prehistoric landscapes from the Cretaceous Period.

They reveal the Flipside.

Now, thirty years after the first Turn, the clockwork is breaking down as one of the world's powers has decided to exploit the phenomenon for their own gain, possibly destroying everything then and now in the process.

A MAN OUT OF TIME
by Christopher Laflan

Five years after the Chinese Axis detonated an unknown weapon of mass destruction off the southern coast of the United States, Special Ops Sergeant John Crider and the members of Shadow Company have finally captured what they all hope will lead to the end of the war. Unfortunately, the population within the United States is no longer sustainable. In an effort to stabilize the economy, the government enacts the Cryonics Act. One hundred years in suspended animation, all debt forgiven, and a chance at a less crowded future are too good to pass up for John and his young daughter.

Except not everything always goes as planned as Sergeant John Crider finds himself pitted against a land of prehistoric monsters genetically resurrected from the fossil record, murderous inhabitants, and a future he never wanted.

CHECK OUT OTHER GREAT DINOSAUR BOOKS

PRIMORDIA
by **Greig Beck**

Ben Cartwright, former soldier, home to mourn the loss of his father stumbles upon cryptic letters from the past between the author, Arthur Conan Doyle and his great, great grandfather who vanished while exploring the Amazon jungle in 1908.

Amazingly, these letters lead Ben to believe that his ancestor's expedition was the basis for Doyle's fantastical tale of a lost world inhabited by long extinct creatures. As Ben digs some more he finds clues to the whereabouts of a lost notebook that might contain a map to a place that is home to creatures that would rewrite everything known about history, biology and evolution.

But other parties now know about the notebook, and will do anything to obtain it. For Ben and his friends, it becomes a race against time and against ruthless rivals.

In the remotest corners of Venezuela, along winding river trails known only to lost tribes, and through near impenetrable jungle, Ben and his novice team find a forbidden place more terrifying and dangerous than anything they could ever have imagined.

PANGAEA EXILES
by **Jeff Brackett**

Tried and convicted for his crimes, Sean Barrow is sent into temporal exile—banished to a time so far before recorded history that there is no chance that he, or any other criminal sent back, has any chance of altering history.

Now Sean must find a way to survive more than 200 million years in the past, in a world populated by monstrous creatures that would rend him limb from limb if they got the chance. And that's just his fellow prisoners.

The dinosaurs are almost as bad.